# Roll! They Cried

Copyright 2006, 2012 by Soren Narnia

ISBN 978-1478259633

## A Riveting Disclaimer

As if I even had a phone to contact them, this book was not written in association with APBA International, Inc. Oh, and the actual game uses the names and stats of real players and teams from the big leagues, not fictional folks, and thus it tends to be more interesting than these pages convey. Go Brewers.

**PROLOGUE: The Night the Warning Track Wept**

At ten-fifteen p.m. on the twenty-first of October in the year 2002, a celebrity of mind-boggling importance to the Hollywood community, whose name, if it were mentioned here, would cause the reader to spontaneously combust with surprise and fascination, went out to walk his dog. The dog, a fragile brown dachshund named Carrots, was quite excited to explore the foreign avenues of residential Lexington, Kentucky, having never before strayed beyond the sunny come-hither curves of L.A.'s Mulholland Drive. The movie star who owned him had popped into Lexington for a quick visit to his elderly and perennially judgmental mother before winging it back to the coast to begin shooting a film of such incredible quality and renown that any revelation of its title here would cause the reader to immediately drop over dead with appreciation and flabbergast. Carrots had just finished sniffing a rusty Yield sign for all it was worth (and then some) when the movie star heard a dim roar rise from beyond the tree line to the south, overwhelming the street's customary tranquility.

"Carrots," Hollywood's favorite screen Virgo remarked, lifting his famous left eyebrow, "my celebrity sense is telling me that something big in happening in the center of town."

He was right. His celebrity sense had not failed him since his dubious decision to produce and direct a trilogy of big-budget films depicting the life of the first Secretary of the Interior, and this time he was zeroed in. Just two seconds after the roar was first heard, a chorus of booing, as if voiced by an entire nation, began to pour like a wave of acerbic lava from downtown Lexington toward the suburbs. The booing was only strengthened by a recent patch of humid air from an unexpected Canadian warm front. It caused Carrots to raise his tennis ball-sized head to the night sky in wonder and dread terror, which was pretty much how Carrots approached every natural phenomenon, including even his meals.

Closer to the bustling streets of the city center, the human booing did not just worry the citizens who populated the coffeehouses, the bars, the ATMs, the Christian Science Reading Rooms of Lexington—it endangered their safety. The booing rose to such a freakish crescendo that the Kentucky Earthquake and Equestrian Center began to receive frightened phone calls about a possible record-breaking tremor. Traffic became ensnarled as people slammed on their brakes, and the brakes of others, to listen. On North Limestone Street, buildings trembled, and a fabricated metal letter fell off a Starbucks Coffee sign and crashed to the sidewalk, causing the place to become a tarbuck's. Down the street at Tarbuck's Coffee, Terrence Tarbuck shook an angry fist and shouted something about trademark violations when the sound of the booing rushed in through the front door accompanied by a throng of scared pedestrians, rattling his knockoff cups and plates and dishes and causing him to instantly stop honoring all Tarbuck Tuesdays discount cards for fear that the end was near. At the intersection of Church and Market Streets, the booing disrupted the electrical circuit inside the blinking yellow caution light in front of Avalon Hill Elementary, causing it to blink almost twice as rapidly, throwing drivers into unprecedented fits of prudence. On West Vine Street, the booing was so apocalyptic and terrifying that two co-workers putting in late hours at a prominent investment firm felt the need to suddenly confess long-dormant feelings for each other, which would have been quite tender and sweet if their feelings were not generally ones of mild disgust.

In less than sixty seconds the city's intelligentsia, including Carrots himself, was able to determine the source of the booing. It wasn't hard to figure out. All of Lexington's eyes went toward the biggest building in town: Goods and Services Field, the forty-five thousand seat baseball stadium that was home to the Lexington Cannons.

Inside that august shrine to America's greatest game except for possibly football, the capacity crowd was just getting started. Game Seven of the 2002 World Championship Series was not yet officially over, but the partisan audience bellowed and screeched to the high heavens to let the rest of mankind know that the contest was done, dead, history, nada. The stands shook violently with their anger and disapproval. Fifteen thousand people would later be treated for eardrum damage sustained during the fifty-two minute twelfth inning, and another twenty-two thousand large sodas (priced reasonably at eight dollars each) would be knocked over by no force other than the nightmarish decibel level. The scoreboard blew roughly forty percent of its bulbs, causing the evening's displayed attendance figure to become, simply, 8.

The ire of the crowd was focused squarely on one Cannons player.

His name was Benjamin Glinton. During the 2002 season he had hit for a solid .272 average with 12 homeruns and 77 RBI. He had stolen ten bases, come through with a pair of game winning hits. He had patrolled left field reasonably well, making up for a weak left arm with solid range. It was his sixth season with the Cannons. His team jokingly called him Sasquatch in ode to a particular game in which he had lurched with almost simian awkwardness toward home plate after stumbling on the edge of third base. After October 21, he would have a very different nickname. Hundreds of them, in fact.

Ben Glinton, a speck of nothingness to the cosmos but a figure of some sudden importance to Kentucky sports history, sat like Stonehenge at the end of the Cannons bench, trying desperately to keep himself from putting his fingers in his ears. Many of his teammates, who had moved far, far away from him, had already done so, but Ben felt that moving the slightest muscle in his body might cause him to crack into a thousand useless pieces. His face was as ashen as Don Knotts's tombstone. He felt the booing of the crowd pierce his feet and his hands like some sort of disrespectful reference to the Crucifixion. The jeers found the On switch controlling his pores, struck it with one mighty swipe, and the flop sweat commenced, running freely down his forehead and neck in a magnificent river whose breathtaking peaks and rapids would be a boon to any northern state's tourist economy. He felt the penetrating glare of embattled manager Greeny St. Clair in his very epiglottis.

Time spun out, and the booing of the forty-five thousand seemed to pass through decades, centuries, and finally eons as Ben tried to mentally will his body to reduce itself to a sub-molecular level and pop out of existence like a soap bubble. It didn't happen. Somehow, just before the crowd's sinister group mind began to weigh the pros and cons of rushing the field in an attempt to literally eat him in one voracious bite, he managed to get to his feet and turn to the Cannons' backup catcher, Joey "Carrots" Williamson, speaking the last seven words he ever would to his teammates:

"I have to go to the bathroom."

No one stopped him. No one could find the words. Ben took two steps down from the dugout into the tunnel and disappeared, moving as stiffly as the tin solder in whatever production of *The Nutcracker* would be most avoided that particular year.

The boos followed him into the tunnel, not letting up for an instant. The tunnel ended at the locker room. His face slack and expressionless, Ben pushed the door open, moving silently past a pair of stunned network news reporters who were still trying to figure out what to ask him and could get out nothing but some odd guttural sounds that sounded like a bunch of Gs stuck together.

Ben shuffled like a thoroughly Thorazined zombie past his locker, more than aware of the gawking stares of the equipment manager and the assistant trainer, who looked up at him from a small screen where the two men announcing the game on national TV were trying to convey to millions of viewers the sense of abject doom inside the stadium. Ben moved past the bathrooms as well and just kept going, as if he were taking a leisurely but strangely nervous stroll on a Tuesday morning before batting practice. He kept his eyes straight ahead.

After the locker room was the training room, where a towel boy stepped out of Ben's way and shoved two small wads of cotton in his young ears to drown out the booing which had penetrated the very earth. Ben said nothing. He looked as if ten liters of maple syrup had been shot directly into his cerebral cortex. It was how he looked one night back at college when he had drunk so many beers that he fell down and skinned his knee when attempting to simply spell his name to impress a girl.

Past the training room there was only a short outer hallway where Bruce Kish, the creator of the team's mascot, stood in his black bear outfit, cradling the giant head under one arm. He started to say something to Ben that sounded like an embarrassed "vuh" but could force out nothing more. His face was beet red in empathy. Ben barely noticed him. He pushed on the door that marked the exit to the Cannons parking lot and stepped through it into the night.

Ben stood still for a moment, inhaling the musk of the sweet autumn air.

Then he started to run. Still in uniform, mind you. He didn't even take his cap off.

He had eighty cents in loose change in his rear pocket where he kept his batting glove. That would have to be enough. The 29 bus to Gratz Park was just coming around the corner. It was going to be close. He had maybe two minutes to get beyond the fence to High Street. He ran like he was trying to beat a throw to home plate. He ran like he had never run before.

The booing inside the stadium drowned out the sound of the door opening behind him. He heard a single male voice shout his name and he began to run even faster. For all he knew, Abner Doubleday himself had appeared behind him in enraged spirit form, bent on taking him down with a single dart from a Tanzanian blow gun for the damage he had just irreversibly caused to the sport of baseball.

The chain link fence was just fifteen feet away. No time to leave through the faraway player's entrance. He would have to climb and throw himself over like that spy dude from the James Bond movies.

"Ben, stop!!" cried the lone voice. "It's me, Harold!"

Ben stopped and turned. Harold Pillick, the Cannons' bench utility infielder (.221, 1 HR, 6 RBI in 22 games in 2002, all career highs), stood under the feeble glow of the lights in the parking lot, waving his arms. Ben started back quickly, but not because of a change of heart.

"Harold!" he shouted. "You've got to get me out of here! Give me your car keys!"

"I don't have them," Harold said meekly when Ben was close enough so that he didn't have to yell and could be heard above the pitiless crowd. "My mother dropped me off today."

"Then come with me," Ben said desperately. "Come on, you never had a career and mine is over. Come with me and we can get away before they rip my arms off and fry them up with butter and lemon!"

"You've got to get back in here, Ben," Harold pleaded meekly. "You're gonna get in a lot of trouble."

"Do you hear those animals?!" Ben shouted. "If I'm not on that 29 bus when it pulls away, I'm a dead man!"

"Oh, you're making too much of it," Harold tried to tell him, at which point dozens of people in the top row of the stadium high above spotted the two of them down in the parking lot and began to yell, pointing and cursing. The news of Ben's exact geographical location spread through the capacity crowd at the speed of light. Now if they could only locate some propane torches and meat hooks, they could get busy.

"This is our chance for freedom," Ben said, panting, his eyes becoming wild and spacey as his last connection to sanity abandoned him without looking back or even leaving a Dear John letter. "Our names are mud in this town. You're the worst player in the history of baseball and I just became the most hated. Together we can start new lives in New Zealand! We can marry Maori girls and never think about this stupid sport again!"

"I don't know, Ben," Harold replied, removing his Extra Small cap and scratching his balding head. "I think you're going to make people even madder."

"Then stay and be damned!" Ben cried, not so much in anger as in soul-searing horror as debris began to rain down from the top row of the stadium, debris that included everything from ice to seat cushions to seats themselves to an actual wheelchair, hurled at Ben by the Cannons' oldest living fan. The last words Ben ever uttered on Cannons team property were "I'm getting out of here while I still have my legs!", at which point he turned, galloped toward the fence, and scaled it with the agility of a well-fed moa, New Zealand's favorite wingless bird. From there it was a mere nineteen foot drop to the pavement. He hit it like a big bag of soggy candy corn, enduring bruises in places better left to the imagination. The 29 bus screeched to a halt twenty-four inches from his face. Fortunately for Ben Glinton, the bus had no working radio to transmit the broadcast of the game, or the driver would surely have finished the job. Ben got very slowly to his feet, having dislocated a useless humerus or two, and threw himself into the bus as if he were diving headlong into the stands to catch a foul ball, which he had never actually had to do.

The bus pulled away just as the national press burst through the door behind Harold in search of the man who had just destroyed the Cannons' title chances in the most phenomenal display of bad baseball the world had ever seen. Harold waved at the bus in a friendly manner and Ben waved back from his aisle seat. Inside the stadium, the New York Guardians sent another three runners across the plate with a moon shot homerun to left that closed out a ten run, ten hit twelfth inning. The booing eventually, mercifully, stopped. Recordings of it in its entirety would soon be sold on the Internet as a CD. Harold Pillick would buy one for his niece because she asked for it for Christmas. From that point on, the CD would be played without commercial interruption once a year on most Lexington radio stations at the exact time the booing had begun on that night in 2002. Once, sitting alone in the darkened Oval Office, the President of the United States, a Cannons fan since childhood, listened mournfully to those sounds and wept silently, considering how he could best use the faith entrusted to him by the American people to deport Ben Glinton to Yemen. Nothing ever came of it. Like all the great men who had held that office before him, the President just wasn't all that much on following through with things.

*Almost as soon as baseball was invented, game designers tried to simulate it for people who didn't feel up to going out on the lawn to play because they didn't like the look of that cloud in the sky. Whether it was with wooden contraptions or marbles or playing cards or tea leaves, kids and adults liked to compete with each other using these simple games as if they were really out there performing in the pro leagues and threatening to walk if their contracts weren't re-negotiated.*

*Among the first board games to approach the feel of a real pro contest were Clifford Van Beek's* National Pastime *and Ethan Allan's* All-Star Baseball. *Gamers could play using the abilities of actual major league players, and were able to feel a manager's joy of throwing a massive tantrum if those players didn't perform in the clutch. Baseball board games began to get ever more sophisticated just as the sophistication level of those who got paid to actually play in the pros began the steady decline which continues to this day. There were some design failures along the way, of course. Games like* Bunt Till You Drop *and Fidel Castro's* Slide, Lying American, Slide! *were quickly forgotten by the public.*

*In 1951, a man named Dick Seitz gave APBA Baseball to the world. APBA (pronounced "AP-BUH" by its fans) quickly became popular with those wishing to re-create single major league contests, series, or even complete seasons. Among its fans were Ed Koch, George H. W. Bush, Jeff Daniels, and Brent Musburger.*

*The nineteen eighties saw the rise of video games, which at long last enabled sports fans to channel most of their mental energies directly into their thumbs. The stimulation of flashing lights and fake crowd noise, coupled with the long dreamed-of ability to program one's initials onto a TV screen, caused many to turn away from board games. But thousands have continued to play APBA, both in leagues and individually in quiet rooms on sunny Saturday afternoons when the pros come to life under the guidance of anonymous managers, with no real limits to what can happen.*

*This is the story of how the game changed one man's life.*

*(Not Brent Musburger's, if you're wondering.)*

# 1. The Psychiatric Profession's Mixed-Result Strike-Back

Three and a half years after the night that he darkened baseball's record books forever, Ben Glinton found himself in his modest bachelor's apartment in Harrisburg, Pennsylvania, searching through his kitchen cabinet for the last of the Fruity Nut Soy Smacks he just knew were still in there somewhere. Once he was able to produce them, at 10:19 a.m., he ate a bowlful with milk and added an absolutely fantastic Entenmann's apple danish on the side. At 11:04 a.m., after accomplishing breakfast, he stumbled back into his bedroom and changed from his favorite gray sweatpants into his favorite red sweatpants, which had been procured at no cost by sending a certain number of proofs of purchase to a major waffle manufacturer. The words AUNT GABBY'S LUSTIN' FORKFUL were emblazoned on the sweatpants in question. To these he added a T-shirt adorned with the face of a semi-popular cartoon aardvark and a ball cap denouncing those who differed with Ben's views on flag burning. The cap would both protect his face from the sun's damaging ultra-violet rays on this summer morning and cover the fact that he hadn't bothered to comb his scruffy brown hair. At 11:27 he seriously considered shaving, and at 11:27 and twenty seconds he left the apartment for the six block journey to The Place He Just Really Wasn't Too Crazy About.

Dr. Smozer's office was in a two-story brownstone that marked the dividing line between the nice section of Harrisburg and the one that Ben had called home for the past eighteen months. Ben entered the office at a little after noon, or about an hour before he usually got out of bed these days. He offered a subdued hello to Bernicia, the moody receptionist whose eye patch seemed to switch from one eye to the other depending on the season, and waited twenty minutes for his appointment to begin. He had a choice of magazines he could read to pass the time. From a stack highlighted by Sports Illustrated, Baseball Weekly, and this year's Street and Smith's major league preview guide, he selected the June 1997 issue of Permafrost Gardening and thumbed idly through the pages, stopping occasionally to look at attractive women featured in advertisements. He tried to remember when he had last gone on an actual date. He recalled there being some snow on the ground. The young woman he'd wooed at the local laundromat had been somewhat impressed at dinner by his tall frame and his claim to be an ex-ballplayer. She'd been noticeably less enchanted with a very long and complicated joke he'd told about the difficulties of physical intimacy between a prune and a walnut. Though the joke was solid gold, and had been confirmed as such by the fellas who worked behind the counter at GobbleDonut, he'd been alone in the world since the moment he delivered its punch line.

"I *know* you," spoke a grizzled voice to Ben's left as he reminisced about unrequited loves gone by. He turned to see a small elderly man gazing at him intensely, and in not too friendly a manner.

"Mmmmmm, no, I don't think you do," Ben replied, unconsciously tugging the bill of his ball cap lower over his face.

"Yes, yes," the man insisted, squinting and leaning further in. "I've seen you on the television—in some negative context if I'm not mistaken."

Ben sighed. "All right, yes, you have," he said. "My name is Glen Binton. I'm the guy that played the first Secretary of the Interior in that trilogy."

The old man's eyes lit up. "Of course!" he said, beaming. "I watched the last ten minutes of it not a year ago. Well done, young man, well done! Such authenticity!" He grabbed Ben's hand with one that felt like a cold moist pancake and squeezed.

"Super, super," Ben said, smiling nervously. A minute later, just as the old man launched into a lengthy, rambling monologue about the history of the Dewey Decimal System, Ben was called into

Dr. Smozer's office. He walked in more jittery than he had been in years.

Dr. Smozer was a rare psychiatrist in that he had vintage monster movie posters from the nineteen-fifties plastered all over his walls and a steady stream of Supertramp hits playing softly on a small stereo system at the back of the room. He was a pudgy man who had chosen to dye his graying hair a fiery red color which tended to frighten children and people with pacemakers. Ben ran his hands though his own sorry excuse for a haircut and sat down across from him.

"Okay, Ben," the doctor began, "today's the big day. How do you feel?"

"All right, I suppose," Ben replied. "Sorry about that bounced check."

"Which one?" Smozer asked. "The one from February or the one from May?"

"May," Ben said. "The one from February was more the electric company's fault. See, they have this thing where they usually cash my check for my water bill on the fourth, but then suddenly out of nowhere they decided to be heartless Nazis and—"

"No matter," Smozer interrupted. "Let's not put off today's momentous task by getting sidetracked on matters of who owes who what money, or who's been mis-dating his checks, et cetera. Shall we begin?"

"Sure," Ben said. "Absolutely. Let's cut right to heart of the thing, let's scale that rock. It's been seven months of therapy, I'm ready to roll."

"Excellent," Smozer said. "I'll ease you into this a bit. I'll let you set the scene for me, and you can even close your eyes if you like and we'll go back to that night in 2002, and hopefully by the end of this session you'll have finally confronted those events head-on and we can move right past them."

"Okay," Ben said, closing his eyes, losing sight of the far wall and Mothra breathing fire over the terrified Japanese populace. "Okay, it was...October 21st, and it was Game Seven of the championship. Full house. Fifty-eight degrees or so. I don't know what the barometer was doing. Rising, I think. Rising? Yeah, that sounds right. Bono sang the national anthem. Pretty good, except he put in lyrics about some free trade deal involving Panama or something."

"Yes, I recall," Smozer said, leaning back in his leather chair and lowering the volume on the stereo somewhat. He stroked his freakishly red beard. "Go on."

Ben swallowed hard. This was going to be tougher than he thought. "Um...things were going pretty good. We got a couple of runs in the top of the second, New York got a couple of runs in the fifth. Curse Williger was pitching pretty well—"

"Curse Williger?" Smozer asked. "Is that the Walter Williger you've mentioned before?"

"Yeah, we called him Curse because of those three awful calls that went against him in the wildcard series the year before," Ben remembered. "Completely changed his personality. Started calling inanimate objects 'bastard', stuff like that. He just plain quit last year. Still sends me Christmas cards. He talks about his wife and kids and then goes off on a violent harangue against umpires and then thanks Jesus Christ for various things."

"I understand," Smozer said. "Continue."

Ben took a deep breath. "So, ah, yeah, Joe Costa scored on a squeeze play and we were ahead 3-2 in the top of the ninth. Our closer came in, Tom Tippett, and, you know, things went on from there, and New York took the title. Shame, that. Good times, though. Good days."

Smozer smiled. "Yes, quite, Ben. But you may have left something out."

"Well, we don't have to do this today, right?" Ben asked meekly. "Why don't I come back next week. I'm a bit peckish right now, not so much up for talking. All I had for dinner last night was a Slim Jim and some turkey stuffing."

"Sorry, Ben. Today's the day. Would you like me to use the dimmer?" Smozer got up, always excited to use the dimmer he'd installed the month before. It made him genuinely happy. The light in the room got six percent softer and he sat down again. Yes yes, that dimmer was all right.

Ben sighed. "Okay. So, yeah, top of the ninth and New York's leadoff hitter doubled. Spike Vail. Most obnoxious baseball player on the planet. Even you must have heard of him."

"I have. I very much enjoy his Office Depot commercials."

"Yeah. great," Ben said unhappily. "He's real sincere in those, too. Really believes in that toner. Not a money-grubber at all. Not in it for the glory, no sir."

"Remember what we said about anger," Smozer advised. "It's the icing on the sheet cake of despair."

"Yeah, I never understood what that meant, but whatever," Ben said. "Vail slid into second, practically took a bow for the crowd even though we were the home team, and then Tom blew the next guy away with that freaky fastball of his. I used to have dreams that thing was coming for me. Except it had a little white disco suit on it, and shoes. Should we talk about that? Because it creeps me out pretty bad."

"Perhaps next time," Smozer said. "You're very close now, Ben. Just tell me what happened next."

"Well," Ben said, trying to scrunch himself more deeply into his chair, "the next hitter was Al Arthurs. Swung on the first pitch. It came my way. I had to drift to my right a bit, toward the line. I had it all the way. And the ball went into my glove and I caught it, and, you know, I began to celebrate. I took the ball out of my glove and I..." He trailed off. His head hurt. He was sweating.

"Yes, what did you do, Ben?" Smozer asked, sensing a breakthrough was imminent.

"Well, I...I thought there were two outs. I thought we'd just won it all. So naturally, I was happy. I took off my cap and I threw it into the crowd. And then the ball...I figured the thing to do would be to throw it into the seats. So someone could have a souvenir he could treasure for ten minutes and then hawk on eBay."

"But there was only one out, yes, I see," Smozer said. "Based on my understanding of the game, it would not have been advisable to dispose of the ball."

"No, it wasn't the best thing," Ben said, opening his eyes and looking to the Mothra poster for strength. On the stereo, the lead singer of Supertramp was warbling about how all he needed was just a little bit of your time for him, a little bit of your life for him.

"Did you, in fact, Ben, throw the ball into the stands?"

"Yes," Ben said, taking a cushion from the sofa nearby and pressing it to his chest defensively. "Just into the first row, though. To some kid. How come I don't get any credit for tossing the ball to a kid? An ugly one, too! I still could have made the play on Vail if that little guttersnipe had given it back when I yelled at him to do it!"

"Easy, Ben, eeeeeeeeeeeasy," Smozer said soothingly. "So, Spike Vail was able to score?"

"Just barely," Ben recalled. "The thing is, some Cannons fan next to the kid yanked the ball away from him and tossed it back to me, but only after he called me an idiot. So technically, there was time to make the play. Except I...except I..." He couldn't go on. He leaned back in his chair and stared at the ceiling.

"Say it, Ben. say it...you're very close."

"I took off my jersey," Ben confessed in a laborious exhalation of woe. "I took off my jersey right after I tossed the ball into the stands. You know, in celebration. So that cost me a few seconds before I realized that there was only one out. And...Vail scored."

"So your throw wasn't on time," Smozer deduced.

"Not on time," Ben mused, feeling woozy, "well, it could have been, I guess. It's just that I was panicky and I threw the ball a bit too hard." He stopped there.

"Where exactly did it go?" Smozer asked.

"Section 10, about fifteen rows up," Ben said. "Box seats, right behind the plate."

"I see," Smozer said. "And so from that moment on, you've been haunted by—"

"Oh, God no, that wasn't what made me so depressed. That just *tied* the game. Jeez, the ninth inning thing could have happened to *anybody.* Happens all the time. My friend from the team, Harold, he once ran out of the dugout skipping and yelling and hollering and jumping on Ted Turocy for getting the last out of a no-hitter when he still had two more innings to go. Ted fell down and wrenched his ankle and had to come out of the game. So let's not hand me the World's Dumbest Man award just yet."

"So there was...a second incident," Smozer said. He had to dig out a second note pad from his desk drawer and shake his ballpoint pen again to get some more ink flowing.

"Yeah, you might say there was a second incident," Ben said, getting red in the face as he gritted his teeth in shame, self-loathing, and something that seemed to recall the buyer's remorse he'd suffered when he bought a ticket to see *Home Alone 3.*

"Okay, Ben, let's confront that second incident head on," Smozer said. "You can do it."

"It was the bottom of the eleventh," Ben said. "Still 3-3. Jason Blaze was on first with one man out. That brought me up to the plate. There was some booing, a lot of it in fact, but I didn't care. I was going to hit a homerun and end the game. I had just made up my mind to do it. I'd gotten into this freaky mental zone where there was just no other option. And the Guardians' pitcher, I forget who it was, some skinny pimply guy, he served up a total baked potato on a 1-1 count and I clouted it. *Man,* did I ever clout that thing. The crowd went nuts and I started trotting. I had never hit a ball so hard and so clean. I couldn't even feel the bat touch it, that's how sweet it was."

"I'm confused," Smozer said. "That doesn't seem—"

"So I started trotting around the bases," Ben said. "I guess I was in my own world a little bit. I mean, I'd never had a feeling like that before. I'd just won the Series. With a walk-off homerun. I was in a daze. I was on top of the world. Rare air, stuff like that. So I wasn't quite, ah, listening to the crowd."

"Couldn't hear them at all?" Smozer said. He had set his notepad down and was staring at his patient as if Ben were an unusual and brightly colored puffer fish gadding about inside a private aquarium.

"Nope," Ben said. He was now gazing into some undefined middle space, resolved to tell it all. He felt nothing anymore. "So when I looked up, I was kind of shocked to see nobody on the team surrounding home plate waiting to congratulate me. I figured there'd be a mob scene there, maybe people flinging themselves out of the stands, flash bulbs, the cops moving in to bash streakers over the head, the whole deal. But I just saw Jason Blaze, mouthing some words I didn't understand. And I saw the Guardians' catcher standing in front of the plate with a confused expression on his face. He was holding his mitt out and I sort of just...walked right into it. That's when I realized I may have made some kind of a mistake."

"Describe that 'mistake' for me," Smozer said. He had closed his own eyes in horror.

"Well, apparently I didn't quite get all of the pitch, because the ball landed on the warning track in left center and it got thrown back in and they got Jason trying to slide. That was the second out. And I was behind him. Pretty far behind him, actually. Our third base coach had been motioning for me to hold up at third but I never saw him. I was trying to be modest, you know. Keeping my head down. So the catcher was waiting for me with the ball for pretty much the whole ninety feet. And that was, you know, the third out. We didn't score. Then in the top of the twelfth, the Guardians scored...let me see...ten. Ten runs. Yeah, they got going pretty good." Ben sighed once more. "Wow. Actually, you know, that does feel like a great weight off my chest. I haven't spoken the words ever. I think that worked. I mean, I'm definitely going to throw up, that's a given, but progress was definitely just made." He leaned back in his chair, ran his hands through his hair once more, and his body became jelly-like, as if he had just come out of the ocean after spending four exhausting hours in it trying to scare people with a fake shark fin.

Smozer looked at him with penetrating eyes. His breathing seemed uneven.

"It was more than ninety feet, Ben," he whispered. "It was *much* more than that."

"Hmmm? Whassat?" Ben asked.

"The catcher had the ball even *before* you got to third base, you mind-numbingly silly man," Smozer said, rising out of his chair and dropping his note pad to the floor. "Haven't you ever had the decency to watch the *tape?* Are you such a cowardly *lummox* that you've been afraid to look at it? Well, I'll show it to you *twenty-four hours a day* if you like, you destroyer of dreams! You crusher of hopes!"

Ben got up too, backing away in terror. "What are you talking about? Are you nuts?!"

"I had four hundred dollars bet on that game, you dunderpate!" Smozer yelled, shaking with an impotent rage that curiously enough made him seem shorter. "I waited fifty-one years of my *life* for the Cannons to win the Series, and you sabotaged it all in *ten seconds!* You are Satan! Get out of my office, Beelzebub! I will not allow you to eat my soul as you ate the souls of all thinking baseball fans! Try not to despoil the history of the game on your way through the *lobby!* Do you think you can manage *that, pea brain?!* DO YOU THINK YOU CAN MANAGE THAT?!"

Ben ran for the door. Smozer tried to deliver a kick to his hind quarters but missed them by about three feet, causing him to lose his balance and fall to the floor. He tried to grab onto the diplomas hanging on the wall to halt his descent but managed only to take them all down with him. The carpet enveloped him, as it had so many times before.

Ben tore through the waiting room, looking over his shoulder to see if Winchester Smozer, M.D., author of *Embracing Insanity*, was coming to murder him, perhaps by boiling him in melted cheese (as had been the case in one of Ben's many recent dreams about Jeff Goldblum). The last thing he ever heard inside that particular building was the voice of the old geezer who had befriended him fifteen minutes before. Now he was telling Ben that as a young man, he had been quite accomplished at wooing the young ladies, and he launched into a semi-coherent story involving a chance meeting with Stacy Keach on the San Francisco trolley system, the point of which Ben would never know.

## 2. Opportunity Knocks, Then Just Leaves Junk Mail

Tick's Bar on South Front Street was generally ranked at the bottom of all trusted consumer lists in the categories of service, atmosphere, and cleanliness, and the place would have almost certainly been torn down long ago had Jim Morrison not once stopped there during a U.S. tour and choked on a pickle. The pickle had been preserved in murky brine and now sat on the bar year after year as an index card taped to the jar described the incident in question and embellished it to no small degree. According to Tick's owner, Morrison had choked in the act of saving Lyndon Johnson's life from a terrorist bullet over beside the pinball machine. Johnson, it said on the index card, had been an "unusually good tipper."

Ben liked Tick's because it was literally right across the street from the front door of his apartment building. Once he had even closed his eyes and walked dead ahead across the street and parted the bar's doorway almost flawlessly, just barely bumping his left shoulder on the frame. Geographical convenience had, over the past fourteen months or so, more than made up for the fact that to order chicken fingers or even an imported beer at Tick's was to embark on a taste journey to the lower bowels of unpleasantness. Plus Harold liked it.

They sat there for a few hours after Ben left Dr. Smozer's office, Ben nursing a Budweiser and Harold, who didn't drink, sipping sweetened iced tea. They were the only patrons in the place except for a goat-faced man of about fifty who seemed to be talking to people who weren't there, pausing once in a while only to press a gentle kiss on the thermostat in the corner of the room. He was a regular too. A plate of soggy French fries sat on the bar between Ben and Harold, who shared them joylessly and berated themselves for not realizing in advance that there was not a chance in hell that Tick's would have ketchup.

"Here's what we could do," Ben was saying. "We could market a cereal that's like, every cereal thrown together. We could just call it Luck of the Draw. It would be the cereal for everyone. There'd be nothing in it that someone wouldn't like."

Harold mused upon it for a moment and wiped his greasy fingers on the front of his shirt, then scratched his balding head, leaving more grease there. His few years away from baseball had made him somewhat lumpy and hairless. Without a cap on his head and a bat in his hand, Harold looked like a bewildered, undercooked corn muffin. Once his mother, in a fit of rage, had told him he looked like a pay phone, and despite the existential meaninglessness of that statement he often found himself staring fixedly at pay phones as his thoughts went to unfortunate places.

"I think the no-frills car is a better idea, if we could get the money together," he said.

"What was that again, I don't remember that," Ben said.

"You know, where we could send Ford or Chrysler the design for a car that didn't have anything but the essentials, you know, for poor people. So there'd be just a steering wheel and a big hump you could sit on, and no heat or anything, no glove compartment, no odometer, no turn signals. The Simplica."

"Yeah, the Simplica," Ben said, eyes narrowing in thought. "That has possibilities."

"I mean, a car can easily go on just three wheels too, there's almost no reason for the fourth one," Harold said, and stifled an iced tea burp. "It's just price gouging, really."

"Whatever we decide, we have to get moving on something," Ben said. "The wolf is at the door. I'm this close to having to find a job."

"Are you serious?" Harold asked in amazement. "You don't have anything left?"

Ben took a sip of his warm beer. "Nope. I just went in the hole for another three thousand."

"Since *Tuesday?* How?"

"There was this guy who explained to me how a lot of money could be made by selling refurbished kitchen appliances to foreign embassies," Ben explained. "A lot of these places are still in the dark ages. They'd kill for modern American technology. Africa and such."

"Oh, man," Harold said, shaking his head.

"Hey, the guy's plan is rock solid," Ben insisted. "You know how many countries Africa has? Every one of them has an embassy, and all the people who work in them want a decent cup of coffee when they roll into work in the morning. But what's gonna make that coffee? Huh? You tell me."

"You're just really not so good with money, Ben," Harold offered hesitantly. "Even I wouldn't go for that one."

"No, the embassy thing is gold, I think," Ben said, and repeated the sentence to convince himself. After a moment of silence, he simply said the word 'embassy' aloud. Harold said it too. Then they said it together, just a couple of times at first.

"Embassy. Embassy, embassy, embassy," they said in unison. It was the most fun they'd had in about two months.


They left the bar after dark, Ben weaving the tiniest bit because of the beer, and Harold weaving a bit because when he got too much food coloring in him his mysterious inner ear problem kicked in. They debated renting a kung fu movie but Harold decided to try and beat his wife home lest she be left alone and perhaps get it in her head to make another attempt at a dinner dish she called "pork loop." They separated in the parking lot and Ben headed down to Walgreen's to buy some cherry ice cream. The evening was looking up. Cherry ice cream plus a jaunty turn through the upper reaches of his basic cable TV channel range was just the low-key adventure he was looking for on this night. His nerves were still a-jumble after the encounter with Crazy RageTime Doctor and a really embarrassing final scene to an episode of *Will and Grace* he'd watched at the bar.

Things seemed to be about to get even worse when he heard some idiot shouting his name from a block away. It was something that happened once a month or so. Since he'd gotten away from Kentucky and settled in Pennsylvania things had gotten much better, but he could still compile an impressive index of the profane shouts recently launched in his direction. The trend these days seemed to be to twist his last name into various disgusting words germane to both the sport of baseball and the act of mating with different animal species, whereas before, people had been content to simply call him vermin.

The voice that called to him now was high-pitched, squeaky, and desperate, not unlike Harold's. Ben stopped, having found that the best way to deal with street hecklers was to acknowledge their insult with a polite wave, then wait for them to turn and move on before flipping them both middle fingers. He saw a skinny dude running fast at him down the sidewalk, calling him "Mr. Glinton" again and again. This was unusual. More unusual still was the fact that between the words "Mister" and "Glinton," there was no reference whatsoever to his own buttocks.

The interloper caught up to him just as he stopped in front of the drug store. The poor guy had completely exhausted his breath in trying to catch up. He stood doubled over, hands on his knees, still repeating Ben's name. The guy was maybe twenty-four or twenty-five years old, still suffering from acne and a boyish face that might as well have had the phrase LEFT LANES GO THRU TO NEBRASKA, THE DAKOTAS crayoned on it.

"Yeah, can I help you in some way?" Ben asked him tiredly. "Sorry I ruined your life with the Guardians game. Try to focus on other things. Family, Jesus, and so forth."

"Oh no, Mr. Glinton, I don't care about that," said the stranger when he had regained his composure. "I want to talk to you about maybe working with you on something."

Ben's brain began to glow in big pulses of neon green. He couldn't help it. Anytime someone came to him with an investment opportunity, he became as pliable as a bowl of warm mustard. Since his semi-voluntary retirement from the Cannons he had lost scads of money on everything from internet cafés to the creation of a children's television show based on the fictional crime-solving adventures of a young Tori Amos. But he knew that it could all be turned around in one great stroke of genius. He had been repeatedly assured of this fact by a little man inside his head who often put similar horrifying ideas into his brain just before turning quickly away and pretending he did not speak English.

"All right, whaddya got?" Ben asked the mysterious Okie in his midst, entering Walgreen's and grabbing a green hand-basket. He wanted to pick up a Whitman's Sampler too in addition to the ice cream because he'd just read on a message board that they'd changed the map on the inside of the box and he thought that was probably a damned lie.

The guy clung to him up and down the aisles like paint on a wheelbarrow. "My name is Roy Skinla," he said, "and I cover Division I-A college football for the Harrisburg Daily Fact Holder."

Ben squinted at him. "That's the newspaper owned by the American Dental Association or something, isn't it?"

"That's only partially true," Roy corrected him, almost knocking over a display of parrot food as Ben rounded a tricky corner and threw some extra low grade laundry detergent into his basket. "Anyway, they found out you lived in the area, and they had the idea to send me out to get an interview."

"Sorry, pal," Ben said, examining the label on some abominable knockoff of Frosted Flakes, "I don't do interviews. Ever. Hold the basket for a sec, I need to dig out six of these beef ramen noodle things."

Roy took the basket, whose minimal weight still made his non-existent biceps strain worrisomely. "I know that, I've read a lot about you. All sorts of things. Wanna know how many post-season stolen bases you had in your career?"

"Um, I'm pretty sure it was none," Ben said, sorting through the chicken ramen, the shrimp ramen, and the pork ramen to get at the ultimate prize.

"Ah, right, none," Roy said. "But I know other things, too. I know you played the Mandy Patinkin part in your high school production of *Yentl*, and that you're allergic to oranges and pears."

Ben got down on his knees and buried his upper torso between two shelves in his quest for stiff processed noodles. "That's really disturbing," he said, his voice somewhat muffled.

"The reason I know all this is because I want to do something far better than an interview." He set the grocery basket on the floor and inhaled deeply. "I want to write your biography."

Ben emerged and stared at Roy as if he were a fingernail he had found inside his chocolate pudding. "My biography," Ben said. "You want to write *my* biography."

"Not only do I want to," Roy said with barely contained glee, "I'm already guaranteed an advance from Running Clam Press if I can give them the first two chapters!"

Ben got to his feet, one noodle packet shy of six. That meant he wouldn't get the full sale price and would have to pay eight cents a piece instead of six. "Okay," he said disbelievingly, "tell me how you possibly managed to extract a deal for the biography of a six-year player who supposedly set baseball back five decades."

"It couldn't have been easier," Roy said, flush with boyish excitement. "I couched it as a story of one man trying to overcome a legacy of shame suffered all because of one night. Failure is a big seller nowadays. You know, real down-low confessional stuff that makes people seem human and foibled."

"Terrific," Ben said, turning away and moving toward the bathroom supplies, letting Roy earn his way by carrying the basket. "Only problem is, I'm not trying to overcome anything. I'm fine with what happened. I thought I wasn't, but since the only two psychiatrists I've been to about it have either gone on trial for mail fraud or tried to kill me, I think I'll just work it all out for myself. Alone. In peace."

"Well, it doesn't have to be a very *dramatic* book," Roy told him, holding the basket out so Ben could drop some blueberry lip balm into it. Winter would be here in only six months. "I just played it up that way to get the advance. The important part is, I'd love to have a major publishing credit to my name and move on to bigger things, and if you're any kind of ex-athlete, I'm sure you wouldn't mind the extra cash. I'd even let you cross out anything I write that you don't like."

Ben wandered up to the cash register and emptied his stuff onto the counter. "Frankly," he said, "I don't even like people knowing I'm still alive. So unless you end the book by telling people I drove off the edge of the Snake River Canyon in a go-cart, it ain't gonna happen." He gave a smile to the cute cashier, who had perhaps twenty years on him. Stranger things had happened, so he figured a smile couldn't hurt. It did; the cashier began to bring a knife with her to work for protection from that moment on.

Roy, not having thought his presentation through much, tried to come up with new angles of attack but couldn't produce much. "You know, I'm a really good writer," he said. "I won all kinds of essay contests in college."

"You say that as if college was in the past," Ben said. "How old are you?"

"Twenty-three," Roy said.

"Not even a master's degree, eh?" Ben chided. "Hired right out of Boise State. Even *I* have a master's degree."

"You do?" Roy said, eyes wide.

Ben sighed. "No, you teenager, of course I don't. I thought you said you knew everything there was to know about me."

"I know enough," Roy said. "Couldn't you look at this as giving a young sports writer the chance to bring the public a side of Ben Glinton they've never known? Don't you want them to see you as a human being instead of a joke? Wouldn't you like to set the record straight?"

"The record is perfectly straight," Ben told him as they left the pharmacy. "I did what I did. It could have actually even been worse. I had a mild head cold that night. I could have sneezed on someone. But I didn't." He frowned. "What was my point again?" He started to move down the sidewalk.

"Please, just take my card," Roy pleaded, and he forced it into Ben's hand. "There's money in it for you. We'd split the royalties right down the middle. "

"I'll tell you what," Ben told him, peering at the card, which simply bore Roy's name and phone number at the newspaper, as well as a handwritten advisory to speak loudly because his line was defective. "You're a good guy, you're a go-getter, you're eleven years old. When I reach the absolute, one-hundred-percent-certain, very very last straw of misery and desperation, I'll let you write about me. Until then, I just want to be left alone unless you want to be my shopping assistant full time." He did Roy the courtesy of shoving the business card into the pocket of his sweatpants and gave him a little salute of goodbye.

"If I don't hear from you in a few weeks, I'll have to pitch a book about Spike Vail!" Roy called feebly after him. "I know he's looking for someone to do it, but I was holding out for *your* story!"

"The biography of Spike Vail, that'll be a big hit!" Ben shouted back as he darted out of the path of an oncoming Volvo. "Part One: How My Ego Swallowed the Staten Island Ferry!"

With that, he was gone. Young Roy stood alone on the sidewalk with nothing to do with the rest of the evening. He walked the streets weighing his options for a good hour or so. Go to a movie? Check out a bar? Hit the health club? He wound up back in Walgreen's for three hours.

## 3. Nothing Good Ever Began in a Beaker

The next day saw a jittery mood settle over a shining industrial complex on the east side of the city. In the middle of the complex sat You Like? Laboratories, a division of Shinjoda Beneficial Industries. From these labs had sprung some of the most innovative products of the twenty-first century, funded by riches from the prosperous Japanese auto industry and introduced to the public by the marketing savvy of two guys who used to work for the Golf Channel. It was not the kind of place where tarnished ex-ballplayers were usually found, but Ben Glinton was in the process of skewing the traditional Shinjoda demographic entirely.

At nine a.m. sharp he stood with twelve other venture capitalists of varying expertise inside Examination Area 7, a cavernous, spotless room filled with gleaming scientific apparatus of varying danger levels. Everyone, including Ben, had donned a suit and tie for the occasion, although Ben's had been pieced together from four different suits, and his shoes did not quite match. The group featured a lot of gray hair; Ben was easily the youngest among them. Each of the investors had sunk at least twice as much money into the research and development of the product they were about to experience as Ben had. Somehow they were able to detect this about him without asking a single question. It was probably the way he always seemed to be scanning the room for some sort of free breakfast layout that gave his relative poverty away. Ben was subconsciously sticking close to a bearded man in his sixties who someone else had referred to as "Professor." Knowing there was someone with a college degree in the group made Ben feel much better about his investment. He tried not to notice the nervous, spectacularly bespectacled gentleman to his left who seemed to be intent on gnawing his fingernails down to his palm.

Two young Japanese scientists in lab coats appeared at 9:07, pushing a table on wheels toward the gathering. Everyone fanned around it. Some objects atop the table were covered by a smooth white sheet.

Scientist #1 offered a quick bow to the group. "Welcome, focused and smiling investors," he greeted them. "We so glad to see you appear standing in front of table with cloth on it today. We have worked pleasingly on product which will be shown to your colorful eyes at this time. Many money has been spent by you, and we wish for you to clash hands in sound to honor both vision and on-time achieving."

Everyone looked at each other, relatively sure they got his meaning, and they clapped briefly and modestly.

"Yes yes, this is where," the scientist said meaninglessly. "Two years before today, we imagine product based on simple observation: beer more vital to happiness of American man than even sun rays or wife love. So we start to come up with various imaginary method to bring beer into him."

Scientist #2 removed the white cloth from the table to reveal three dinner plates. On each sat a tasty-looking item of old-fashioned American comfort food. There was a nice fat steak with red juice leaking out of it, a plump hot dog nestled in a toasted bun, and a peanut butter and jelly sandwich cut diagonally, crusts untrimmed. Off to the side there was a six-pack of what appeared to be normal bottled beer, but as Ben and the other investors knew, there was nothing normal about it. It was, to put it simply:

"Magic Thrill Beer," said Scientist #2, lifting one of the bottles from its plain black cardboard casing. It had no label yet. "Inspiration is a similar item, beloved by your country, which cover ice cream in bowl, then harden into chocolate shell for mouth consumption."

Everyone in the group applauded again and crowded in a little closer as the idea that would soon make them all billionaires entered its final phase of production right before their lusty stares. Scientist #2 twisted open the bottle and let the cap drop onto the table. He then tilted the neck gently over the wiener sitting unsuspectingly on the plate within its maternal bun. Beer-ish liquid dribbled out in a docile stream and covered the hot dog from head to foot. The crackling of fizz was seen and heard. An ambrosial smell hung in the lab, that of rich, well-aged hops walking straight up to the meat of a dead pig and saying *Let's dance, baby face.*

Scientist #1 grinned and pressed his hands together in anticipation. "Now you remain quiet and wait less than time it take to flush average toilet," he said. Ben felt the same tingle in his feet that he had felt when the petting zoo he'd partially funded opened on that very first day back in March, accepting a wave of excited children. There had been nervousness, excitement, and dreams of riches that day too. It had ended with nine pre-schoolers being treated for mysterious ear rashes. Ben had quickly lost ninety percent of his twenty-five hundred dollar investment, but that initial rush of discovery and naked greed had been worth every penny.

After fifteen seconds or so, Scientist #2 lifted the hot dog off the plate and held it out to a woman investor with steely eyes the size of BB pellets. She took an impressively ambitious bite of the hot dog, which now bore a thick yellowish coating of totally immobile beer sauce. After giving it three or four chews, she nodded excitedly. "It's delicious!" she announced. Everyone applauded one more time in relief and appreciation of this vital moment in history. After hundreds of years of unfulfilled promise, beer had at last become a condiment, and it involved not just a refreshing taste but a chemical reaction of some kind, making it educational as well. It was immediately clear to all of the investors, Ben included, that none of them would ever again know the cruel indignity of having to live more than fifty feet from a major ocean.

"Now you all try beer on expensive sizzle steak," Scientist #1 urged them with barely contained glee. The man with the eyeglass lenses as thick as a standard Bible stepped forward, and a knife and fork were thrust into his hands, which shook now not with fear but excitement. Scientist #2 had already smothered the steak with Magic Thrill Beer, and it was all he could do to wait a full fifteen seconds before he could pounce on it.

"What a time to be alive," the Professor noted to the gathering.

"If we could cut the waiting time from fifteen seconds to twelve, we're looking at a thirty percent margin jump," noted someone else, and there were general frumphs of agreement.

The bespectacled man jammed his fork through the hardened beer and into the luscious steak, commencing to saw the knife back and forth across its tender surface. Almost instantly, a curl of smoke rose up from it. At first Ben thought it was an optical illusion, or maybe leftover vigor from the original grilling, wherever that had taken place. But no, there was more smoke as the knife cut boldly through the beer shell.

"This is very odd," said the guinea pig with no small measure of concern.

"Do not worry," Scientist #1 said. "Reaction of steel and ingredients in beer shell combine to create danger amount of intense heat, but everything all right."

"But I can feel my fingers getting hot," the man replied even as he kept cutting. "It's getting uncomfortable."

Scientist #2 smiled and shook his head. "No alarm to be caused today or any other day. Natural phenomenon when we dabble with necessary."

Ben, who had opened another one of the beers and begun to raise it to his lips, bent over to get a better look at the steak and nearly had his eyebrows singed when the thing suddenly erupted into flame. Teeny-Eyed Woman yelped and Frightening Glasses Man's arm flew up in the air, his shirt cuff on fire. He waved it around madly and began to run in a tight circle as Scientist #1 dashed over to the wall to grab a fire extinguisher which hadn't been inspected in nineteen years.

Bedlam ensued for the eleventh time that month inside the lab. The investors backed away in horror as the man's arm, and soon the rest of his body above the waist, was covered with expired blue foam from the extinguisher, which the scientist controlled with the precision of a gunslinger. He had obviously had to go through this drill before.

"No, you no drink in natural state!" Scientist #2 suddenly yelled at Ben, who had ingested some of the beer from the bottle in his hand. "It cause lung deflation, make scary ghosts in vision!" But it was too late; by the time the bottle had been snatched from Ben's hand, he felt a little funny and needed to sit down. There seemed to be two of everybody, and everybody's double had a stretchy orange head.

Now the first scientist had trained the fire extinguisher on the offending steak itself, but he was having a dickens of a time actually crushing the flame. It had a fondness for the beer shell and really seemed to thrive on its every molecule. There were shouts of anger from the scurrying investors and threats of both lawsuits and vomiting. The man in glasses had collapsed in a chair, dazed and covered in foam that smelled like the inside of a camel. Ben was lucky enough to find the comfort of a chair before every color in the lab inverted at once, causing him to lose his balance. At the same moment, the ghoulish aftertaste of the beer treated his taste buds to a sensation comparable to the experience of licking a television screen.

"I don't feel so good," Ben said almost pleasantly, having lapsed into a mild sedative state of shock as the wildly unnatural ingredients inside the beer helped itself to the good stuff which controlled his cerebral cortex. An eighty-year old captain of industry who was now officially out a half million bucks tried to catch him but lacked the upper body strength to do so. Despite news accounts to the contrary which would appear the next day, Ben did *not* lapse into a coma. He merely fell to the floor in a quiet, well-behaved heap. Even bare seconds before he lost consciousness for the next forty-five minutes, he still clung to the childlike belief that You Like? Laboratories had a hit on its hands.

"Hey, that guy's stealing microscopes!" someone shouted, pointing at the Professor.

"That's absurd!" the Professor cried, backing toward the nearest exit. Two of the objects in question fell out of his sports jacket and his eyes got round and panicked like a raccoon's. He turned and ran for it as both Shinjoda scientists chased after him vengefully. This was the thanks they'd gotten for going through the charade of mangling the English language just to conform to their investors' clichéd image of them as dedicated but simple-minded Japanese tech nerds. When they caught the Professor, they'd have to restrain themselves from beating him silly with their master's degrees in American gothic literature.

The notes and materials that went into the creation of Mutant Beer Sauce were quietly burned that afternoon as Ben Glinton lay morosely in his hospital bed. He was kept under observation for several hours and advised to stay away from carbonated beverages and incandescent lighting for six months. He pretended to be a homeless Swede so as not to have to pay his bill.


He was trying to make tater tots on the stove in his dirty kitchen the next day as he called Roy at the newspaper.

"This is Roy," his future biographer answered the phone within his cubicle, whose third and fourth walls were still on backorder at the Gettysburg warehouse. It was the first call he'd gotten in several days. He assumed it would be his editor demanding an explanation for another disastrous typographical error.

Ben shook the frying pan in which he had condemned so many tater tots to uneven browning and turned the burner to Xtra Hi to bring the revolting process to a conclusion once and for all. "This is Ben Glinton," he said. "I've decided that the book thing you were talking about the other night at Applebee's should be done after all."

"I think we were at the Gap," Roy said, "but this is terrific! I promise you, you won't be disappointed. What made you change your mind?"

"The children," Ben said solemnly. "The children have a right to know what really happened that night at the stadium. Future generations. I saw a kid on the street yesterday, and I wept. Now, about that money you mentioned..."

"Yeah," Roy said, literally moving to the edge of his seat with excitement, "I just have to submit a couple of chapters to Running Clam Press and they'll get the financial ball rolling. It shouldn't take me long to whip those into shape."

"So Running Clam Press is the best you could do?" Ben asked, dumping his wee potato cubes onto a paper towel, which the grease from the pan devoured in about two seconds, leaving the cubes sitting on the surface of the countertop itself. "I've never heard of them."

"Well, they mostly publish zoology textbooks," Roy told him, "but they're anxious to move into other areas." Pressed for time as he spoke, he was also trying to type up an article about a high school lacrosse player who had lost a pinkie toe to a huge chunk of hail, and he realized he had just spelled the kid's name wrong three different times in three different ways, somehow forming three different derogatory terms for Europeans. He decided to turn his attention entirely to the man who was going to make his fortune in the cutthroat world of cheapie sports biographies.

"So how do we get started on this masterpiece?" Ben asked as he poured himself some ginger ale. He had a disturbing mental image of his face plastered on a book jacket and gawking idiotically out the display window of a bus station gift shop.

"Actually, if you have a minute, there's just some quick background info I want to get," Roy said, flipping open a notepad. "First of all, where were you born?"

"Rochester," Ben told him.

"Okay. And you were originally drafted by the Montreal Edmontons, right?"

"Right. Interesting organization. Their press guide was always quoting from the Koran."

"And from there you were traded to the Cannons system."

"No, there was actually three weeks in there when I played for a team overseas," Ben recalled dimly. "In England. The West Brighton Curvers. I remember the club folded after eight games. They never scored a single run. There were rumors of a curse."

"But right after that, the Cannons signed you."

"No, after that the Curvers' entire roster was bought by a two-team winter league in south Texas and our name was changed to the Equatorial Baseball Brigade. We all came back to America, played ten games or so against the Plano Minutemen, lost them all, scored two runs. After that I mostly gave clarinet lessons for a couple of years."

"Oh, this is good stuff," Roy said, scribbling furiously. "Do you think any of the semi-pro guys you played with are still around to be interviewed?"

"Strangely enough, I know exactly where they all are," Ben said. "The winter league disbanded and the players pooled their money and produced a musical that ran for about two years on Broadway. They're all working for Sony now."

"Great!" Roy said. At the height of his note-taking enthusiasm, Gary Wayne, the bullying oaf from Horoscopes, walked by and threw an empty Big Mac wrapper onto Roy's keyboard, muttering "Here ya go, Iowa Boy" as he did so. That Gary Wayne really mushed his marshmallows. Roy would show *him* one day.

Ben didn't like where all this nosy research was going. He popped a tater tot into his mouth and chewed cynically. "So is this going to be one of those nice sepia-tinged sports bios about overcoming this and that and the other thing," he asked, "or are you going to spend half the book talking about that night against the Guardians? I'll back out if this turns out to be a hatchet job, or if there's all kinds of babbling from my ex-wife, not that you could ever track her down in the Israeli army."

"Oh no, honest to goodness no," Roy assured him. "I mean, they told me the unflattering bios sell about fifteen times better than the nice ones, but I said I wouldn't do that kind of thing. I wouldn't want anyone doing that to me. I remember when I was in seventh grade, and I passed my yearbook around for people to sign, and some girls wrote nasty things about the sweaters I wore, and I just felt so—"

"Yeah, well, there's no need for us to dwell on things that happened to you two weeks ago," Ben said. "I guess I'm just looking for some kind of evidence that you're not going to *In Cold Blood* me.*"

A bell went off inside Roy's head and on the microwave oven in the break room at the exact same time. "I've got it!" he exclaimed. "I was going to open up the book with the crowd filing into the stadium that night of game seven, but as a good faith gesture, why don't we start it off by showing you today, doing charity work? Right from the first page it'll get people to like you. How does that sound?"

Ben squeezed the grease from another tater tot and looked up at the ceiling quizzically. "Um, charity work?" he asked, trying not to sound completely flummoxed.

"Yeah," said Roy. "You still have a hand in all that from your playing days, right?"

"Um...yes, very much so," Ben improvised. "Of course. A lot of people think we do all that stuff for the photo ops and because the teams make us do it. But the exact opposite is true. I'm still up to my rubbery butt in charity. I actually have something tonight. I should be getting dressed, in fact."

"Great, I have off tonight!" Roy said, prematurely smelling both a Pulitzer Prize for non-fiction and an Oscar for Best Screenplay, Material Adapted from Another Medium. "I can show up wherever you're going and cover it, and chapter one will be halfway done."

"Yes indeed," Ben said, swallowing the last of his lunch. "That's definitely the way to go. I've got to find the address of the place on the internet, and then what I'll do is call you back and tell you where to meet me."

"Okay, I'll be here all day," Roy told him. "If I'm not at my desk, I'll be in the break room, and if I'm not in the break room, I'm just down at the soda machine and I'll be right back."

"Super. Bye."

"Bye!"

Ben hung up the phone and rubbed his unshaven face. For the third time this year, a harmless lie to someone he'd just met was going to cause him to have to create a fake charity. But no, he vowed to himself, *this* time he wasn't going to waste his precious money having fictitious banners made or hiring students from the local community college to portray blind people. This was getting out of hand. He would put on his thinking cap and methodically grind out a solution, in just the same way he used to methodically grind himself out of a batting slump by waving his bat wildly at any pitch that was even remotely close to the plate. Obviously the whole process would go much more smoothly if a two-hour nap refreshed his brain clankings, so he started planning for that right away.

## 4. It's Easy to Fool People if You Have a Heart of Darkness

Ever-reliable, ever-pliable Harold lived three miles away from Ben in a very nice new suburban enclave called Windemere Hillswallowsea. Ben got in his weepy Ford Escort at six-thirty and weaved and swerved over there without calling first, as was his usual modus operandi. Harold was almost never engaged in anything important anyway; after work he just tended to come home, kick up his feet, and age poorly. Ben left his car in the driveway and trotted up to the front door, grabbing the mail on his way in order to score some good neighbor points. He did not realize it was outgoing mail. He knocked several times, tapping one foot impatiently.

Harold eventually opened the door and poked his head out. "Oh, hey Ben," he said. "I can't come out and do anything tonight. We have the police over here talking to us about those two weird ritual murders that happened in the neighborhood. It's pretty scary."

"Well, that's fairly horrifying," Ben agreed, "but I have myself a bit of a dilemma," Ben told him. "I told you about the guy who wanted to write my biography, right?"

"Yeah, that's great!" Harold said with a smile devoid of all irony. "When does that whole process start?"

"Tonight, in fact," Ben said. "Which brings me to my point. Does your kid still have the flu?"

Harold tilted his head, not certain he had heard Ben correctly. "Gordy? Um...yeah, he's in bed. Temperature's down to almost normal, though. He'll probably go back to school tomorrow or the next day. Why?"

Ben rubbed his hands together. "Yeah, I'm gonna need him to pretend he's dying of something so that my biographer thinks I'm visiting him as a charity case."

Harold, who had heard descriptions of far stranger schemes tumble from Ben's lips in recent years, simply looked pained. "Ben...can't this wait? I want to hear what the police have to tell us. The murders keep getting closer to our street..."

"It won't take too long, and the guy is coming over here in like fifteen minutes. All you have to do is tell Gordy to keep kind of motionless in bed and look sick and pale. He's unnaturally skinny, isn't he? I seem to remember him being unnaturally skinny. With a little bean head."

"Well..." Harold began, "...what are we going to tell Deenie?"

"Just tell her I'm visiting Gordy out of concern, you know," Ben offered.

"She's definitely not going to believe that," Harold said.

"Then we'll say you invited me over for dinner. You haven't eaten, right? What are you going to have, I'm starving anyway."

"I don't know," Harold said with tangible fear, "but I saw her scooping out a melon and putting raw turkey into it. This was the solution you came up with? A lie? Using Gordy?"

Ben pouted. "I am not a theoretical physicist, Harold. I am not an expert in space geometry. I never claimed to have an IQ of six hundred. I'm just a guy who's trying to keep from having to get a job and has to trick some sportswriter into thinking I'm a good person to do it. I don't think a court in the world would put me in jail for not graduating from Yale with a degree in computational mathema—"

"Okay, *okay,"* Harold said, stepping back to let him inside. "We can try something, maybe it'll work."

"Just one thing," Ben said. "I don't think this guy is gonna recognize you from the Cannons, but your last name's on your mailbox. That should probably come off there."

"Those letters would have to be scraped off, Ben," Harold said. "It's next to impossible."

"Okay, so do you maybe have a black marker, one of those thick ones?"

"I doubt it."

"Harold, you work for a company that makes them. I know they give you a case every Christmas."

Harold closed his eyes. "If this goes wrong somehow, Deenie might not let me hang around with you anymore. She keeps giving me these ultimatums."

"If, schmiff," Ben said, stepping in and closing the door behind him. "Let's get this done, we'll have dinner, then we'll go bowling and ask about that Dented Lane Special you've been wondering about for so many years."


"Hi there, Gordy," Roy Skinla of the Harrisburg Daily Fact Holder said to Harold's son a half hour later, after the eleven year old had been briefed and debriefed and issued a written quiz about his responsibilities regarding the evening's shameful deception. The always adventurous Gordy had agreed to play along on the condition that his father take him some upcoming weekend to the National Ice Cream Museum in Scranton, whose cafeteria featured a banana split that levitated. Roy and Ben and Harold stood beside his bed, looking down at him in carefully measured pity and empathy as he cowered beneath sheets bearing the faces of some superheroes whose licensing fees had definitely seen better days. One of the men was wondering what sort of heartless, absent God could possibly strike down such an innocent young lad with Kretzig-Beckler Syndrome, while the other two were trying to remember whether it was Jim Kretzig or Bobby Beckler who batted ninth for the Norristown

Conjurers of the Lesser Pennsylvania Instructional League from 1997 to 1998. Either way, Roy had bought the illusion hook, line, and sinker. He hadn't seen much real pain in his sheltered twenty-three years and had never even been to a funeral, so he was pretty overwhelmed as soon as he set foot in Gordy's room.

"Hello, sir," Gordy replied to his greeting, offering up a weak hand which Roy shook ever so gently. Gordy's mouth sported not one but two thermometers. Harold removed one of them and examined it with a worried look on his face.

"Yes, ninety-eight point six," he said with a sigh. "Very worrying. I'd better call Doctor Yastrzemski sometime this month."

"Doctor Yastrzemski, good man," Ben added, nodding assuredly. "I've met him many times during my charity visits to the eye ward."

"I'm hungry, Dad," Gordy said, a little off-script but still convincingly. "Can I have a hot dog?"

"I don't know if your system can take that right now," Harold said. "Maybe when your visitors leave. Look here, son, this is baseball superstar Ben Glinton. Your wish has come true!"

Gordy did his best to pretend he didn't know this kind-hearted stranger at all, though he had of course met him several times at the house. Ben was best known to Gordy as the man who had spent an admirable amount of time one afternoon adjusting the basketball hoop in the driveway so that he could attempt a slam dunk just like his real hero, T.K. "To Dunk a Mockingbird" Corkiston. Other memories of his father's slightly younger, slightly messier friend included an accident-enriched overnight campout at Shenandoah National Park and a birthday party at Chuck-e-Cheese's during which Ben had loudly declared the pizza to be the best thing he had ever tasted in his life.

"Hello, sir," Gordy said. "Have you come to watch me deal with the pain?"

"There'll be no more pain in your future, kid, not if I have anything to say about it," Ben predicted boldly. "By summertime I just know you'll be out of this bed and tossing around a baseball of your own to kids much, much sicker than you."

"So, he just sent you a postcard asking you to come and you showed up?" Roy asked Ben, taking his notepad from his vest pocket.

"I have a policy, don't I, Gordy," Ben said, patting the child's head, which had been treated with warm water to produce the desired shiny effect. "Any kid who wants me to visit him on his deathbed, I'm there. Right, kid?"

"Yay!" Gordy said, starting to enjoy himself. This had all the fun of telling his Mom and Dad that he was too sick to go to school, but with even more adults in the room to lie to.

"I guess it's easier when the kid happens to live three miles away," Roy noted.

"Three miles, ten miles, no distance is too far for a young fan," Ben said. "Kid, how'd you like an autographed cap?"

"Okay," Gordy said. He tried rolling his eyes around in his sockets briefly to improve his performance but then stopped when he thought it would be a little too much like that awful Keanu Reeves guy. God, he was just so *terrible.*

"What are the symptoms of Kretzig-Beckler Syndrome, for my notes," Roy asked Harold quietly, most disturbed by the rolling of the child's eyes.

"I've been reading about it in my off hours," Ben said before Harold could say something to queer the deal. From his back pocket he took a Cannons cap which he had bought at the mall that afternoon and scribbled his name on it. "It can be anything from a chronic light fever to an unquenchable desire for meat, as we just saw."

"Eventually his kidneys begin to migrate unless we give him constant penicillin," Harold offered.

"Medicine," Ben said sadly. "It can cure sickness, but nothing else." He handed the hat to Gordy.

"This logo is out of date," the boy noted. "They got a new one last year."

"Yeah, it really helped, too," Ben said cynically.

A quiet moment passed. Harold leaned over and put the hat on Gordy. Ben had been clever enough to get the extra large one to make his head seem the size of a grape.

"Well, we should probably be thinking about wrapping this up," Ben said. "There's no need to excite Gordy too much."

"Why don't we play a game?" Gordy asked, sitting up in bed.

"Ah, well, yeah, you know, Mr. Pillick doesn't need a bunch of strangers hanging around his house all night," Ben said. "You take care now, Gordy. You know where to reach me. Obviously you do, because that's how you contacted me for this charity visit. It's not exactly a state secret where to find me when people are in need. I practically have a website."

"But Mr. Glinton, if you played a game with Gordy for a couple of hours, my wife and I could have an evening together when the police leave," Harold suggested.

"Why are the police here anyway?" Roy asked.

"The Pool Skimmer Strangler," Ben informed him. "He's getting kind of close."

"Why don't we stay?" Roy suggested. "I really have nowhere to be, and I could use some quiet time to compile an outline for the book."

"Please, Mr. Glinton?" Gordy asked. "It would make me get better so I won't die so fast."

Ben plastered an icy grin on his face. "Ah, yeah, anything you say, kid. I'm sure someone somewhere will record *Scarface* for me." He elbowed Harold, who was already on his way out the door. Ben made a mental note to destroy his friend's life sometime this week, preferably before daylight savings time began. As Roy sat down in one corner, rolling up his shirt sleeves, Gordy scampered out of his bed with alarming energy.

"Be careful there, Gordy," Ben advised him nervously, "use your spine spasms wisely, because they could, you know, disappear all at once."

"He doesn't seem that sick, really," Roy said softly to Ben as Gordy dug through his closet, which bore pictures of various baseball superstars, none of them Ben Glinton or even anyone who even shared either one of his initials. "I think it's possible his father tricked you just to get you to come over here."

"Yeah, that guy has some shifty eyes, there's no doubt," Ben agreed. "I hate to cause trouble, though. One round of Yahtzee and we'll be out of here."

Gordy emerged from the messy closet with a colorful box that seemed a little too heavy for him. He set it down on a card table beside the bed. "Let's play APBA Football!" he said. "I'll bet I can beat you."

"Football, yeah, sure," Ben said. Gordy sat down in a green plastic chair beside the card table. With no other chair available, Ben lowered himself onto the edge of the child's bed. "What do we do, do we make one of those little paper things and push it across the table and try to get it to hang over the edge? That's what we used to do in school."

"No way," Gordy said, removing the top of the box and pulling out what looked to be hundreds of playing cards, a group of large charts, and an artful representation of a football field. "You have to play a whole game like the pros do, and call all the plays and like that."

"Hmmm," Ben said, thinking that Parcheesi would have been more suited to his taste. He had really put a hurting on some Parcheesi people in his day.

"First you have to pick a team and fill out your starting offense and defense," Gordy said, taking red and white dice from the box and setting a scoresheet and pencil in front of Ben. "I'm gonna be the Miami Stimuli because they won the Super Bowl last year."

"Well, that doesn't seem totally fair, but whatever," Ben said, sorting through the stack of rubber banded cards. "I guess I'll be the Portland Rabids. Good cheerleaders."

"Oh man, you're in trouble," Gordy cackled as he began to sort through his team. "They have the worst linebackers ever."

Ben shuffled through the cards in his hand and saw all the names of last year's Rabids represented. Below each name was listed the player's position and a simple grid of red and black numbers. "So how does this work?" he asked. "All the players do different things, they're not all the same?"

"Right," Gordy said, dividing his players between offense and defense. "The better players have higher ratings and stuff. After you write them down, we kick off and then we choose plays and roll the dice and go by the player ratings to see how much yardage they ran for or whether a pass was complete and stuff."

"Good God," Ben said, worried. "For every play? How long is this gonna take?"

"As long as it takes for me to kick your butt!" Gordy said cheerfully. "I think I'll start Brien Martin at quarterback instead of Jello Anthony. It's not fair that Brien Martin never got to start just because he kept throwing to the other team."

Ben did a double-take when he came across a wide receiver's card bearing the name Spike Vail. "Oh God, I forgot he plays *football* too," Ben groaned. "Hey Gordy, he has an 'A' on his card, what does that mean?"

"It means he's real real good," Gordy said. "Just like he was last year."

Ben shook his head and dropped the card off to the side of the miniature football field, which Gordy was adorning with a little plastic yard marker. Sighing and feeling his whole night go up in smoke little by little, he began to go through his cards to select a starting lineup, going out of his way to leave Spike Vail out of the equation.

"Hey Roy, do us a favor and grab us a couple of Yoo Hoos or something from downstairs," Ben said. "I got a sick kid here who needs hydration."

"Sure," Roy said and disappeared eagerly, way too excited to be out of his apartment for the evening. His roommates were both jerks, and girls still avoided him like the plague for his boyish face, freckles, and habit of constantly smiling when this life was so obviously such a miasma of despair.

As soon as Roy was out of the room, Ben looked at Gordy sternly. "All right, kid, is there like a super-speed version of this game we can do so I can get out of here?"

Gordy shook his head and straightened his cards and looked through the playing boards until he found one bearing various kickoff results. "Dad said you had to stay a while so he and Mom can kiss and stuff or he'd tell that man you're with that you teach people how to read on Saturdays. He even picked out a place you would have to show up at."

Ben gritted his teeth. "Pillick, you weak-hitting snake," he whispered. "All right, all right. Let's just move this along, huh? I'm thirty-five years old, I don't feel like playing board games with my nights. I have pillows to cry into."


11:38 p.m.

Ben Glinton was hunched over the miniature football field on the card table before him like a man who had just bet his life savings on Red 21 at four in the morning and was waiting for the poker-faced croupier to spin the roulette wheel. The remains of five empty Yoo Hoo bottles sat at his left elbow, and at his right elbow was the scoresheet which described in exhaustive statistical detail the night's third and final football showdown between himself and the eleven year old budding tactician Gordy Pillick. Ben's Houston Mudthumpers were down to Gordy's L.A. Smooths 27-21 with almost no time remaining on the game clock, which was represented by full and half slash marks on the sheet.

"Come on, Ben, pick a play and stick with it," Roy Skinla was telling him from twelve inches away. A couple of hours before, he had taken a chair from the kitchen and set it up as close as possible to the action, and he now seemed almost as hypnotized by it as Ben himself. His eyes darted from Gordy to Ben and back again. Gordy had selected his defensive call and now could only wait for Ben to either complete his freakish comeback or fail trying.

"Don't pressure me!" Ben hissed, wiping his forehead for the seventh time in eighteen minutes. This foolish rube from the Midwest didn't seem to realize how much he had scratched and clawed not only to get back into this game but to win the last one and draw even with Gordy, one to one. Gordy's willingness to throw deep on third and short and give the ball to obscure running backs again and again had flummoxed him for the past five hours. Oh, the kid was going down for good all right. It had to be done. This last play—a 4th and goal from the runt's 6 yard line—had to assure it. It *had* to. Meanwhile, Gordy, cool as a Fender guitar case, just sat there smugly.

"What is that incessant *tapping* sound?" Ben blurted out just as he was getting comfortable with selecting an intended receiver.

"Um, Ben, you're doing that with the pencil," Roy pointed out.

"Okay, okay, we're moving, we're moving," Ben said, taking three deep breaths. "I still have one time out left, right?"

"Doesn't matter if you don't score on this play," Gordy said. He had changed into his polka dot pajamas at about nine, and given up any pretense of illness at about ten-thirty. Roy had not really noticed.

"Okay," Ben said. "I know your feeble little child's brain can't handle the fact that I could possibly run straight into the line in this situation, but that's just what I'm gonna do, mini-man. Inside run, Jeff Downey, and let's see your defense, short stack!"

Gordy grinned and bounced up and down in his plastic chair. "I played a nine man line!" he shouted. "Gotcha!"

"Oh, you little neckless *imp,*" Ben said, picking up his dice shaker and rattling the contents within, a sound that had become hauntingly rhythmic to everyone in the room and to Deenie Pillick, who just wanted to get some sleep but could hear that infernal *chicka-chicka-chicka* through the wall every single time. She vowed to redouble her efforts to believe that her husband's irritating friend Ben had some minor but influential part in everything from rising divorce rates in the United States to the disturbing rollbacks of individual freedoms in Vladimir Putin's new Russia.

With a decisive flick of the wrist, Ben released his two zealous dice upon the table as an imagined capacity crowd rose to their feet in agonized suspense. The dice crashed selflessly into one of the empty Yoo Hoo bottles and caromed back onto the football field. The red one settled showing a 6, while the smaller white one kept spinning defiantly, causing Ben's eyes to glow a fiery orange as his blood pressure rose to levels previously not known since his last dozen or so phone fights with his ex-wife. In his tortured mind he imagined his running back (16 carries for 86 yards so far) daring to dart to the outside with brilliant improvisation and stiff-arming the entire Smooths secondary in an attempt to hit paydirt. Roy put his hands to his head and sucked his breath in as his mouth formed a gaping O.

The white die came to rest. It was a 2. Ben felt his lungs leap into his mouth as he checked Jeff Downey's card to see what the injury-prone and devoutly petulant running back did for him on this Play of Plays. Downey gave him a simple numerical result of 18, usually good for an admirable chunk of yardage when referenced on the playing boards. But in his simple, uneducated peasant's heart, Ben knew a bad moon was rising.

"Inside the ten against a run defense, that's only a 4 yard gain!" Gordy cried, confirming it on the Inside Run chart. "No score! I win!"

"Ouch, so close!" Roy said, laughing and patting Gordy on the head.

*"You sons of bitches, I'll kill you all!"* Ben cried inappropriately, and flopped back onto Gordy's bed in coniptic pain. His knees rose up and slammed against the underside of the card table, causing the cards, the dice, and the football field to jump up in

the air. The empty bottles rolled off the table and onto the carpet. Gordy cackled and clapped his hands.

"That was fun!" Gordy said. "You probably shouldn't have punted on that last possession. I should probably go to bed now."

"Yeah, we've really kept the kid up, Ben," Roy said, standing up, stretching, yawning, and collecting his feeble attempt at an outline. He had not taken a single note since the third quarter of the first game played tonight, when Ben had performed a most curious victory dance upon seeing his team block a field goal, a dance which Roy didn't think he'd ever be able to describe in mere words.

Ben remained motionless on the bed, staring at the ceiling like Martin Sheen contemplating the mysteries of Saigon in the opening scene of *Apocalypse Now.* "It's wasn't me," he muttered to no one in particular. "Pat Premo is the worst quarterback in the history of the world. It wasn't me."

"You're the one who started him," Gordy noted, trying to push Ben off the bed but managing only to roll him onto his side. A bit of drool threatened to escape from the defeated coach's mouth but was unable.

"It's just a game, Ben," Roy said, grabbing one of Ben's wrists and hauling him up to his feet. Like a prize fighter at the end of his endurance, Ben wobbled a bit but managed to remain upright, if only for cosmetic reasons.

"A game...yes," Ben said, obviously meaning just the opposite. "We will go into the night now, and forget all about it." The soot-streaked coal-stokers who lived in his brain were doing their best to shovel in enough fuel to get it up and running again, but there seemed to be a severe unexplained jam in the works. Ben allowed Roy to guide him out of the room as if he'd just undergone an appendectomy and was wearing a blue gown and plastic slippers.

"See ya!" Gordy said to them both, and in the next moment he had turned his lights out and dashed under his covers once again to dream the easy sleep of the victorious. He replayed his players' finest highlights in his mind as he drifted off, augmenting them with the exclamations of booth announcers who cautiously guaranteed Gordy a spot in the Hall of Fame as soon as he left elementary school.

Roy didn't like the look of Ben's face as they walked down the stairs into the living room. The five hour session of APBA Football seemed to have possessed him unnaturally from the very first moments. There had been a wicked gleam in his eye as he sorted through the players' cards, taken the dice shaker in his hand, kept track of passing and rushing yardage on the scoresheet. Every simple coaching decision he had made had been prefaced by intense silences and bouts of pointless pacing. Ben's irritation with having to play the game had quickly given way to utter immersion, as if he had forgotten how to differentiate between an actual sport and the miniature one that had only been created to pleasantly expend some spare time. Ben had given Roy the details of his most recent financial setback during halftime of game two when Ben had finally allowed Gordy to briefly break the action in order to go to the bathroom. Perhaps that final humiliation had done something to him somehow, made him unable to accept any more defeat of any kind. More bothersome still to Roy was the feeling that he himself had been overcome with as the games went on into the night. He had found himself gazing at the proceedings with rapt attention...and he'd been touched with a tingling feeling of competitive drive that he had not experienced since that dark night in May of 2001, of which he would tell no one, no one *ever...*

"Try not to wake up Mr. Pillick," Roy forced himself to whisper to Ben before his mind could touch upon a most unpleasant memory. In the living room, Harold was sitting slumped over in his easy chair in front of the TV set, which had been showing *The Goonies* when he fell asleep, but with the late hour had segued delightfully into softcore pornography. Ben caught sight of a bikini-clad woman making eyes at a brawny man in dirty mechanic's overalls as the two of them stood in the Sistine Chapel before he and Roy suddenly found themselves outdoors on the front step. For a moment Ben was genuinely confused as to how it had gotten dark. It seemed to him they had pulled up to the house just an hour or so before.

"I wonder," he mused as Roy put his sport jacket back on, one which was almost two sizes too big for him, "I wonder if that company makes a baseball game too, by any chance."

"I don't know," Roy said, yawning. "But, um, Ben, do you by any chance have a gambling addiction or anything like that? Not for the book. I'm just wondering."

"Don't be silly," Ben said. "I just like to take my board games seriously, that's all. Ask the fallen who have dared take me on in

Clue. I do regret telling the kid after that blocked field goal that I was going to eat his brain stem with crackers and grape jelly, but hey, I used to be an athlete. We get carried away."

"Yeah, I guess," Roy said. "I'll call you tomorrow afternoon, okay, and maybe we can meet up and I can ask you some more questions and we won't get so sidetracked."

"A baseball game...yes," Ben said to the night air, totally ignoring Roy and remaining on the front step as his biographer drove off through the neighborhood that NBC's *Dateline* would soon call "a brimming cauldron of hot tasty death" upon the Pool Skimmer Strangler's shocking capture. "What a thing *that* would be," he added for good measure. Eventually he crossed the lawn in his reverie and began the long walk back to town, which he completed almost halfway before he realized he had actually driven to Harold's that night and had left his car in his driveway. He was forced to blow five dollars on a cab ride back. Deenie P. Pillick happened to see him return for his car through a bathroom window. She called him a doofus and an 'ankle-mouth' under her breath and went back into the bedroom, where her increasingly doughy husband, an ex-ballplayer who at least knew how to comport himself somewhat, slept on, unaware that his best friend's life had just changed irrevocably and in somewhat silly fashion.

## 5. See, If Only You Could Plug it in Somehow and Make it Light Up, Then You'd Really Have Something

APBA International did in fact produce a tabletop baseball simulation for sale on the American consumer market, and had for the past fifty-five years or so. While this was a statement that should not have too dramatically affected the existence of an adult male of average intelligence and abilities, in Ben's case it was very soon to become a fact of Big Bang-level significance.

He found out about the baseball game through his explorations in Foolish Human, Your Doom Is Assured, a local board game shop located above a volunteer fire department on Chestnut Street. He had been in there once before, to buy some replacement Boggle score pads as a Christmas gift for an uncle he truly despised on every conceivable level, but now he had a far loftier sense of mission as he entered the musty, dimly lit single room that comprised the store and was greeted by Bill Butters, the shop's proprietor. As always, the weighty, fifty year old Butters was seated at a rickety gaming table in the middle of the room across from a man familiar to habitual patrons as Six-Sided Sid, a very tall, nervous fellow who always had a cigar in his mouth and who had last eaten a meal shortly before the inauguration of Gerald Ford. The men had taken a break from engaging in a complex simulation of an incredibly obscure military campaign that took place during three hours of the Boer War to wax poetic on the vicissitudes of the Australian army circa 1899 as they drank warm Sprite and generally lived life at one eightieth of the speed of regular humans. Ben waved off Butters's offer to help and just said he was looking around, not wanting to witness the sight of the man trying to hoist himself out of his folding chair.

Ben nosed through the shelves filled with war games, games involving the building of interstellar colonies and declaring war with them, games in which one did battle with everything from zombies to mutant bananas, and games in which no one fought at all; these last usually had a thick layer of dust on them. Ben spotted APBA Baseball sitting beside a display case offering dice you could see through. This, it seemed, was the Master Edition, an apparent upgrade from the one the casual public bought, offering more managerial challenges. To his surprise, the box revealed that the company was based out of Lancaster, just a mouthful of miles away. He grabbed the game and noted that the box contained player cards from the most recent pro season. He took it over to the cash register, which looked as though Bill Butters had scavenged it from Boer War surplus.

"I don't suppose that you have any older card sets for this game," Ben said to Butters.

The shop owner tilted his head back at a dramatic angle and appeared to scan the ceiling tiles for the answer to the question. "Let me think now," he mused. "Seems to me that a young fella came in here a few weeks ago wanting to trade an older card set for the new edition of Alien Salt Mine. That's the one where you supervise the construction of an alien salt mine on Neptune."

"No, no, no, you supervise the construction of an alien salt mine in Salt Mines of Lankhmar," Six-Sided Sid scolded him severely. "Alien Salt Mine just lets you *plan* the mine."

"I think I know the difference between Salt Mines of Lankhmar and Alien Salt Mine, you wheezing freeloader," Butters countered. This wasn't true; when it came to the alien salt mine construction genre of board games, no one could hold a candle to Sid's acumen.

"So he had an older card set he wanted to trade, eh?" Ben interjected impatiently.

"Yeah," Bill Butters said. "In fact, I don't think I got around to pricing it yet. Let's see..." He peered below the counter and laboriously knelt down to fish around below it. In seconds he had come out with a long thin cardboard box. He opened the top to show the 600-odd cards therein, all in excellent condition. He picked one out at random. "Dean Patino," he read off the card. "Says he hit .336...that could only have been—"

"2002," Ben said right away. He had struck paydirt. "How much for the set?"

"You got any games to trade?" Bill Butters asked him. "I'd take ten dollars off if you had a copy of Sherlock Holmes: Railroad Tycoon. Can't seem to get it from any of my distributors."

"No, just cash," Ben said, unable to drag his eyes away from the box of cards. In that moment he would have given this big tub of goo his shoes, his windbreaker, his mother, and his coupon for a free medium soda at Arby's with the purchase of any regular roast beef sandwich, a coupon that was good not just locally but *nationwide*.

"Name your price, local merchant," he declared, unafraid of the consequences. "I have a long day ahead of me."


Ben drove home as fast as he could but made himself wait to pore through the player cards until after he had examined the contents of APBA Baseball itself. He dumped everything on his kitchen table at about noon, poured himself some stale lemonade, and got to work. As with the game Harold's son had obviously cheated at somehow the night before, this one was colorful and simple to learn while offering him a multitude of managerial options. He could call for stolen base attempts, sacrifice bunts, intentional walks, play his infield in, pinch hit, change pitchers with abandon, try for a hit and run, et cetera, et cetera. In other words, all the strategies that he had suggested on occasion to Greeny St. Clair only to get a bitter frown in return. The man had not been the most adventurous of managers. It was said that Greeny hadn't looked at a baseball rulebook in decades, and that if no one had remembered to tell him that it wasn't legal anymore for batters to request certain kinds of pitches from the mound, he would still be yelling out for slow underhand changeups right down the middle.

Beginning today, all that was in the past.

Ben read over the rules of the game and then turned to the box of player cards. He thumbed through the 2002 teams, seeing the names of so many of the players he had known and competed against. Here was Dave "Three Bean" Barton, a Pittsburgh Pilots shortstop who in 1999 had hit three consecutive batters in the head during a spring training game. The nickname, printed right on the card, had stuck to him even after he had literally changed his last name to Frankenstein in an effort to distract people from his old stigma. Here amongst the roster of the perennially bottom-dwelling Milwaukee Suds was the card of Lee Wykes, a free-swinging catcher whom Ben had roomed with during his two years in the minors. For years it had been incredibly obvious to anyone with even a single functioning eye that Wykes could be struck out on any pitch in at the knees, yet pitchers kept trying to get him out high. The day they realized their folly, Wykes knew, was the day he would have to go to work in his father's cement trussing and fabrication business. That day came in 2002. The card representing the efforts of Boston Harbors journeyman starter Bryce Eldynk showed his birth date as being 1965, which Ben knew Bryce had lied about. In 2002 he had actually been a whopping 46 years old. He couldn't believe he had been getting away with it. What the card did reflect quite accurately, Ben would later discover as he played the game, was that Bryce had the strike zone accuracy that season of a blind man pushed out the top window of a ten story building and forced to drink a fifth of whiskey on the way down. And of course, here was Spike Vail's card, revealing that he could play almost any position and play it with a very high numerical rating. Ben growled, actually growled as he put the card back in the stacks. He didn't like the looks of all those 1s on it. If they meant something good for the player, as they did in APBA Football, then Spike Vail was regarded by the hard-working folks at the game company as quite the legend indeed. His nickname, "Lord God and Creator," stood out officiously in bold type.

He paused for a moment when he came to the twenty-odd player cards representing the Kentucky Cannons team that had pushed the New York Guardians to game seven of the championship series before...well, before things didn't pan out quite as people in the south wanted them to. Ben closed his eyes and wondered at this incredible feeling he had. It was as if the years since his retirement from baseball had all been leading up to this moment. The only time he could remember feeling this sort of elation before was when he was sixteen years old and his father had foolishly given him the keys to a company car so that Ben could run out and "just grab *Native Son* from the library." The total cost of chain-hoisting that car's twisted hulk out of Black Stump Swamp a mere fifteen minutes later had cost the Glinton family no less than two vacations to Knott's Berry Farm.

Ben went through the roster card by card. The names of his teammates, reduced conveniently to inert and silent data, were more familiar than the condition of his own toenails. Joey Williamson. John Kuchar. Clyde "The Dingo" Ringo. Even Harold was there. Harold "Wannabe" Pillick, shortstop and second baseman. Ben took a moment to make a mental note of the physical appearance of Harold's card so that he could quickly recognize by sight what symbols and numbers comprised a truly terrible player.

He finally came to his own card. He lifted it up before his eyes as if it were the beautiful shiny diamond that Harrison Ford had swiped in the opening sequence of *Raiders of the Lost Ark.* He was listed as an outfielder rated a 1. Checking back over the rules, he realized that this was not such a flattering description of his fielding skills. That was okay; he had never claimed to be a marksman with the ball. He was delighted to see that his twelve stolen bases kept him from being rated a slow runner. His statistics from 2002 were even shown. He could have cried out to the world that he had really batted .274 that year and not .272, and had been denied those two precious points by an official scorer who'd had it in for him ever since he'd referred to the man in an interview as "dumber than a box of snot." Ben took a quick look around the kitchen to make sure no one was watching him, and then ran a finger over the numbers on his card, touching them lovingly. It was him! It was Ben Glinton!

Then his eyes fell on the nickname assigned to him by the card makers and his face went beet red. **Benjamin "The Blemish" Glinton** read the words below the date and town of his birth.

"Oh, that's real nice, you ankle-mouths!" Ben shouted in the unsanitary stillness of his kitchen. Just for that, he had no intention of ever, ever buying an APBA T-shirt off the company's website.

The orange phone hanging from a nail beside the refrigerator rang at that moment, and Ben rose to answer it still holding his card. "Hello?" he said.

"Hi Ben, it's Roy Skinla," said a voice over a scratchy cell phone connection. "Sorry if you can't hear me so well, I'm at some place called Meat Colony 604 grabbing some lunch before I have to go cover a soccer game somewhere. It's a church league, but it's actually pretty cool."

"Yeah, what's up?" Ben asked him, noting that the pristine condition of his card suggested that the kid who had owned the set before him probably never used Ben once. He hoped the little pants-wearer had problems in life.

"I was just starting to collect some basic background info on you for the book, and I wanted to get some quotes from some of the guys you used to play with. Are you still in touch with any of them?"

Ben was about to automatically speak Harold's name but then caught himself. A whole night of deception almost went right out the window. "Actually, not really," he told Roy. "Most of those guys kind of turned on me after that night in Lexington, you know. Good riddance, too."

There was a sudden burst of static on the other end of the line and when Roy came back on he apologized. "There's this big ugly guy in line who just cut in front of me," Roy said softly. "Why do people have to be such jerks?"

"Couldn't tell ya," Ben said, reading over the playing charts that came with the game, one for each men-on-base situation, and casting an eye on the sheet of Master Symbols, which further honed each player's skill ratings. "Anyway, I think you'll probably have to call those guys direct if you want stories from them."

"Yeah, okay," said Roy. He paused briefly to place an order for a burger and fries at the counter. Ben heard enough keywords to figure out that Roy was trying in vain to get the employees of the joint to prepare his meal in some kind of imitation of healthy eating. At Meat Colony 604, this was a practical impossibility. Many had died. "So," Roy continued, "do you suppose to find some of those guys I could call the Cannons office and maybe talk to a guy in...would it be called Personnel? Or Media Relations? Or no, wait, would they maybe, um, get mad if I called? Maybe I should just write."

"Not on such intimate terms with the big leagues, are you, Roy," Ben said, quite amused.

"Well, you know, I hope this book will be my entry into that world, I guess," Roy said. "The guy who covers the Wilkes-Barre Sky Turks for the paper gets free passes to the games sometimes. Man, that would be aces. Anyway, while I have you on the line...your old high school told me that it wasn't you who played the Mandy Patinkin part in the Drama Club production of *Yentl*. It was some kid named Phil Riviere. He was in the Wisconsin phone book so I called him and he claimed he took over the part after Barbra Streisand herself called the school and asked that you be replaced. Do you want to set the record straight on that?"

"Could we do this later, Roy?" Ben asked. "I'm on the verge of something over here. Might be important material for the book, actually. Big doings in the works."

"Oh, great!" Roy said so loudly that it created a burst of static on the other end.

"Yeah. Why don't we get together at the Meat Colony for dinner after your little soccer show and I can tell you what's going on."

Ben could detect a definite note of anguish in Roy's voice. "Okay, I guess I can eat a salad then, that'll balance out this hamburger."

"No salads at the Colony," Ben noted. "Well, not according to the traditional definition. Meet me there at eight."

"Sure," Roy said, and beeped out.

Ben set the phone ringer on Mute and sat down again. He spent another ten minutes or so reading the various board results and just rolling the dice again and again, seeing what sorts of feats his card was capable of producing. He had never had so much fun with batting practice. He hit grounders, fly outs, singles, the occasional double. True to real life, homeruns eluded him. After a while he got up to use the phone once again. Though the game could be played solitaire, he desperately needed someone to square off against to begin Phase One of the Secret Project Only He Could Now Understand. An insatiable thirst for competition began to brew in his stomach like a hot fresh batch of Magic Thrill Beer. Needing a warm body to fill in as opposing manager, he commenced to do what he had done so often: relentlessly hassle Harold Pillick to take the afternoon off work, drive over to the apartment, and just do whatever Ben said without too much complaint. It was a scheme that still worked at a percentage far higher than Ben's record of getting on base safely in his six-year career with the Cannons.

### 6. Why Ben Was Never Asked to Teach at Stanford

"Oh, you little kidney-necked floor-sucking *finger-foot!*"

Ben's face turned a high-gloss red for the eleventh time in as many minutes as his dice, bounding recklessly from the little yellow cup squished in his left hand, promptly came to rest on his kitchen table and offered only certain death. He cast a baleful eye at the card of one Dan Patterson, the 2002 Cannons' erstwhile second baseman, and knew immediately that the self-satisfied punk who used to refer to himself as "the ultimate ladies man" had just popped out weakly to third, ending the game. Harold clapped his hands and emitted a childlike yelp as his Las Vegas Jacks closed out the series 4 to 1. He swept his roster off the table as he heartlessly nudged Ben's base runners, represented by tiny red discs, off the playing diamond set between them.

"I'm giving the series MVP award to myself," Harold said happily, checking over the five heavily notated scoresheets he and Ben had plowed through over the course of the past three and a half hours as the afternoon light dissolved into dusk outside the grimy kitchen window.

*"What?"* Ben asked, mouth agape. "Okay, first of all, *I* was managing the Cannons, not you, Opey. Secondly, you may have noticed that I put you into the lineup for exactly one inning in game three, and only because Clyde Ringo got hurt turning that double

play, and I pinch hit for you! With Bud Pibble. A *pitcher,* if you'll recall. A *devout Christian* pitcher."

"Doesn't matter," said Harold. "I won the series, so I get to pick the MVP. And it's me. Harold Pillick."

"Thank you for identifying yourself," Ben said dourly. "What a wipeout of a series. What ridiculous luck you had." He gazed at the boards bound inside the playing booklet as if he were gazing upon a faraway Tahitian sunset from the port of Detroit, dreaming of an island that might have been.

"I wonder what the real turning point was," Harold mused, sifting through the scoresheets. "Of course, there wasn't a *real* turning point, since I guess you were kind of never really in it, but I think it was that homerun Jose Herequiquez hit with one man on to seal Game Four. You probably should have intentionally walked him, especially in TriBiOmniCom Park."

"I'll intentionally give a free pass to a hitter when starfish play dominoes," Ben said. "As for the reasons for your alleged victory, I think it has more to do with the humidity in here warping my dice. Did you notice I rolled a lot more fours with the red one than seems normal? Watch. Watch." He shook his dice out across the emptied playing field but the result did not exactly confirm his theory. "Damn you!" he cried out at this betrayal. On the cardboard field, an imaginary grounds crew took a pause from sweeping the dirt between second and third to shake their heads sadly.

"I don't think the dice are a problem," Harold sighed.

"No, I'll bet you, because my hands were sweaty from making cookies and I kept, like, holding the dice in them while I was waiting for you to make your interminable pitching changes and completely pointless double switches."

"I may have gotten a little lucky sometimes," Harold admitted, "but you keep making some strange decisions. You keep trying to steal bases at the wrong times, you stick with your starters too long, and you never bunt."

"Bunting is for the frightened and the lost!" Ben countered. "Every time Greeny used to make me do it, I died a little inside. I mean, are we men or women?"

"You keep forgetting to factor in the fielding ratings too," Harold added, trying to sound as diplomatic as possible. "Your runners keep getting thrown out at the plate because of it. And what about the lefty-righty percentages, which you—"

"Enough, houseguest," Ben cut in. "Your victory was fluky and will be forgotten by everyone who was here to witness it." He began to examine the Bases Empty chart for typographical errors which might overturn the results of the series. Damn the APBA people for their proofreading excellence!

"Your biggest mistake was not putting your own card into the lineup," Harold said. "I just don't understand it."

"I told you, I don't want to jinx myself," Ben said with the utmost seriousness, picking up his card from the spot beside his left elbow which represented the Cannons bench, where Lee Harris and J.J. Portsmongerfield also lingered, unused and forgotten despite their admirable foot speed, which might have been able to nudge in a run during the Cannons' disastrous eighth inning meltdown in Game One. In that frame, Ben had somehow started with the bases loaded and nobody out only to push no one across the plate. The numbers on his own crisp white card shone out pristinely in red and black, virginal and plenty ready for the Show.

"Jinx yourself?" Harold said, getting up to grab another one of Ben's famous oatmeal raisin cookies from the plate on the counter. "What does that mean?" He broke his cookie in half. Deenie would kill him if he had no appetite for tonight's dinner, which would be something called brown noodles with wheat fingers.

"Oh Harold, childlike, innocent Harold," Ben said, "don't you understand what we've walked into here? This is baseball, man. Baseball reduced to miniature, but baseball all the same, and these cards, even your pathetically ineffective one, are *us.*"

"Well, they're the *baseball* us," Harold said, sitting again and putting his full roster of players back into their petite envelope. "The real world us has it a little bit harder."

"Exactly my point," Ben said. He took the APBA box into his hands and admired the artwork thereon. *"These* us-es are immune to history, and to the vermin scum who keep criticizing we who gave our lives to the sport."

"I gave three years," Harold said. "They paid us pretty well, didn't they? And there was always food around. So many snacks!"

"Not the point. I've got a plan, Harold. A plan for this game, and for us." His eyes gleamed like the ragtag collection of quarters that made up his laundry fund.

Harold put his sneakers on, ready to leave. "Does this plan involve you throwing away the last of your money?"

"Probably," came the reply as Ben stared into space, the gears of his mind clanking and clanging. "All the pieces aren't quite clear yet. Come on, let's play a quick best-of-five. The Channel 8 *Seinfeld* block doesn't start for another couple of hours. You be New York, I'll be Portland."

"Deenie isn't going to like that," Harold said. "As it is, I have to go into work on Saturday now to make up for this half day. Do you maybe want to come with me, you could talk to my boss about applying for that copying department job."

"Saturday I'll be deep in study," Ben said. "I have much to learn before I dominate this game like I dominated everything Pop-O-Matic in elementary school."

"I don't think just reading the rules over and over is going to make you that good," Harold observed. "I'll keep playing you, but maybe you should line up some other opponents."

"Other opponents, yes, that's not as patently stupid as it first sounds," Ben said, ushering Harold to the door. "There must be someone out there who can show me why the dice aren't rolling right. We probably should have rolled them into the box instead of on the table."

"Or you could stop calling for a hit and run when you don't really need to," Harold offered, zipping up his windbreaker. "There's this book called *Baseball for Your Brain* that's good if you want to figure out all that stuff. I read it when I was in Double-A."

"Hello, Harold, I've been playing baseball since I was in seventh grade, I think I know when to put on a hit and run. I can't be blamed if Dennis Rendall couldn't hit worth a lick."

"Whatever you say," Harold said. "See you later."

When he was gone, Ben retreated into the stillness of the kitchen. He dashed off his July rent check, post-dated to the following weekend so as not to destroy his savings, and then, while cooking up some spaghetti, spattering the walls behind the stove with great dollops of marinara sauce, he immersed himself in APBA Baseball again. It was going to be a long night.

It didn't end till 3:43 the next morning, as a matter of fact. In that time, many an anguished screech was heard in the apartment as Ben lost again and again playing the solitaire version of the game. He lost with six different teams, by blowout, nail-biter, extra inning marathon, and a couple of head-hanging 6-2 affairs he probably could have made closer if he had only stopped calling for his base runners to steal on Fritz LeMetzelaars, an otherwise forgettable starter for the Jersey Tollmen whose move to first was deadlier than the bite of the fiercest flightless moa in all of New Zealand. But Ben learned much in the wee hours of the night of July 10. And at no point did he look again at his own card, which remained snugly nestled in the Kentucky Cannons team envelope. The jinx, he kept reminding himself, the jinx. He would smack himself silly if he ruined his destiny before the time was just right to do so.

## 7. Their Eyes Were Watching *Tron*

On page 1217 of Dr. Daniel Snydersugar's best-selling 2004 self-help book, *Unscrewing Yourself Up,* he describes what he refers to as the Ten Percentile Theory of behavior modification. It states that human beings as a whole tend to conform to a certain range of habits and behaviors, and what we define as "normal" is that spectrum of common actions which most people rather wisely adhere to. Snydersugar advises his readers to make a list of any habits and behaviors which it is safe to assume that less than ten percent of all people engage in regularly. This could be everything from owning a tarantula farm to being addicted to milkshakes to eating tree bark to painting one's face on a regular basis. Anything one does routinely that falls into that ten percentile "abnormal" range, the respected doctor claims, should be examined carefully, because these are the things that may well be responsible for stunting our emotional and intellectual growth.

Ben had never read that book or heard about that theory, and thus felt free to post the following advertisement on the internet upon waking up from his long night of tabletop gaming:

**SERIOUS APBA BASEBALL ENTHUSIASTS WANTED** to come over to my place in Harrisburg and play competitively. No Spike Vail cards, please. My famous oatmeal raisin cookies will be served. Limit 2 per person.

The replies he got back were encouraging, after he spent some time filtering out the people who wanted to sell him condos, pre-marital relations with THE HOTTEST NOTARIES EVER!!!!! and a disturbing number of people who offered to play the game with him only if he in return would, at some point in the future, sit with them up to their waists in gelatin. After only a day or so of planning the first meeting of the club Ben had in mind, he was ready to host a gathering of strangers in his home for the first time since he was twelve. This time, though, the absence of chicken pox-riddled pre-teen brown-noser Richie McLiggo would all but guarantee success.

"Welcome, APBA managers," Ben greeted his new friends when all were congregated in his cramped living room on Wednesday night, "to a refuge where we can all enjoy this fine pursuit I myself just discovered. I hope we can make this a regular get-together, especially if I can get a bigger apartment without those big freaky sinkholes in the parking lot. Sorry, I really should have warned you about those before you took that last right onto Knibler Court."

The eight or nine faces in the room applauded Ben briefly as he stood before them. Roy was there too, having been lured to the event by Ben's promise that it would all be essential material for the book. The gathering was spread out among four mismatched card tables he had snagged from Goodwill. Most of them had brought their own game sets and they all seemed anxious to begin. Cans of discount soda were everywhere. The company that made it, American Thirster, had actually shut down years earlier and Ben had been lucky to find two cases of the stuff sitting abandoned beside a pet shop dumpster just hours before.

"Now I must tell you," Ben announced proudly, "that you've all been a little bit deceived. I am not a complete baseball amateur, having played in the big leagues myself for several years for the Kentucky Cannons. You might have heard of me. My name is Ben Glinton."

Blank stares and polite smiles came Ben's way. Someone near the back of the room coughed. A hand was raised to Ben's right and he nodded in that direction.

"Um, are you the Ben Glinton who played in the 2002 series against New York?" asked a portly man of about fifty.

"Ah, yes, yes I am," Ben said hesitantly.

"Okay, just checking," the man said, and with that, he got up with no further comment, scooped his game under his arm, and walked toward the front door. In a moment he was gone.

Ben swallowed hard, trying not to look too mortally embarrassed. "Yes yes, that was all such a long time ago. A different era entirely, really. Ah...yes, sir, do you have a question?"

Someone else had raised his hand, and now this man stood up as well. "Are you the Ben Glinton who rented out a room on Woodland Avenue in Lexington a few years ago and had a dog named Crinkles who had horrible barking and urinary problems?"

Ben swallowed again. "Yes. That's me."

The man got up with no further comment, scooped his game under his arm, and walked toward the front door. In a moment he was gone.

"Okay," Ben said determinedly, "now that the naysayers are gone, we can all have some fun. But first, why don't we go around the room and introduce ourselves, starting to my left." Ben sat down.

A bald man with glasses and a bit of a belly stood up with a young boy of about twelve. "Hello," the bald man greeted everyone. "My name is Earl Shavey. I've been playing APBA since 1969, and recently I got my son here into the game. His name is Jake. He's actually going to graduate high school this year, several years ahead of schedule. He's already been accepted to Hofstra. I used APBA to teach him about statistics and probability, and, well, he took the ball and ran with it, so to speak, ha ha ha ha, heh, ha, yeah." He laid a fond hand on his son's shoulder.

The boy spoke in a tremulous voice that still seemed to be a decade or so away from puberty. "Sometimes I use baseball players from this game as characters in my Dungeons and Dragons campaigns," he said. "And I found a way to use APBA results to predict trends in arctic weather patterns."

His father laughed nervously. "He really likes baseball a lot," he said somewhat apologetically, and they both sat down.

The next person to stand up was a good bit younger than Earl Shavey and a fair bit older than Jake. He wore a stained, tie-dyed T-shirt bearing the face of Jerry Garcia, and catastrophically ripped jeans. His messy Jesus hair cascaded beside his sunburned face. "Hi, my name is Rick. I play APBA instead of computer games out of respect for the modern Luddite movement."

"What are Luddites again?" Ben asked.

"Luddites," Earl's nerdy son piped in, "are people who don't like technology."

"He speaks the truth, man," said Rick. "Computer games retard the brain. Also, APBA is constructed from wholesome materials like paper and dice. Plus I love baseball. It's really slow and boring, like the movement of the earth, which we should all respect. I also will only listen to games on the radio. Seeing the actual players stifles the imagination. The absence of imagination is what led this country down the path of war and away from nature's prophecy."

"We appreciate the sentiment," Ben said. "Um, next?"

Roy looked around him, embarrassed that everyone was now staring at him. He stood up quickly. "Oh, hi, I'm not really an APBA player per se, I write for the Harrisburg Daily Fact Holder. I'm working on a biography of Ben here, but I'll be glad to join in if anyone's short an opponent, it looks like fun. Um, real quick, does anybody else's soda taste a little funny, kind of like duck sauce maybe?"

There were general nods of agreement, but no solutions were offered.

"My name is Emmitt Templeton," said the next player to stand, a stocky, professorial-looking chap with a head of wavy gray hair. "I've been playing the game since I served in Vietnam."

"Emmitt Templeton the three-time Pulitzer-Prize winning novelist?!" little Jake Shavey asked excitedly, pushing his glasses higher up his nose.

"Yes, that's right," Templeton replied.

"I've read the entire Ottoman trilogy!" Jake exclaimed. "I asked my teacher if I could do my book report on volume two instead of *My Side of the Mountain.*"

"Well, it's not my best work," Templeton said coolly. "It's a wonder it was ever accepted for publication. A trifle, really."

"Wow, how do you find the time to play APBA when you write all those novels and win all those awards?" Earl Shavey asked.

"I use the game as a stress-reliever," Templeton said. "The sound of the dice shaking clears my mind. I finished my cycle of novels about the Civil War draft riots in between a project to simulate the 1997 playoffs. The results were most gratifying. Most gratifying."

The last person left in the room didn't seem to want to stand. He sat low in his chair and nervously fingered the box in front of him. "My name's, um, Walter," he said from underneath the bill of a St. Louis Steamers baseball cap. "I figured I should get a hobby at some point, and this one seemed pretty cheap. So, yeah, that's pretty much the whole story."

Ben thought for a moment, peering at the guest. "Do you have a last name?" he asked.

Walter looked around nervously. "Last name? No. Why would I have one of those?"

Ben stood to get a better look at the mystery man. "Wait, I *know* that voice. Where do I know you from?"

"We went to the same high school, I think," Walter said, his eyes still invisible under his cap. "I sat behind you in Band. Go Panthers."

"Walter Williger!" Ben said, snapping his fingers. "Curse, is that *you?*"

The man tore off his cap and dropped it on the table in front of him.

"Yeah, okay, it's me."

"Curse Williger of the Cannons!" Earl Shavey said, impressed. "I know why Ben Glinton dropped out of baseball and out of society, but how come *you* did? You were terrific!"

"Yeah, dude, what was up with that?" Rick asked. "My father used to call me a loser and tell me I quit everything like Curse Williger. No offense."

Curse, only thirty years old, still handsome as the day was long and fit as Ben was getting flabby, spoke reluctantly. "It was the damn umpires," he told the group. "And those calls in the series in 2002. After I complained about those in the media, I could never get another break from the umps. I had to become a total power pitcher just so those goons couldn't cheat me out of the corners of the plate. I just got sick of it after a while. End of story."

"Wow," Jake said, wide-eyed. "For 2002, you're rated an A (Y)(ZZ) with a 2 fielding rating and even an instant homerun on a roll of 66," he said. "That's the last really good card you ever had from APBA."

"I know," Curse said. "This game is the only baseball I feel like playing now. There *are* no bad calls in it. Everything's totally honest. If I pitch and lose, it's because I sucked, not because those scheming umpires took it from me. I just like doing this more than the real thing."

"Quite a poignant tale," Templeton observed. "I would consider it an honor to play against you, with yourself as the starting pitcher."

"All right," Curse said, his mood lightening. "Right now I only have the year 2003 card set, when I was mostly in the bullpen because I was working on my new mechanics, but I have a C rating as a starter. I'll give it a shot."

"I suggest we play freeform for a while, against whoever we feel like," Ben told the group, "and then a little later we can go playoff-style, one and done, until we crown a champion. I've come up with a prize for tonight's winner. Get ready, people: the man who captures the title walks out of here with a lightly used VHS copy of *Tron.*"

A buzz of either excitement or total indifference went through the room, and the players began to arrange their contests. Cards were brought out, pencils were sharpened, and boards laid down. Soon the room was filled with the sound of rattling dice and CD recordings of radio broadcasts of historic ball games that Harold had lent Ben. Ben sat out this first round of casual games, content to walk from table to table to observe what was going on and to make barely appropriate comments on strategy and sudden turns of fortune. He was a little dismayed at everyone's facility with the rules and the way they made managerial decisions so casually and confidently. There was a disturbing lack of blowouts and gaffes.

At about eight-thirty, Ben made a list of playoff pairings. Roy sat out, wanting to work on his notes. As soon as teams of roughly equal abilities were decided on, the three pairs of competitors went to battle while Roy took Ben aside.

"I'm a little confused as to what this might have to do with the book," Roy said. "This is fun and all, but isn't it just a bunch of guys hanging out and playing a game?"

"Baby steps, Roy, baby steps," Ben told him. "You are witnessing the beginning of a process which will end with a terrific climax for the book."

"Okay, I trust you, I guess," Roy said, sipping his soda and trying not to grimace. "By the way, I called your mother for some background information about your childhood. I think it's probably only fair that we reveal somewhere near the beginning that your real name is Herschel Gury Locknagel."

"That's a long story," Ben said. "No one will be interested. I have some anecdotes about working at Dairy Queen when I was a teenager that'll completely blow people away."

"We haven't talked yet about how we're going to approach that night against the Guardians," Roy said delicately. "Any ideas?"

"Soon it'll be a moot point," Ben said. "Keep your eyes on the proceedings."

Ben sat down to take on Rick head-to-head and started off well, thanks to a couple of quick homeruns which even his managerial shakiness couldn't keep off the scoreboard. When Rick tied up their game by using the dreaded small-ball skills of the Minnesota Ice Eaters, Ben started to panic, and by the seventh inning, he was making strange roster moves and inserting pinch-hitters so fast he was in danger of completely exhausting his bench. Then a miracle happened: Rick took out his fatiguing starter and replaced him with the best middle reliever the Ice Eaters had, an illegal Estonian immigrant who wasn't very good at all, and back-to-back rolls of box cars produced four runs for Ben's Orlando Sun Snakes. Just like that, he had won the game. His head swelled to the size of California itself.

"Piece of cake," he muttered, and tilted back in his chair so far that he momentarily lost his balance and threatened to topple over backwards.

Nearby, Emmitt Templeton, a painfully slow player who tended to shake his dice in hypnotic rhythm before every single roll and contemplated every maneuver with the facial expression of Boris Spassky considering moving his decoy bishop to his queen's unguarded flank, edged out Curse Williger by a score of 2-1. Curse's

APBA self pitched valiantly, but Templeton seemed to know exactly when to take chances, which put him in a position to score both his runs on sacrifice flies. The men shook hands cordially when their game was over. Ben then overheard Curse swearing an axe-based bloody vengeance on God himself. Across the room, young Jake Shavey beat his father 6-4, despite having a weaker team, on a freak error in the twelfth inning. His father emitted a very mild curse word and apologized profusely to the boy, wondering aloud if he should even be allowed to raise a son while possessed with such a rampant potty mouth. He excused himself to call his wife and beg her forgiveness, which, as usual, was not forthcoming.

Jake was given a bye in the semi-finals due to strength of schedule and the fact that he had to dash off a quick homework assignment before heading for the last round. Templeton and Ben squared off, and Ben drew a slightly better team. Templeton uttered a series of moody harrumphs as his hitters proved unable to make contact through five full innings, and Ben, delirious with the possibility of actually winning back-to-back games, got more and more animated as his Detroit Run Dogs hit bunches of singles to get two runs across. After a homerun, things got only worse for Templeton. Ben was ahead 3-2 in the ninth inning when he made the boneheaded mistake of not bringing in some defensive substitutions to back up ace reliever Solomon Sodd. An error put a man on first base, Templeton flashed the hit and run, and suddenly there were runners on first and third. But without any help from Ben, Sodd struck out three batters in a row to send Ben to the finals, one game away from keeping his stained and smelly VHS tape.

That left Jake and Ben. The others gathered around. The hour grew late.

Jake beat Ben 12-1 in thirty-seven minutes.

It all happened so fast. Ben had no idea what really transpired. He made three bad moves in the second inning, once again refusing to walk anyone, then falling asleep to the possibility of the squeeze play, then playing the infield in rather than give up a single run, a mistake of pride that built a slippery slope toward a seven run explosion. Five runs followed in the third. Ben had put his faith in his players' overall batting averages over the fact that the opposing pitcher was dominant against lefties, and batter after batter tanked. When his final batter lined out to short, Ben reached for the dice again, certain it couldn't possibly be over so fast. The eleven o'clock *Friends* block on Channel 13 hadn't even started yet.

"Okay," Ben said to Jake, trying to control his interior agony, "you can have *Tron,* but you'll have to re-spool the tape yourself. Why don't we go just one more time, and make it a little more interesting. I've got thirty bucks that says I take you out, little man."

A sudden hush fell over the room and Jake's dad dropped his blessedly empty soda can onto the carpet. Rick's mouth formed into a silent, horrified oval. Even the penetrating eyes of the normally unshakeable Emmitt Templeton went wide. "What? What?" Ben asked. "Okay, it's a kid, if he doesn't have thirty bucks, I'll take a bicycle in fairly good condition."

"People don't really *bet* on APBA," Earl Shavey said. "It just...isn't done, really."

"It diminishes what we do, Ben," Templeton added. "We try to keep it pure. That's what separates APBA from the tawdriness of professional sports and the cutthroat myopia of fantasy leagues."

"Fantasy leagues, man," Rick said distastefully. "No accounting for defense, no sense of game strategy, no appreciation of role players, no dice shakers. Leave me out of it, dude."

"Well, how intense are we allowed to get?" Ben asked, stunned. "Is there no money to be made in this game?"

"Not really," said Earl.

"Come on," Ben said. "Surely somewhere in this great land of ours there are players who want to take it to the next level. If not for cash, then to at least lord their victories over the heads of the losers. If you can't lord, what's the point of any of it?"

"If it's a more hardcore strain of players you seek, I think I might have an idea where to begin looking for them," Templeton said. "They tend to not dwell on message boards. They're more serious than even that. When I was researching my four novels about the Negro leagues, I met a man who lives in Philadelphia...I don't even know how to really describe him..."

"Is he really serious about this game?" Ben asked, covertly pushing the scoresheet presenting the facts of his awful loss to Jake out of sight. "Because I need to find the absolute masters for a little competition I have in mind."

"Serious...oh yes, he's serious," Templeton said, narrowing his eyes in memory. "I could go through my notes from back then and possibly find an address..."

"Yes!" Ben said. "Now we're rolling."

"Tell us about this competition, man," Rick said. "Sounds like fun."

"I can't just now," Ben said. "You'll all be kept informed of the developments. Our next meeting will be on Friday night, and there may be chips. That's not confirmed yet. Actually, forget I said anything about chips. Just be here at seven."

### 8. Our Nation's Fabled Interstate Highway System Earns its Keep

Only one more meeting of the Independent APBA Collective of Metro Harrisburg was held before Ben found himself in the passenger's seat of Harold's 1999 Toyota Camry on a shiny Saturday morning, headed east on 76 with Roy Skinla in the back seat. A bare week had passed since the first gathering which had tipped Ben off to the existence of some fabled Others who might aid and abet his education and passion for the board game he could barely afford. Since then he hadn't made any progress whatsoever excellence-wise, but in simulating a mini-season as manager of the Florida Winsmiths, he had at least gotten down the basics of keeping statistics on the scoresheet. His record in that mini-season: 7 wins, 21 losses. The Winsmiths' actual record that year was 103-59. The discrepancy would have been alarming enough to cause any serious APBA player to confiscate his set and donate it to a worthy charity.

"So, you learned the game from watching *This Week in Baseball?*" Roy was asking Ben from the back seat, trying to write down his answers to various biographical questions between the Camry's tremulous encounters with assorted potholes.

"Yeah," Ben replied. "I heard that theme they used to play over the end credits and I got chills. That was also my introduction to classical music. I started watching the show for the highlights but my mother thought I was just waiting for the theme to play again. So she signed me up for clarinet lessons and I never got to play baseball till I was fifteen."

"Wow, that's good stuff!" Roy said, scribbling furiously.

"Very soon it became totally obvious that no classical music was nearly as good as the end theme to *This Week in Baseball,* and I sold the clarinet on the sly. I told my mother I dropped it down a grating."

"And, um, what was the first team you ever played for?"

Ben thought for a moment. "That would have been the Sewickley Savings & Loan Banjo Boys. It was a four-team league. It just about disbanded because we got three straight days of rain and the field wouldn't dry out. Then our coach disappeared. All they found was the canoe he'd been fishing in on Lake Meade, completely covered in enriched flour. It was on *Unsolved Mysteries* a few years ago."

"It wasn't flour, it was baking soda," a voice said from the seat beside Roy. The voice belonged to young Jake Shavey, whose attention had been buried in a book of Richard Feynman's lectures. His appearance in the car was not so bizarre as to make the scene completely implausible. When Ben had told his father of this day trip to Philadelphia to meet with a supposed intellectual wizard of the APBA arts, Earl had asked if Ben could take Jake to the Mutter Museum of Medical Curiosities and maybe also the latest Rodin exhibition. Ben saw the opportunity to make twenty dollars and had seized upon it.

"Flour, baking soda, either way that guy wasn't going to be teaching any more kids to rub yogurt on their gloves to soften the webbing," Ben said. "He used to send the kids who were really bad into deep, deep left field and call the position 'zone sentry'."

"Aw, rats, my pencil broke," Roy said sadly. "Can we stop somewhere and get a new one? We were really on a roll there."

Ben, who had been making up about half of the facts he'd been offering, was only too glad for a brief respite to collect his thoughts and hone the lies he'd created to make his life sound somewhat interesting. It had already taken a half hour or so to explain why Harold, whom Ben supposedly did not know and whose son he had visited out of pure altruism the week before, was not only in the car with them but had revealed himself to be an ex-Cannons player. The tapestry of falsehoods they'd had to weave to alleviate Roy's suspicions of foul play had been worthy of preservation in some sort of Fabrication Hall of Fame. "Yeah," Ben said, "let's get you a pencil and grab some hamburgers or something too. Keep your eye out for a Checkers or something."

"I can't eat hamburgers," Jake said, closing his book and leaning forward so that his head floated between Ben and Harold. "My mom says the glurbinates will stunt my growth."

"There's a Fat Chicken Mountain up ahead," Harold said, turning on his blinker.

"Go through the drive-thru," Ben said, "we have to keep an eye on the time."

"Why are we going to Philadelphia anyway?" Jake asked. "My dad said it had something to do with APBA."

"You got that right," Ben said. "I've got a plan."

"But why couldn't we go in *your* car?"

"Because the state of Pennsylvania has something against my emissions pipe," Ben said bitterly. "Harold, do me a favor, spot me a few dollars so I can get a number 4 value meal. It's incredible, it's like the best thing anybody has ever eaten."

"I'll buy you two of them if you just tell us what this plan of yours is," Harold said, getting in line at the drive-thru. Jake expressed an interest in waffle fries and Roy, after checking out the menu and once again resigning himself to eating poorly, opted for the Heart Healthy grilled vegetable sandwich with no condiments, which, according to the dietary chart beside the order speaker, possessed four days' worth of saturated fat. The more time he spent in Ben's company, the more and more his life span dwindled.

"The plan," Ben said, looking toward the horizon like the captain of a voyage into unknown lands where the cities were rumored to be made of gold and mermaids swam about day and night, sleeping with anything that moved. "Okay, I'll tell you. Are you ready? Here it is. I propose, my friends, nothing less than—"

"Yes, ah, hello, how are you, can I get a number 4 value meal," Harold was forced to interrupt, leaning out the driver's side window, "a number 7 with no pickle, a number 6 with the pickle on top of the bun instead of inside it, a large waffle fries, four medium root beers, and a Silly Cone. Just the cone please, I don't want the ice cream in it."

"As I was saying about the plan," Ben said. "What I intend to do is, and I am absolutely serious about this, is—wait, didn't I tell you I wanted a moon pie? Did I not clearly say moon pie?"

"And a moon pie," Harold added. An electronic squawk asked him to drive around to the second window.

"Maybe we should wait till I get a pencil so I can write this down," Roy said.

"Why do you need to write it down?" Jake asked. "The guy inside the restaurant knows what the order is now."

"I mean the plan, not the order," Roy said.

"I think I might have a nub of a pencil in the glove compartment," Harold offered.

"How much of a nub?" Roy asked.

"My PLAN is two-pronged, for anyone who cares to listen," Ben said.

Harold opened the glove box as he stopped beside the delivery window. "You know, maybe I shouldn't even call it a nub. That's being generous."

"I'd like to eat a moon pie, but my Mom says they're full of all kinds of bad stuff, and she reads articles all the time," Jake said.

"It's important to learn to eat well as soon as you can, Jake," Roy said. "You wouldn't think it to look at me now, but I was fat as a kid, and it really made life tough in school."

"*You* were fat?" Jake asked, amazed. "Wow. How did you get so skinny and small? You're like a boy, or a really tough girl."

"I had a plan," Roy said. "Do you want to hear it?"

Ben closed his eyes and put a hand to his forehead. "Sally save my Skittles," he muttered under his breath.

"We could have gotten a number 5 for a dollar cheaper if we had all agreed to get cherry Cokes," Harold mused regretfully. "Oh man. Oh man. See, that's the kind of thing that if you keep an eye out for, the money really starts to add up."

In the Middle East, unrest continued.


"We're going to stage a tournament," Ben told them when the car was back on the highway, headed more or less where they were intending to go. Jake had fallen asleep immediately upon starting in on his lunch, doing nothing to dispel the rumor (proved in a court of law three years later) that Fat Chicken Mountain's waffle fries were absolutely drenched in Thorazine. "We're going to stage the biggest APBA tournament in history. It will be so big that it'll be covered by all the major sports networks. At this tournament, I will advance to the highest level of competition. I will manage the 2002 Kentucky Cannons." He paused only to take a loud slurp from his warmish root beer, the straw nestled in the corner of his mouth. "My opponent, whoever it turns out to be, will manage the New York Guardians. And as God as my witness, in front of the crowd that turns out to watch, I will absolutely trounce that sucker, and you can bet your butt that my card will be in the lineup, batting cleanup. Any questions?"

There was a moment of silence inside the car. Harold appeared to silently replay Ben's words in his mind from beginning to end, trying to find just one or two rational concepts he could work with. Roy chewed on his pencil nub, started to say something, and then stopped. He looked merely confused.

"But Ben," Harold finally ventured as they passed road signs pointing the way to downtown Philadelphia, "what's the point?"

"The point is, I need to do this," Ben said. "I don't expect you to understand. You had your career. It started, it went on for a few years for no particular reason, and when it ended you shook hands with everybody and went home to your lawn and your wife's gory Tom Savini meals. I wasn't so lucky."

"You can't go back in time, Ben," Harold cautioned. "You should maybe just forget it all ever happened."

"Easy for you to say, Pillick. Guardians fans didn't pressure their city council to name a wetlands preserve after you for pretty much handing them the world championship. I have to live with that every day."

"This kind of sounds like a lot of work, Ben," Roy added, just trying to be helpful. "How do you know you'd even win? If you lost, wouldn't you feel even worse?"

"Failure is not an option," Ben said tersely, then rubbed his chin. "What movie is that from? Isn't there some movie where Ed Harris says that?"

"*The Hours*," Harold said.

"I will win because I'm going to spend the time between now and the tournament getting as good as anyone has ever been at this game," Ben said. "There's no reason excellence should be worth more on a real playing field than a cardboard one. A champion is a champion. If I work just as hard as mastering APBA baseball as I did at playing left field, the results I get are just as meaningful."

Roy did his best to write this down on his notepad, smooshing his pencil nub this way and that. What came out on the page looked like the writing of a mildly talented monkey. "Interesting, I can sort of see your point," he said.

"I'm not real sure *I* do," Harold said. "And how are you going to arrange a major tournament and get it covered by the sports channels? They don't have much interest in something like this."

"They will if I tell them that Ben Glinton intends at this tournament to reveal for the first time exactly *why* he destroyed game seven of the 2002 series," Ben said, and looked casually at his fingernails, waiting for their reaction.

"You mean you did it on *purpose?"* Roy asked, bending forward excitedly. "Is *that* what you're saying?"

"No, not on purpose, per se," Ben said. "But there's a very specific reason that things happened in that inning the way they did. I've kept it secret for four long years."

"It was drugs, right?" Roy guessed. "Drugs? What kind?"

"It wasn't drugs, and thanks for letting me know what you think of me, Roy," Ben said. "The only way the world will finally understand what went down is if the reporters are at the tournament when I explain it. The Nineteen Thousand, Four Hundred and Fifty Dollar Tournament of Valiants, I will call it, because fellas, that's exactly how much I'm going to walk away with when I make the Cannons trounce the Guardians. In other words, exactly one 2002 world championship series winner's share."

"Twenty thousand dollars for winning an APBA tournament?!" Harold said, almost lapsing into shock and getting into the wrong lane to turn onto Market Street. "Are you *nuts*, Ben? Where do you think you're going to get that money from?"

"That particular piece of the puzzle has yet to fall into perfect position," Ben admitted. "I think it'll involve another day trip, possibly on Monday. Who's in? Roy?"

Roy almost leapt off his seat in excitement. "Now I see what you meant by the great ending for the book!" he said. "It's got irony, drama, and weirdness. If you could really win with your own card in the lineup, beating the same team you gave the series to with your incredibly bizarre, incredibly awful, unbelievably stupid play—I mean, you know, no offense, Ben, but they'll be talking about it for hundreds of years after we all die—and on the very same day that you manage to win, you stand up and tell everyone what really happened that night..."

"You never told me anything about this before, that there was a reason for it," Harold said. "How come I'm just hearing about it now?"

"I don't tell you *everything*, Harold," Ben said. "Jeez. We're not Betty and Veronica."

"So where are we going on Monday?" Roy asked, almost as bouncy as Jake got sometimes when his parents took him on Saturdays to the Erie County Library of Botanical Abstracts.

"To the mean streets and mystical vistas of Pittsburgh, Pennsylvania," Ben told him. "But first things first. Harold, we should have turned left about three stoplights ago. And if Jake's not gonna wake up, there's no reason we should be letting his fries get cold."

## 9. Non-Quantal Pathozones in Differential Calculative Combines Utterly Independent of Their Associative Rudimates

They dropped him off in front of a tenement-ish brownstone on a street named after a famous American slave owner who was definitely a tax cheat and may very well have been a serial killer and deadbeat dad. As soon as Harold pulled away, having arranged to pick Ben up again in front of the crack house on the corner next to the bullet-riddled sub shop, a homeless man came up to Ben to ask him for spare change. Ben gave some to him, at which point the homeless man recognized him and gave him thanks for the donation not of the seventy-five cents but of the 2002 championship series to his beloved New York Guardians.

"Boy, you sure did make some mistakes that night," the homeless gent noted.

"Yeah, I'm sure *your* record is spotless," Ben countered, and the guy walked off. The lottery ticket he bought with that three-quarters of a dollar fifteen minutes later wound up netting him $23, 411.

Ben climbed some chipped and mossy steps to the front door of the building before him, and seeing that the gaping, jagged hole in it would make for an easier entrance than actually pulling the door open, stepped through into a hallway decorated lovingly with graffiti of such spectacular profanity that Ben actually took a moment to memorize some new words. Then he went to the end of the hall, avoiding the bicycle and refrigerator parts strewn across the floor, and knocked on a blue door which had been highlighted in black marker with the number 104. The 4 was woefully off-center. And based on the numbers on the doors of the other apartments on the floor, it should have been 108 instead.

"Come in!" he heard a voice call out, and he opened the door and entered. The apartment inside was dark but not quite forbidding. It just looked like someone was more or less allergic to the concept of electric lamps. The place was cluttered, that was for sure. Books were piled everywhere. Ben saw a man standing in the middle of the living room with his back to him, carefully ironing a pair of pants. The man turned and smiled.

"Hello, Mr. Glinton," he said. "I'm happy to meet you." Fergus Hibbert came forward with a nervous smile. He was about forty, sickly pale, and wearing a T-shirt advertising a poorly received animated motion picture that no one had thought about much since the actor who had done the voice for the dancing hippopotamus mysteriously drowned in his soup in 1996.

"Hi," Ben said. "So, Emmitt Templeton tells me you're a serious APBA player." He leaned a casual hand on the edge of the ironing board and it came to rest in a moldy peanut butter and jelly sandwich.

"Oops, sorry about that, not a lot of room in here," Fergus said. "Here, wipe your hand on these." He lifted the newly ironed pants and offered them.

"That's okay," Ben said.

Fergus frowned. "Yes, it wouldn't make a whole lot of sense to sully these, would it, since I just spent half the morning smoothing them. I have an interview for a research grant tomorrow, you see, and I have to look my best. That's why I'm sort of modeling this T-shirt today, to get a feel for it."

"Super," Ben said. "So you're a real scientist, then?"

"Since I was nine," Fergus said, unplugging his iron. "This grant will allow me to study non-quantal pathozones in differential calculative combines utterly independent of their associative rudimates."

"Terrific. Does that mean anything I would understand?"

"Oh yes!" Fergus said, beaming. "The end result will be the completion of a seven month project to make the APBA Baseball sacrifice bunt booklet eleven percent more accurate on fields with artificial turf!"

"Hmmmm," Ben said. "Seven months."

"Well, I would have liked to have spent ten, but you know, I've got to pay my bills," Fergus said, gesturing for Ben to follow him over to a large, poorly painted table on which Ben spied the first evidence of the scientist's pro-APBA leanings. An older version of the Master game was set up for solitaire play. Ben noted that the boards were yellowed and grimy, and had been handled so often that the edges were completely rounded. A white path had been worn away on the baseball diamond due to so many red plastic chips moving from home to first base and onward. Around the game were piled several spiral-bound volumes marked with handwritten titles like HIT AND RUN CHART 1992, VERSION 9 and BALLPARK EFFECTS ON FOUL BALLS TO THE FIRST BASE SIDE and PINCH HIT PROBABILITY, ALL PLAYOFF SERIES SINCE 1941. The volumes tended to be thicker than any book Ben had ever tried to read except, of course, for Harry Potter.

"Since my ideal avenue of research ended some years ago," Fergus told him, "I've focused my energies on APBA. So many possibilities for modifying the game to simulate as closely as possible the real thing! First I had to completely break down the mathematics of the Basic game to know exactly what I was dealing with. That took a mere year and a half, after which I was ready to really get into it. I began with the batting tables, of course, because I thought I detected a very slight advantage given to hitters who tended to strike the ball to the left side. Here, look at the first analysis I did." From one of the stacks of booklets he pulled out one with a cherry red cover. Ben noted with some amusement and some horror that Fergus had drawn a little picture of a baseball player beneath the words MID-RANGE BATTING RESULT

DISCREPANCY ASSESSMENT, RUNNERS ON FIRST AND THIRD. Ben leafed through the dozens of pages of mathematical formulae, feeling a little dizzy.

"I played 1700 games to test that initial hypothesis," Fergus said. "Always the same two teams of course, to make the results more reliable."

"Of course," Ben said, smiling nervously and taking one very small step back away from Fergus. "Says on the last page here that your findings were incorrect and that you scrapped the idea."

"Yes, most disappointing," Fergus said. "That's when I turned to re-working the stolen base system. After 840 games, I really had something I could work with. My results brought the accuracy within .0139 percentage points of those from the actual 1994 season."

"I see," Ben said, putting the booklet down. "So, ah, you don't really play competitively, then. Or even, you know, for fun."

"Goodness no," Fergus said. "Oh, I did at first, of course, but then when I saw the possibilities to make the game mimic the real thing to the absolute letter, I couldn't simply ignore them. Everything must be taken into account, from wind patterns over certain parts of certain stadiums to the tendencies of some players to round first and third bases on greater arcs than others to the possibility—rare, I grant you—that a pitcher could stub his toe jogging in for relief and possibly reduce his Master grade level by a full point. Did Emmitt tell you of my magnum opus, the Unusual Play Omnibus? There are seven volumes thus far. They take into account and make it possible to reproduce every rare play that has occurred in the big leagues since 1904. I couldn't access the game data before that year, much to my chagrin."

"Oof, that really sucks grapes," Ben agreed. "So, ah, exactly how long does it take for you to play a single game using all your modifications?"

"Oh, not more than nine or ten hours," Fergus said mildly. "Sometimes if I'm in a hurry, I won't use the Player Mood formulas."

"Player Mood formulas?"

"Indeed. A player's private life can have as much effect on his performance as many other factors, a fact sadly not reflected on the standard APBA card. So I went back through the years and studied newspaper clippings of all the controversies to which I could assign a rudimentary mathematical card alteration, and then, when I could, I accessed public records of divorces and deaths of close relatives to further tweak a player's abilities in months that I believed his play was affected by these events. For instance, poor Stookie Sullbarb of the 1928 Richmond Rivermen...remember the public outrage against him when he was ticketed for loitering during the break between the end of the regular season and the beginning of the playoffs? If you play a game on any day within two weeks after that fateful September night, it causes one of the 8s on his card to be downgraded all the way to a 24...an instant ground out to short! Can you imagine?"

"Oh yeah, I can imagine," Ben said, all of a sudden silently regretting his long-ago decision not to carry a handgun with him at all times for protection. "So does this mean that you own pretty much every card set APBA ever produced?"

"But of course," Fergus said, nimbly darting between the clutter all around him towards a giant rack of bookshelves in the corner of the room. Ben hadn't noticed it because the light in the room didn't even come close to reaching that far back. Fergus turned on another lamp and there they were, going up to the ceiling, every card set there ever was, a veritable landslide of yellowish team roster envelopes, each year noted with a slip of paper taped to the shelf directly above it. "And do you know, Ben, I've found out something quite interesting about your 2002 card in particular."

"Oh yeah?" Ben said, staying where he was. The bookshelves looked kind of wobbly, more wobbly even than Fergus's brain.

"In certain on-base and out situations, your card from that year is deceptively effective," Fergus informed him. "In fact, given just the right circumstances, you hit almost twelve points higher than you did in real life. And then there's the printing error, which of course you already know about."

"Printing error?"

Fergus ran a finger along the shelf where cards from the most recent turn of the century were located. From beneath the roster envelopes he removed a folding accordion card on which the Master game player symbols were printed. Fergus walked over to Ben and pointed out his name in the Kentucky Cannons lineup.

"There it is," Fergus said breathlessly. "You are not listed as a pull hitter, but rather as a straight-away type. It very much improves your effectiveness against righties. A blatant and shocking typo produced not by the APBA company itself, oh no, but rather by a deranged man named Hentley Harkaby. In 2001 he invented a poorly received tabletop baseball simulation called Hey Batter Hey Batter Hey Batter Hey Batter *Swing!* The failure of it caused him to go quite insane, break into the APBA building in the middle of the night, and make an attempt to sabotage their card printing process. He failed miserably except for making you a straight-away hitter and causing the name of the Guardians' ace relief pitcher, Jeff Morone, to become rather comically misspelled."

"Most excellent," Ben whispered reflectively. Things just kept getting better and better for his plan, if you ignored the fact that it had taken him to a dangerous tenement in Philadelphia where he was now being offered a corn chip from a snack bag whose expiration date was June 1985. "No thanks," he said to Fergus. "So, this kind of thing is making you more happy than...what was your original 'ideal avenue of research' again?"

Fergus walked away from Ben, gazing up toward the ceiling in fond memory. "When I was a lad of thirty and on sabbatical from M.I.T., I was just months away from perfecting the ultimate machine. A contraption so valuable to the enrichment of humankind that it would have changed life as we know it forever. Yes, Ben Glinton... I speak of a time machine."

"No way," Ben said, taking a few corn chips from the snack bag after all. "Now *that* is cool."

"Cool as school," Fergus mused. "I was about to become the first man to literally travel through time. I expended more intellectual energy and super-sophisticated particle acceleration analysis on that pursuit than all the other scientists in the world put together. But in the end, I realized I had done some long division wrong and eighteen years of research went down the drain. I moped about for a time with species studies deep inside the Amazonian rain forest, taught a semester or two in advanced hypothetical geometry at Princeton—you know, totally wasting my life—and then one day at my mother's house I was poring over some of my old childhood toys and I came across APBA Baseball again. I was never going to be able to build my time machine, but here was one right in the palm of my hands. With it, I've been able to journey throughout the twentieth century re-creating some of history's greatest sporting contests."

"You know, if you want to re-create events from the past," Ben told Fergus, "there's all kinds of historical war games you can obsess over."

"Oh God, those damn things are too complicated," the theoretical physicist replied. "Ever pick up one of those rulebooks? Gack."

"Yeah," Ben said, "good point. Well, it's been nice meeting you, Fergus. I've got to go now. I think maybe you're a little too serious about the game for what I have in mind, which was just a simple competition that I really want to win." He shook Fergus's slightly greasy hand and started for the door.

"Let me give you something first," Fergus said, taking one of seven ballpoint pens from the pocket of his tattered chinos and jotting a note down on the back of a bubble gum wrapper. "This is the address of a man who can really, truly help you if you want to merely become great at the Master game and not the Uber-Master game as I play it. I've never told anyone where this man can be found, and he would certainly have my head if I gave his identity out without good cause, but he is the ultimate APBA guru, a mind so skilled that no one, as far as I know, has ever been able to beat him on a consistent basis, even given the game's reliance on the music of chance."

"Okay, yeah, that I could maybe use," Ben said, taking the wrapper and squinting at the chicken scratch scrawled upon it.

"If you're playing against anything but the Nynaxitron APBA supercomputer at the University of Chicago, which I helped design, I can all but guarantee you that if you agree to submit to this man's program, you will not lose any tournament, and maybe not even a single game."

"Terrific!" Ben said. "How come I'm so special that you're giving this to me?"

"Because we're like brothers, Mr. Glinton," Fergus told him, looking forlornly at his giant shelf o' player cards. "Two men who reached for the sun only to be stricken down at the last moment, condemned to a life far away from the reach of the cruel mockery of the scientific community—or in your case, the overwhelming majority of the general public. It's too late for me, but maybe you can regain your former glory somehow. I wish you all the best."

"Thanks, man," Ben said, stepping out into the hallway. "I hope you can afford a nicer place sometime."

"Are you sure you don't want to stick around and play just one game with me?" Fergus asked. "I've been working on some new pitcher fatigue charts which take into consideration a player's perspiration levels. I created them through watching hundreds of hours of videotapes."

"No thanks, I've got to get going," Ben said. "Maybe one day I can come back and you can show me some of the stuff you've whipped up for APBA Football."

"Definitely. Take care, young man," Fergus said, and closed the door behind Ben, then turned and allowed himself to be enclosed once again in the dimness of his skanky living space.

"Holy crap," he said aloud, eyes wide. "There's an APBA *Football?*"


## 10. You Can't Stop Hentley Harkaby; You Can Only Hope to Contain Him


Ridiculously far away, in beautiful, sunny, but irritatingly cold-at-night San Francisco, a tall, stupendously muscled individual was sitting at a table at the back of a bustling downtown convention center signing his autograph at fifty bucks a pop to all who presented themselves with shirts, caps, bats, and what-have-you in hand. This man's name was Spike Vail, and he was considered the third best baseball player alive, behind two guys whose stats weren't necessarily better but who had not publicly demanded five trades in four years and thus presented a more favorable image to the sports writers of America, Roy Skinla included. Spike, thirty-six years old and the owner of thirteen professional batting records, flashed his trademark smile to every fan who approached the table. He had, for upwards of two hours now, done a credible job of seeming like the ultimate nice guy who had mesmerized the nation with both his play on the field and in three recent Hollywood action films. Each of these films, in which he had starred with an animated duck named

Pepito, the most hard-drinking, hell-raising example of law enforcement waterfowl ever depicted on the big screen, had been savaged by critics and grossed successively less money, but kids still seemed to enjoy them. Hordes of people wandered around the cavernous convention center in search of memorabilia and stars who would adorn it with their signatures. Many held free soft pretzels shaped like the newest New York Guardians' superstar, Im Ho Ngoc Thy.

"You're my hero, Spike!" a boy of nine said to Spike as he held out a New England Nevers pennant for him to sign.

"Thanks, tike," Spike replied. "You're not gonna grow up to challenge my homerun record, are you?" he added with a wink.

"No sir!" the boy piped. "I want to work for Greyhound!"

"Aces," Spike said. When the boy was gone, Spike turned to his agent, a severe-looking young woman whom Spike had never seen crack a smile. "Didn't you send someone to get me a Chunky bar like an hour ago?"

"I'll make some calls," the woman said ominously. "If you don't get that Chunky bar in the next five minutes, we'll sue this place into the ground."

"Um, okay, that sounds a little mean, but whatever you say, Daisy," Spike said. He kept signing his autograph and making polite chit chat with the public, wondering if he would ever be able to free himself from the masses today. He had scenes to shoot for his next two action films, *Maximum Fracas* and *The Death of Pepito*, in about three hours, and he had lots of lines to memorize, most of them consisting of subtle variants of the sentence "Let's get the hell out of here."

Just as Spike's right hand was getting sore, a fresh-faced lad of about ten came up to the table, his father beside him. "Can you sign your APBA card, Mr. Vail?" the boy asked, holding it out to him.

Spike took the card and examined it, fascinated. "What is this again?" he asked the boy.

"It's your card from APBA Baseball," the boy informed him matter-of-factly. "You know, the board game."

"Hmmmmm," Spike said as Daisy leaned in beside him to take a severe look at the object in question. "Judging by all these numbers here, it looks like the game is pretty involved."

"Not as good as the one we put *your* name on, surely," Daisy assured him. In addition to Spike Vail's Happenin' Homerun Derby for video game systems, Spike had also lent his name to a baseball simulation for children called Back Back Back Back Back Back It's Gone! It consisted entirely of a single chart and ten possible play results. The game had been briefly recalled the year before due to the sabotaging of one of the print runs by a crazy man named Hentley Harkaby. The damage had caused the strikeout on the play chart to instead cause a pitcher to give up something called an intentional triple.

Spike signed the card and gave it back to the kid, whose father grinned as the boy danced off with wild excitement, having actually met the man whose posters festooned his bedroom walls. On the PA system, a bored voice announced that a special baseball bloopers DVD was going on sale for ten minutes only, one that featured the infamous swallowed mitt accident from this year's All-Star game.

"I assume we're getting a little money coming in from allowing my name to be licensed for use in this ABBA game, right?" Spike asked Daisy.

"APBA," she corrected. "I'll look into it. There's no reason we can't get you a bit more. I'm sure they'd cave to any demands we cared to make."

"I wonder," Spike said, deep in thought. A man of about forty gave him a T-shirt to sign but Spike absently wrote his name on the man's forearm instead. "I'd like to learn more about this board game," he went on to no one in particular. "How am I assured that they're portraying me as good as I really am? We'll have to make absolutely certain of it. If not, I don't think I can live with that...I'd hate to raise a ruckus about it, but I suppose I'd have no other choice..."

Spike's Chunky bar came two minutes later. It was the kind with raisins—yes, yes, most ideal for his purposes.


## 11. Selected Meat Products Available by Request


Pittsburgh, Pennsylvania, population 335,123, home of the steel industry and Heinz Hall, birthplace of Jeff Goldblum.

Ben had been traversing the state so thoroughly over the past couple of days that he barely knew which way was up anymore. It was one of the advantages of not being employed. He emerged from Heav-Y-Valu-Rack Discount Clothing and Heel Repair on Monday afternoon wearing a sleek new blue suit, one that had been heavily discounted after it was discovered that some of the stitching seemed to accidentally spell out an anti-Semitic phrase. Just as in his unfortunate hour back at Shinjoda Beneficial Industries, he felt like an idiot in the suit, unfamiliar as he was with most clothing that could not be bought at a sporting goods store. The fine garment even seemed to hide his very minor but growing beer belly, and that was something he just could not abide.

"You look great!" Earl Shavey told him as Ben crossed the sidewalk and entered the little park that sat beside a downtown shopping center. Earl was wearing a suit himself, one of many he owned and felt completely comfortable in. Around him stood Roy and Rick and Curse Williger, each of them similarly dressed. Curse's suit was the one he used to wear on road trips with the Cannons, and Rick's had been bought from a thrift store back in Harrisburg. His pants were about eleven inches too short. He had tied his long hair back for the occasion but had not managed to shave. All in all, the package worked just enough to fool the eye into thinking he was as much a Republican as he was a recreational incense-burner and unconditional tree-hugger.

"Yeah, dude, it's like night and day," Rick said to Ben.

"I just have to remember to hold onto the receipt so I can return this thing in three hours," Ben said. "Okay, is everybody about ready?"

"Just about," Roy said. "Can we go over our roles again?"

"Well, there are no real roles per se," Ben told them, "and I don't think anyone's going to have to actually speak. You just need to look official, like you might work for my company."

"What's the name of the company?" Earl asked.

Ben was at a loss. "Oh yeah, we need a name. Um...Earl, what's that outfit you work for?"

"The United Soy Sauce Coalition," Earl said with an audible tinge of pride.

"Okay, we won't be trying any variation of that," Ben said. He stepped over to the picnic bench the fellows had been sitting at and picked up the first APBA card he saw. They'd of course managed to squeeze in a condensed game with Rick's set while Ben was shopping for his suit. The card belonged to one Don Thoney of the Orlando Sun Snakes. "All right, I am the owner and CEO of the sports merchandising firm of Thoney, Orlando, and Dawn," Ben said. "Wait...what the hell happened here?" He realized that several of the player cards, the baseball diamond, and the playing booklet had been torn into small pieces, while dice were strewn across the ground and one of the shakers was actually dangling from the lowest branch of an elm tree behind his head.

"There was an incident," Curse said quietly. "I apologized, and we should probably just leave it at that."

"Curse was beating Rick 2-0 in the bottom of the ninth and the Guardians hit back-to-back-to-back homeruns," Earl reported. "Curse got a little...mad."

"I have a rage problem and I've admitted it," the ex-pitcher said, the frighteningly huge muscles in his chest and upper arms flexing tensely as his fist squished a scoresheet.

"I remember," Ben said.

"Man, you should start eating organic," Rick advised. "Eat brown rice instead of white. It'll totally change your outlook."

"Well, if you can get through the next hour without smashing anything to pieces, we should be all right," Ben said. "Let's walk over to the TDSN Building and make ourselves some money." They all turned and headed east, resembling a disorganized pack of gangsters who looked like they still might live with their parents.


The Thunder Dunk Sports Network was founded in the year 2001 as a more energetic alternative to other 24-hour cable sports channels which, in the opinion of true diehard fans, did not take hype nearly far enough. TDSN boldly added a number of unique wrinkles to its televised contests, including a constant rock and roll soundtrack accompanying the comments of the announcers in the booth, the application of live strobe motion effects and color-altering lenses to spruce the action up visually, and an attention-deficit updates technique which assured that the viewer did not have to arduously keep watching the same game without whipping around to others every ninety seconds. Purists may have taken issue with the way

TDSN gave its viewers neither the highlights nor even the scores of small market pro teams, or the way they had dumped all hockey coverage in favor of dodge ball, blackjack, and extreme mountainwater riverboarding, but the profits spoke for themselves. Their brand new building in downtown Pittsburgh was all silver and steel and giant murals depicting nothing but touchdowns and homeruns—the only two types of plays allowed by corporate decree to be shown on their hourly sports reports.

Ben and the rest of his "staff" navigated their way through the building's enormous revolving doors and checked in with the receptionist in the lushly carpeted lobby, where a Def Leppard song was blaring through a set of plainly visible speakers on the front counter. The receptionist was a part-time underwear model currently displaying so much skin that the group, whom she simply directed to the main elevator, wandered disoriented into a janitor's closet. They eventually found their way out and were soon whisked upwards to the thirtieth floor.

"How did you manage to get a meeting with Thor Rollins anyway?" Earl asked Ben, impressed and all a-tingle just to drop the name of one of sports media's flashiest personalities.

"Oh, the name Ben Glinton still has some currency in the sporting world, my friend," Ben replied, omitting from this sentence the story of how his elderly grandfather, General Crustus Glinton, had saved Thor Rollins's great uncle from an incoming German shell in 1943, and how Crustus had never let the man forget it.

"Back-to-back-to-back homeruns," Curse muttered under his breath behind them. "Great, just great. This whole city's gonna burn if I don't get out of here quick."

"Brown rice, man," Rick said. "Mind, spirit, united."

The ride ended. It was approximately a seven mile walk from the elevator down the hallway to Thor Rollins's main office (he had seven). Ben pushed open a door that was also an aquarium filled with tropical fish and poked his head into a room two-thirds the size of O'Hare Airport. Unlike O'Hare, though, this place had its own Nathan's Hot Dogs in the corner.

"Come on in, fellas!" the ridiculously blonde-headed Thor Rollins shouted from behind his desk, where he was standing and shooting baskets on a miniature clay court. He wore blue gym sweats and a red headband. Ben and the others walked across the carpet, which was cut and colored like artificial football turf and marked with yard lines. Thor's giant desk was in the end zone. YOU GOT THUNDER DUNKED, giant white letters said inside of it to football players who would never actually touch them. His panoramic picture window overlooked the city and sunlight poured in so dramatically that the man was virtually just a five foot eight inch silhouette before them.

"Ben Glinton," Ben greeted him, and they shook hands cordially before Thor gestured for them to sit down in the many chairs provided them.

"Glad to meet you. You boys want anything to drink? We have everything, including Orangina. Or Andrew over here can whip you up a hot dog. Hot dog, anyone?" He pointed at the little kiosk in the corner of the office, where a bored employee in a folded paper hat read a newspaper and looked up only slightly at the mention of his name.

"I think we're all fine," Ben said. "Ready to do some business."

"All riiiiiiiiiiiiiiiight," Thor said, sitting down heavily in his opulent chair, which was probably older than he was. "So what have you got for me to televise, Ben?"

"Well, there's going to be a tournament," Ben said, leaning forward and clasping his hands while the others sat awkwardly, remembering not to say anything under penalty of death. "A cash prize is going to be awarded for athletic excellence. And at this tournament, I'm going to reveal the true *secret history* of the night of October 21st, 2002, when I pretty much single-handedly ruined my team's chances of winning the world championship."

"I was at that game," Thor said. "The Cannons didn't have much of a chance anyway, really. Your bullpen was just about depleted."

"Oh no, I think most people would agree that I alone completely destroyed us," Ben said, trying to sound modest. "And I think the public has shown a definite interest in wanting to know why someone of my intelligence would do something so phenomenally stupid on the baseball field."

"Could be," Thor said, twiddling his fingers and leaning back in his chair. "So what sort of competition are we talking about? Is it extreme? We could always use more extreme. Our ratings reports show that people especially like to watch men either hoisting or crushing things these days. Something involving either one of those activities would be great."

"Our idea is as extreme as it gets," Ben said. "We want your network to sponsor, are you ready for this..." He drew the sentence out for effect, inching ever more forward on his seat. "...an APBA tournament!"

Thor put a finger to his lips in contemplation. "I know what that is, I think," he said. "Isn't that a board game?"

"Correct!" Ben said, smelling blood in the water. "One of the true tests of managerial intellect outside of the real thing."

"Yeah, I used to play that," Thor said with a fond smile of remembrance. "Me and all the kids in the neighborhood used to get together after school. I recall trying to replay a whole season once all by myself, but I lost my set somewhere. Good times, good times."

"And those good times continue today," Ben told him. "I and the others in my firm here have done some preliminary market research, and we have found many people who still live on the thrill of competition in this, um, realm. We want to stage a tournament in Las Vegas, put up a huge cash prize, and lure the press in with the promise that I, Ben Glinton, will both win the tournament *and* reveal the secret of my catastrophic failure, live and unscripted for the cameras."

"Was it drugs?" Thor asked. "It was drugs, right?"

"That's what I thought originally," Roy offered.

"It wasn't drugs!" Ben snapped. "What it was will blow people's brains right out of their noses."

"Yeah, brains, okay," Thor said, clasping his hands in front of him on his desk. "The thing is, though, where's the *sizzle?* Where's the *edge?"*

"You have your pitcher give up back to back to back homeruns and watch a dude physically attack his opponent, *there's* your sizzle," Ben said. "I know a guy who practically broke a picnic table in two not a half hour ago."

"Or suffer the heartbreak of thinking you've hit a run-scoring ground ball to second only to find that an X-graded pitcher just turned it into a harmless strikeout!" Earl offered, desperate to be helpful.

"Mmmmmmmmmmm," Thor said. "Yeah, I just don't know, fellas. We've sponsored video game tournaments before and we made a bundle, but board games, they're kind of slow and quiet, you know what I'm saying? Not very Generation Y."

"Well," Ben assured him, "we're only going to need twenty thousand dollars as a prize, plus the costs of running the tournament, plus hotel rooms for me and the staff of my company, plus we're going to need card sets for all sorts of seasons of course. And food. And drinks. Maybe tickets to a magic show as a random giveaway."

Thor sighed. "It's just too much of a risk, Ben. Thunder Dunk Sports puts the emphasis on the Wow factor. We have a saying here: 'If you can't scream it, don't bother saying it.' We're committed to presenting only the biggest events and the hippest doings. I'd like to hear the secret of why you tanked the series and all, but we're living in a video game world now. That's what the kids want to hear about. The sound of dice rolling isn't going to cut it. You put Monopoly or Risk in front of some kid today, they're going to fall asleep reading the instructions. Have you seen the graphics on Thunder Dunk Salary Cap Derby 2006? The players' faces seem a little bit smooshed and watery, I know, but a third of all at-bats are dingers. A *third!* Plus we've introduced the home plate dance. It's the end zone dance concept brought to baseball! That's what we're into."

"That doesn't sound very realistic," Rick noted.

"Realism is the *last* thing we want to put on TV," Thor said. "Ever tried to actually watch a real baseball game all the way through? I wouldn't recommend it if you're operating a motor vehicle."

"You make good points," Ben said, crossing and uncrossing his legs, "but the tournament I envision will feature one thing the young audience can't seem to get enough of. A thing known as Spike Vail."

"Spike Vail, eh?" Thor said. "You could guarantee he'd be involved?"

"Oh, easily," Ben lied shamelessly. "He and I are good buds from back in the day. We almost both played for Guardians." Instantly seventy percent of his brain went to work on isolating the lie, studying it for cracks in the foundation, and applying cheap rubber cement to those cracks in the form of follow-up lies which would at least get him another meeting with this TV doofus at a later date.

"Spike Vail is a start," Thor said. "How else could we pep this puppy up?"

"How about girls?" Roy suggested, having no idea what he meant by it. He often tended to think about girls, being wholly unable to get one since junior high school. His failure to find a date sometimes manifested itself through the way he found himself issuing a simple verbal statement of their existence. It brought him some comfort.

"Hot girls play APBA now?" Thor asked. "How the hell did *that* happen?"

"Marketing," Ben said quickly. "It's all about marketing. You should have seen the chicks who showed up when I started an APBA group. Man oh man."

"What else?" Thor said, getting interested. "Spike Vail, hot girls, maybe a little co-sponsorship by a certain whiskey manufacturer that owes us a favor...it's starting to come into focus..."

"Bands, of course," Ben said. "It's the only reason people watch the Super Bowl anymore. Long-haired deadbeats singing unintelligible lyrics about their love lives. Ooh yeah!"

"Bands!" Thor agreed, slapping his hand on his desk. "We can turn it into a total rock and roll party, like we did with the British Open! Yes!"

"And naturally, losing a game is not what gets you booted from our tournament," Ben said, taking one last grab at the big brass ring. "You're out only when the viewers *vote* you out. The panel of judges which harshly critiques your play will sway the voting of course, but the opinions of the slack-jawed rubes at home are what thin the herd and keep the long distance and text messaging charges funneling money through the back door."

"You, sir, are a genius!" Thor cried. "The slack-jawed rubes are *always* the linchpin! It's like you've read our corporate mission statement top to bottom!"

*"No!"* blurted a strong, deep voice to Ben's left. Curse Williger stood up in his ungodly uncomfortable gray suit and glared at Thor Rollins with eyes of fire and ominous C-chords resounding in his voice. "I'm not going to stand here and watch you cheapen the game I love! You're going to give us that money and you're going to put the cameras on a bunch of nobodies playing quietly and respectfully!"

"Ah, Ben, this man works for your firm?" Thor asked, offended.

"In the mailroom," Ben said. "We brought him on the trip because he has one of those big folding street maps..."

"My whole career, guys like this cheapened baseball!" Curse raged. "Helmet cams, interviewing managers in the dugout in the middle of the game, making us wait longer between innings to start pitching so they could cram more commercials in...somebody's got to take a stand!"

"Hey pal," Thor challenged, "this ain't PBS; we're actually *trying* to keep people's attention. I don't think adding some swooshing noises when stats pop up on the screen ever killed anybody."

"You're making sports fans dumber and more impatient than ever," Curse told him. "Well, the board game *we* play that's so boring to you just makes you smarter. Smart enough to get the hell out of here."

Ben stood up and put a hand on Curse's shoulder. "What my colleague is saying, obviously, is that we're willing to explore every possible option to make the tournament as viewer-friendly as possible, including putting in some kind of murder mystery."

"I think Curse is right, dude," Rick said to Ben. "TDSN is filled with impurities. Sports-wise."

Ben pointed an accusing finger at each one of them except Thor. "Why did I hire you people for my firm?" Ben demanded to know. "Who are you really working for? *Who sent you?"*

"Let's table this for now until you can get your staff under control," Thor said. "Meanwhile I'll have some employee or the other get in touch with Spike Vail's people and see if maybe there's something worth talking about at some point."

"Spike Vail has no idea who we are, that was a total lie," Curse said. "He's too busy strapping a microphone to his jersey so people at home can hear his stupid chit-chat in the dugout. Come on, guys, let's get out of here before we get sucked into some rotisserie league." He turned and headed for the exit.

"Whatever you've heard about Spike Vail's spontaneous dugout comments to his teammates being completely scripted by interns is totally false!" Thor said, suddenly red-faced. "Who have you been talking to?"

But they had already more or less departed, except for Ben, who leaned over the desk to shake Thor's hand. "Great talking to you," Ben said. "I think Curse is mistaking you for an uncle he used to have, there was some bad blood there, so give me a call." With that, he turned and slunk out of the office. He thought briefly about grabbing a hot dog on the way out, then decided it probably wouldn't help his chances of striking a deal.

The others stood quietly beyond the door that was also an aquarium, looking sheepish, including Curse. When Ben emerged, he merely looked them up and down with vague distaste and then started down the hallway.

"Sorry, Ben," Curse said. "But come on, this whole place is all wrong for us."

"I think I agree," Earl added. "By the time the tournament started, we probably would have forgotten what it was all about, with all those cameras and those network goons around, and that TDSN theme music playing in our heads all the time."

"Which they completely ripped off from Grand Funk Railroad," Rick noted. "I can prove it."

"I'm not speaking to any of you until I've safely gotten a refund for this suit," Ben said as they all got into the elevator. "Only then will I listen to more of your plans to destroy my dream. And only after we've eaten something. I'll be choosing where that meal takes place, if you all don't mind. I was thinking about Hamburger Vampire, unless there are any sudden, unpredicted, and irrational objections."

The others offered no resistance, though there was more than one silent seed of opposition to the Hamburger Vampire idea. As far as fast food burger places with supernatural themes, it was not one of the best.

"So," Earl said gently, "what's the next move?"

Ben gazed intently at the little display of lights tracking their downward progress through the Thunder Dunk building. "Well, I'm going to need some serious time for reflection and logical thinking," he said. "The meetings and gaming sessions will go on in my apartment as usual, but you probably won't see me for a couple of weeks...maybe three. There's a place I go when I need to really sit and carefully sort things out without making rash decisions. It's a little farm my family owns. I'm going to go there and analyze the situation, and only after I examine every possible alternative will I return and inform you what we're going to try next. If you don't hear from me, don't worry. It only means that I'm taking my time, looking at everything from every conceivable angle, so that we don't make any more critical errors in judgment."

## 12. Eighteen Hours Later, Ben Pulled Up In Front of Harold's House After Spending A Great Deal of Money He Did Not Have on an RV and Deciding They Were All Headed on the Spur of the Moment to Las Vegas

Eighteen hours later, Ben pulled up in front of Harold's house after spending a great deal of money he did not have on an RV and deciding they were all headed on the spur of the moment to Las Vegas. When the entire APBA Collective, having been summoned to Harold's place by a series of mysterious late night phone calls from Ben, saw him pull up to the curb, their jaws dropped at the spectacle of Ben honking like a crazy person and accidentally clipping both of Harold's trash cans, sending them bouncing across the lawn. He killed the engine of the off-white, rather grotesque-looking mechanical beast—TRAVEL OPTION was the name brand of the RV, stenciled in silver and unfamiliar to them all—and hopped out, grinning from ear to ear. The group came hesitantly forward, Earl putting a protective arm around his son's shoulders for fear that either the vehicle or Ben himself might suddenly lurch forward and crush them all.

"Have you ever seen anything so beautiful?" Ben said, turning with them to admire his purchase. "It's like the freaking Eiffel Tower if you stuck a bunch of wheels on it and put in a bathroom."

"Ben, what have you done?" Harold asked. He could psychically feel his wife's horrified gaze beaming suspicion down upon the lawn from an upstairs window. "Where did you get the money to buy this thing?"

"A little invention called plastic," Ben said. "I had almost completely forgotten I had a Discover card until you told me about that co-worker of yours who had to declare bankruptcy last month. I went down to Shammy's Showcase of Definitive Rides and grabbed this puppy almost as soon as I saw it."

"But why?" Harold asked. "You already have a place to live."

"Well, actually I really don't," Ben said, "because it turns out my building's getting demolished at the end of the week, but that has nothing to do with it. We're all going to Las Vegas for the tournament—and we're leaving today, if possible."

"Las Vegas?" Rick said, bewildered.

"I'll tell you of this wondrous turn of events while I give you all a grand tour of the place you'll be sleeping in as we head across this great land of ours," Ben said, and opened a door into the RV, jumping in with aplomb. With great reluctance, Harold stepped in, followed by Earl, Jake, Rick, Curse, Roy, and Templeton, who actually seemed more impressed than any of them. It had long been his secret dream to journey across America in an RV, making notes as he went for a two thousand page novel about the more uninteresting parts of the nation's highway system.

"Check it out," Ben said, sweeping his arm across the interior of the somewhat cramped mobile home. "Just barely enough room for everybody, if two people improvise with the sleeping arrangements. There's a fridge, a tiny little stove, a dining room table where we can eat and play APBA, and a TV. Three hundred thousand miles on it, but it purrs along like a cat after a roast beef dinner."

"You, um, expect us all to drop our lives and head off to Las Vegas?" Harold asked.

"Sounds like fun, Ben, but I don't get any vacation time at the paper until I work there for two years without using a sick day," Roy said.

"I don't think my wife would be too crazy about a trip like that," Earl added.

"I'm ready to go!" Jake cried, opening the mini-fridge and sticking his hand inside. "It's cold! It's really cold!"

"Las Vegas," Ben told them, "will be the site of our tournament, to take place one week from today. I've already called the Lucky Ape Hotel and Casino and arranged for the use of their conference center, and I've bombarded the internet with news of the competition. I've also alerted dozens of media sources via e-mail— thank you, Kinko's of South Harrisburg. Wheels have been set in motion. Wheels, gentlemen."

"What about the prize money?" Roy asked. "Oh, wait, you found a way to put that on the credit card too! Superb!" He whipped out his tiny notebook to quickly jot down the details of this scheme for the biography.

"No, no, that didn't happen," Ben said. "There was only enough room on the card to buy the RV."

"So how has the prize money issue been settled?" Templeton asked.

Ben smiled wide and threw his hands up in the air. "Beats the hell out of me!" he said happily. "But if I could buy a sweet RV and set up the tournament in all of four hours, that last part won't be too much of a problem, I don't think."

"You didn't go on the internet and already promise that money, did you?" Harold asked, closing his eyes in terror.

"More or less. Come on, everybody, let's go for a spin around the block and see what this little darling can do." He fired up the engine, which sounded a little like the stuttering of a faulty Commodore 64 hard drive.

Harold turned. "That's it, Ben, you've gone off your rocker. I'm telling Deenie that—"

"Okay, we're just pulling away from the curb here," Ben said, and they were off before Harold could escape. The others grabbed seats as quickly as they could before the sudden swerve knocked them off their feet. Bundles, a dozing neighborhood cat who belonged to no one in particular—but who had, in fact, been silent witness to the latest attempted atrocity by the fiendish but rather inefficient Pool Skimmer Strangler—yelped at the oncoming goliathan and scampered out of the way, vowing revenge as much as any cat could manage it.

"It's going to take me a little while to get the hang of operating something this size," Ben noted as he came within inches of sideswiping a passing Jetta. "Maybe when we cross into the Midwest we can start sharing the driving duties."

"Tell us again," Harold said, rubbing his temple, "why we're expected to do this crazy thing?"

"I've anticipated all your possible objections," Ben said, "and it's like this. All of us in this awesome vehicle share one thing in common: we've just about exhausted the possibilities of making something exciting happen with our lives. We're all tied down to our jobs and our wives and kids, and our youth is rapidly running out."

The obvious fallacy of the very foundation of Ben's argument was grasped within a quarter of a second by every person on board the ship, and confused glances were exchanged. Roy, Rick, Curse, Jake, and Templeton were about to speak up with wishes that they not be so hastily included in his hyperbolic statement, but Ben had already moved on to point number two.

"Secondly, what are the chances of a bunch of guys from different backgrounds, but all sharing a passion for one thing, getting together for a genuine road adventure with guaranteed excitement at the end of it? Isn't that the kind of thing that you remember for the rest of your life? And how many of us have had any adventures in our adulthoods worth remembering? I played big league baseball for years, and even that's all just a blur of bad hotels and foul balls to the right side."

This, none of them could truly deny. Roy scanned his memories of his few post-college years for any hint of excitement outside buying an iPod and getting a single promising response to one of his many internet personal ads. The girl had turned out to be a shrewish co-worker with a face like an angry squid. Templeton thought about all the arduous weeks, months, and years in front of his manual typewriter, producing work after work of undeniable brilliance but sleepwalking through awards ceremony after awards ceremony. To Earl, adulthood had meant the responsibility of providing for his family and raising Jake in absolute terror that the boy might wind up with anything less than a 1700 on his SATs or fall in with that rough crowd which went to movies and rode bicycles. Harold's mind flashed with images of his receding hairline and of his front lawn, whose maintenance had utterly consumed him over the past few years. Rick had had some good times at World Bank protests, but he had never actually been arrested, which saddened him to no end. What did you have to do to get the attention of the cops nowadays? Strangle somebody with a pool skimmer?

"Thirdly," Ben said, "if we don't all go at once, on the spur of the moment, we'll hem and haw and think of all kinds of reasons to put it off and put it off, and eventually we'll start to want to stage the tournament within one mile of where we live for the convenience factor, and somebody will get the sniffles and want to back out, and somebody else will have to go attend their mother-in-law's half-sister's new baby's circumcision, and somebody else will remember that they promised to stand in for the lead actor in some local production of *The Caine Mutiny Court Martial* with an all-deaf cast—you know, all the excuses that make us boring adults with no spark for risk in our lives. Well, *I'm* not going to become that guy. Will you?" He made the mistake of looking at Jake when he delivered this last line, but then quickly shifted his accusatory gaze to Harold.

"I have not done something spontaneous in twenty years," Templeton said, taking out his pipe. "I had a chance to jet off to Africa when *The New Yorker* asked me to go write a piece on Angola, but I said no. I didn't think my knees would like the dry climate."

"We could see some crazy stuff on the road," Rick said optimistically. "The real America, too, probably, before it was destroyed by corporate greed and synthesizers."

"I guess it would be essential for the biography," Roy said. "I suppose I could convince my boss somehow..."

"Oh, could we stop at the Robert Oppenheimer Museum?" Jake asked, bouncing on his hands excitedly.

"I don't think this would be any sort of journey for a young boy," Earl said, trying to contain Jake's emotions. "I suppose my wife would let me go, Ben, she's always saying I should spend some time alone and as far away from her as possible."

"Hell, I'm in," Curse said. "I got nothing going on. My anger management group is always trying to get us to interact with other people more. They're a bunch of worthless stupid spineless ugly jerks, but I guess it makes sense. And I really want to win that tournament, too."

"That just leaves you, Harold," Ben said, putting a hand on his best friend's shoulder. "How about it? This is the part where you think about it for a minute, and then you look at everyone's faces, and then you give in, and then everyone lets out a cheer. So yeah, do that now so everyone can get home and start packing."

"How in the world do you think Deenie would let me bounce off to Las Vegas for a week or two?" Harold asked.

"How strong is your marriage?" Ben asked him.

"It's really strong, you know that," Harold said, somewhat embarrassed. "We love and trust each other completely."

"Then you should take off before she wakes up tomorrow and just leave a note on the counter," Ben urged. "A bond like yours can easily survive some modest hijinks like these. Just be sure to leave her some flowers and a promise that you'll romance her like mad when you get back."

"Isn't that the same technique that made Pippagail finally divorce you?" Harold asked. "When you snuck off for four days to go see that taping of *The Drew Carey Show*?"

"Pippagail divorced me because of a mutual decision that she was the Devil," Ben said. "Now before this stoplight turns green, I want your answer. And remember who was the best man at that sick wedding you let Gordy stage for his hamsters, and who was your only real friend on the Cannons, save for that suck-up Craig Tomarkin."

Harold thought about it for a minute and then looked at everyone's faces. Ben was leaning forward in anticipation, slowly allowing the RV to creep forward into the intersection. Someone honked and he pressed harder on the dangerously loose brake pedal before he killed somebody.

"If I go with you," Harold said, "you have to baby-sit Gordy whenever he needs it for the next full year."

"Done!" Ben said. "A delightful child. Wish he was my own."

"And you have to stop calling me Turkey Boat when we're around other people. I don't even know what you mean by that."

"Done. I wasn't sure either."

"And Roy has to say nice things about me in your biography. I wasn't much of a baseball player, but there's no reason people can't know that I tried to be a nice person."

Roy shrugged. "Sure, Harold. I've already written good things about you. I won't forget that you tried to set me up with your sister, either. Too bad she doesn't go for the unmanly type."

"She may change," Harold said. "She's a little crazy."

"Then we have an entire platoon of soldiers ready to head into ultimate battle!" Ben cried. "We're leavin' for Vegas tomorrow at noon!"

He did not get the eruption of applause and backslapping he had expected; it was more like the general murmur of half-hearted approval one might hear when a public library's acquisitions board agrees to buy a new copy of Dean Koontz's *Watchers* to replace one that some young punk had no intention of ever returning. But it was good enough. Ben tooted the RV's horn once for good measure, utterly terrifying a ninety-one year old woman who was making her way through a crosswalk, and the names of the TRAVEL OPTION's crew were cemented into dubious decision history. The TRAVEL OPTION itself had a very minor catastrophic breakdown at the edge of Harold's street as they returned to the house, but for a Luddite, Rick displayed an impressive knowledge of the unsightly heap's electrical system and he managed to get it up and running again by swapping a few fuses and re-routing two cables whose purpose was somewhat of a mystery and whose aroma of charred pork would remain worrisome. They were all to meet at Ben's apartment the next day with as much APBA paraphernalia as they owned and with the absolute minimum of other personal possessions. Most of the group was haunted that night by frightening dreams that seemed to foretell a horrific fate beyond the Rocky Mountains and warned them vividly not to get in any motorized or even hand-propelled vehicle with Ben even one more time. These were shrugged off as being caused by high-carb meals and the plan rolled on apace.

## 13. Provoke Not the Wrath of Mrs. Sippingcorb

As it turned out, Harold's beloved wife was more than happy to let her husband travel to the wilds of Nevada with a bunch of his friends. At first Harold thought this was most disturbing, especially with a murderer running loose in the neighborhood, but Deenie explained that she meant to seize the opportunity to take their son for a week-long journey to colonial Williamsburg, the one and only travel location Harold had refused to visit in all the years of their marriage. It was actually the sole issue on which he had stood his ground in any aspect of life since the mid-eighties. He justified his hatred for colonial Williamsburg with obscure arguments about the inauthenticity of some of the exhibits and attractions, but in reality, he was possessed by an unnatural terror of the clothing worn during that period of American history. The sight of a tri-cornered hat or a white bonnet made him break into a sweat, and catching a glimpse of any sort of monocle or beige button-up vest made his heart race with fear. He would go to his grave someday never understanding the cause of this affliction, or even revealing its power over him to anyone but Ben. As it turned out, his failure to accompany his wife would allow her the unexpected freedom to attend all sorts of incredibly boring colonial cooking demonstrations, condemning Harold to even more years of experimental meal ideas which he would suffer in morose silence.

Even more surprising was the presence of one Jake Shavey on the ride to Vegas. His mother, who had been secretly worrying that the boy's uneasiness around natural sunlight was getting to be a chronic problem, agreed after much discussion that he would be better off driving across America for two weeks than holed up in his room with his ant farms and old issues of *The Economist,* provided his father didn't destroy him by exposing him to the various horrifying elements that cavorted about the west. Earl Shavey hadn't actually mentioned the words 'Las Vegas' in his plans, replacing them with the term 'fascinating and historically significant dry-mining ghost town of Delmar' at the most key moments, and while this half-truth certainly saved the trip for both of them, Earl was certain it would condemn him to an afterlife in hell.

"Okay, let's see what you think of what I have so far," Roy was saying to Ben as the two of them sat in the RV's dining area while Rick guided them towards Ohio on Sunday afternoon. They had been on the road for about three and a half hours and the dining table had seen no actual food action but more than a few APBA games, with Templeton and Jake getting into some hot and heavy dice rolling craziness involving all-star teams they had drafted from scratch. Templeton had tried out some new managerial theories of his, including spreading his best hitters throughout the lineup instead of bunching them at the top, and playing with wild aggressiveness on the base paths. Jake had countered his gambits by playing straightforward ball and he had taken two games out of three when Templeton and most of the others on board had decided to chill out and simply gaze at the scenery that passed them by as Rick drove them along at speeds well above the legal limit. (In his heart, he knew that the best hope they had for getting all the way across the country in this disastrous dinosaur was to just floor it and hope that sheer forward momentum would counter the engine's many failings.) There would be plenty of time tonight for everyone to play some experimental games they had always wanted to try, in which they would throw the best players among all their card sets against the absolute worst, just to see what happened. In the meantime, Roy had produced all his notes for Ben's biography in preparation for a good hour or so of brainstorming about how best to approach the touchy subject of the night of October 21, 2002.

" 'The October air was arduous in the bottom of the eleventh inning as Ben slithered into the batter's box,' " Roy quoted from his notes. " 'With one out, the opportunity for Jason Blaze to purloin second base was definitely there for the taking, but Greeny St. Clair had confidence in Ben's power against Rick Shelrik. With only a single run necessary to etch the names of all twenty-six of the Kentucky Cannons into the history books, and with Ben desperate to make up for his amazing gaffe in the ninth, everything seemed to be falling into place. When Shelrik fell behind 1-0, the boos around the stadium were replaced by a syrupy quiet.' "

Ben thought about it. "Not a bad start," he said. "But there were really only twenty-five of us on the roster. We were one man short because Mike Morgan suddenly retired after Game Four when he got a MacArthur Genius grant for all his isotope research. Strange, strange guy."

Roy upended his pencil and erased some words, adding others, then read on. " 'The 1-1 pitch was a fast ball right down the middle, but Shelrik had forgotten to add any zing to it and it zanged instead. Ben swung and cranked the ball deep to left field. The crowd leapt to its feet in excitement. Ben launched into his homerun trot halfway to first base, knowing for sure that the series was over, that he had redeemed himself, and that a pageant of jollity would swarm him when he touched that final rectangle in the dirt. The fact that there was no sudden roar from the crowd, which should have come when the ball sailed over the fence as he rounded first, apparently did not register in his spacious mind. He trotted on, oblivious, already tasting the champagne that awaited the Cannons in the clubhouse.' "

"Our owner didn't allow alcohol on the property," Ben said. "He filled the champagne bottles with lemon juice. Even if we had won, there wouldn't have been any carbonation in them to spray anybody with. We would have shaken them up, pointed them at each other, popped the cork, and lemon juice would have dribbled out. And they call *me* an idiot."

Roy did a little more erasing.

" 'Upon rounding third base, Ben sensed something was amiss,' " Roy continued. " 'He saw only Kevin Hanley, the Guardian's catcher, standing dumbfounded at home plate, holding the ball in his mitt. Ben walked right into it with all the force of a snail bumping into a stop sign. Dozens of photographers captured his expression at that moment. That infamous photo would become the cover of Terence Von Sneed's exhaustive and Nobel prize-winning ten-volume history of the twentieth century, bumping images of both the battles of D-Day and the first moon landing.' "

"To be fair, I did make an effort to jostle the ball out of Kevin Hanley's mitt," Ben protested.

"Are you sure?" Roy asked. "I was watching that game, and it didn't really look like it."

"Oh yeah," Ben said. "When I realized what had happened, I slapped at that glove pretty hard."

"Positive?" Roy asked shyly. "I've read accounts of the game, and no one ever said—"

"I'm not sure how he held on to the ball with the whacking I gave that mitt, in fact," Ben interrupted. "You gotta give him credit. He just wanted it more."

"I brought a tape of the game along," Roy said. "Maybe when we get to Las Vegas we can pop it in and—"

"All *right,*" Ben said, slumping in his seat, "I didn't even remember to try to knock the ball out of his glove. Happy? My God, is there *no* positive spin you're willing to put on that play, or anything about that night? Have I not promised you homemade macaroons tonight?"

"I'm just worried that no one will think the book is honest if I start fibbing a little here and there," Roy said. "And then no one will pay any attention to the rest of it."

"Okay, look," Ben said with resignation, "I agreed to let you write whatever you wanted about that night. I agreed to let you spend two full pages on how I failed my Camp Wampum archery test the first three times I took it. I agreed to tell you about how I missed a series in Toronto once because I got my finger stuck in the keys of an accordion. So how about at least letting me pick the title for this monstrosity?"

"Oh sure, I can live with that," Roy said. "Any ideas?"

Ben put his hands up in a primitive framing gesture. *"Standing on the Misty Mountain of Hope: Baseball, Society, and Ben Glinton's Struggle to Overcome the Odds,"* he said.

Roy chewed the end of his pencil. "Sounds a little long," he said. "For the spine."

"How about *Assault in Lexington: America's War on the Ballplayer Who Tried."*

Roy had been writing Ben's thoughts down, but he stopped long before Ben even got to the colon on this last one. "Sounds a little bit...self-pitying," he said.

Ben thought for a moment. *"I Never Wept for My Uncle."*

"Ooh, what does that mean?" Roy asked. "Is there a good personal story there?"

"No, I just can't stand the man," Ben said. "What if we do a play on words, like combine 'Glinton' with 'rocket ship' or something like that?"

"I'll work on it, but it could be tough," Roy said.

"Well, no time to work on it tonight," Ben said, "I've got a surprise for everybody." He stood up. "We're headed to a ball game, people!"

The others looked around from their daydreaming with raised eyebrows.

"Ball game?" Templeton said. "Where?"

"It's off to see the Cleveland Oarsmen battle the Oakland Raftermen in fairly meaningless mid-July action," Ben said. "I bought tickets in advance, so we're all gonna go and turn that stadium upside down!"

"I haven't been inside a baseball stadium in two years," Curse said. "Should be interesting."

"All right, the Cleveland Oarsmen!" Jake said. "I used their lineup in my science project about how foul balls shorten a player's career!"

"I haven't been to a game since I was a kid," Rick said as he steered them down the road. "It got so commercial. Like, when are they going to just start painting ads for porn on the field, you know?"

"I haven't been in a while either," Ben said. "In fact, even going near a stadium makes me a little sick. This should be interesting. Rick, take the next exit. We've been suffering on the road for too long!"

The stadium in Cleveland was pretty much a duplicate of every stadium built in the last fifteen years. Its much-heralded and extremely expensive throwback look would, of course, be mocked and whined about in another few decades just as the cookie cutter stadiums of the sixties and seventies were, but for now, people seemed to be enjoying themselves as they entered the park, confident that their vote to publicly fund the place had finally given the middle and upper classes a new neighborhood in which to buy designer sheets and eat at Fuddrucker's. Ben and the others made their way up to the nosebleed seats holding pretzels and sodas and hot dogs and beer as a cozy summer twilight settled in.

"How does it feel?" Roy asked Ben as they leafed through their programs, hoping that their number sequences on page 77 would win them the seventh inning giveaway and fund the prize money for the Vegas tournament.

"So far, so good," Ben said. "My breathing is even. Pulse rate okay. Nobody's recognized me. How about you, Curse?" He leaned forward and looked down their row of seats at him. Curse had pulled his cap way down low over his eyes.

"Seven dollars for a small beer; these people should be forced to eat a time bomb and dropped into a hive of wasps soaked in arsenic," he commented.

They stood for the anthem and the game began. In the top of the first inning, there were two hits, two walks, three visits to the mound, a pitching change, a meeting in the infield, a disputed call, eleven tosses from the pitchers to first base (only one of which was a genuine pickoff move), an equipment swap, a re-sweeping of the batter's box, and fourteen foul balls. The inning took twenty-seven minutes to resolve.

"Oh my God, is baseball really this boring?" Ben asked wonderingly as a Coldplay song boomed on the PA system. "I don't watch it, I just played it. People just have to sit here for three hours? Is it possible?"

"How come the next half inning hasn't started yet?" Curse asked no one in particular. "Why are we waiting? It was one thing to toss the ball around between innings, but jeez, I never thought about how you have to pay to watch it."

"It's kinda weird how a new reliever gets to throw a bunch of warm-up pitches," Rick noted. "Like, shouldn't you practice off the field? Can't you be prepared when you come into game? Aren't these guys professionals?"

"Did you see the way everyone was stepping out of the batter's box after every pitch?" Ben asked. "Did I do that? Oh Lord, if I did that I am so sorry, people."

"Seems like you should only get so many mound conferences," Earl mused. "They don't give you unlimited timeouts in football."

"And in basketball, just try asking for everyone to stop what they're doing so you can adjust your equipment or adjust your jersey," said Roy.

"The action of the game itself is indeed somewhat obfuscated by vast stretches of nothingness," Templeton noted. "But it is the nothingness that gives us time to ruminate, appreciate the stillness, the strategy, the je ne sais quoi that makes baseball what it is."

"I suppose," Ben said. "Still, seems like we could wrap this baby up in about an hour fifteen if everyone would just make an effort."

"Jake, what are you doing?" Earl asked his son, who had set aside the remains of his ten dollar chicken finger combo meal and removed a box from his backpack.

"I want to play a game between these teams with APBA at the same time," he said, removing the game components. "If I hold it all real careful on my lap, I'll bet I won't spill anything."

"Cool," Rick said beside him. "I'll hold the field and keep score if you want. Actually, why don't you let me manage the Oarsmen."

"Oh, is that the most recent card set?" Templeton asked, leaning in for a look. "You've got your work cut out for you, Rick; last year's Oarsmen had no bullpen before Steve Queeby arrived."

"True, but I think I can hold my own, as long as Mike Mars pulls his weight with the bat for once in his life," Rick said, opening up the Cleveland team envelope and beginning to construct his lineup as Jake produced two dice shakers.

"Fellas, you're going to play APBA when you have an *actual* game unfolding right in front of you?" Roy asked.

"In the time it takes these jokers to get to the seventh inning stretch, we'll have finished a double-header," Rick said. "All right, let's see here...you gonna start a left-hander, Jake? 'Cause if you are, I have some decisions to make."

"If you're talking double-header, I want in on the second game," Curse interjected.

"I'll hold the sacrifice booklet, Jake," his father offered. "Looks like you might have a little trouble balancing it all."

"You know what would be a big help, Roy, is if you supported the box on your knees so we could toss the dice in it," said Rick. "Thanks, that'd be great." He handed the box to Roy, who took it without protest. He looked to Ben, who merely shrugged and sank a little lower in his seat.

As the game on the field went on, the spectators around the group became a little confused at the way their shouts of glee and excitement were often at odds with the actual action down below them. Ben did his best to try to focus on the real game, wanting to get his money's worth, but by the fourth inning, when a 9-0 Oakland lead promised a marathon of quiet pain for all ticket holders, he pretty much gave up and devoted his attention to the way the cards on Jake's lap were creating a back-and-forth, 4-4, thirteen inning duel in which Street Smith, the Cleveland third baseman who had been traded over the winter, knocked two doubles and a triple to rally his team time and time again. Meanwhile, Smith's actual self just four hundred feet away was suffering through a forgettable 0 for 4 night, stranding men on base like it was going out of style. In the sixth inning, with the score on the field 12-1, people began to empty out of the stands, and everyone but Ben and Roy moved down a couple of rows, not for a better view, but because it gave them a little more room to stretch out with the second game of their double-header. Even though that one was a total blowout, it was completed well before the fat lady sang for the true life Oarsmen.

"Thank you for coming to tonight's game!" the PA announcer said to the remaining fans at 11:19 p.m. "We hope to see you again soon. And on the way out, ladies and gentlemen, let's hear it for two former stars who have joined us tonight: Ex-Cannon Walter Williger..."

There was scattered applause from around the park and the giant video screen in center field showed a live shot of Walter's cap-covered face as he finished off the last of his second beer. He lifted a weak hand in a wave, not bothering to take the beer away from his mouth.

"Oh crap!" Ben cried, getting to his feet. "Come on, everyone, hold on to the person next to you and get to the highest row you can! Don't make eye contact with anyone! When they say my name, put your fingers in your ears and just wait for it to end!"

"...and former Cincinnati Chewers standout Jim Lucas!" the announcer finished. There was louder applause for the hometown hero as Ben froze with one leg over the row of seats in front of him. He looked around, stunned.

"What the hell?" he said as he was ignored by the thousands of people filing for the exits.

"Looks like you lucked out, Ben," said Earl. "They missed you."

"What am I, a ghost?" Ben said, offended. "I didn't even wear a cap. Is my face so forgettable?"
"Don't you *want* to go unnoticed?" Roy asked.

"Not anymore, we need publicity for the tournament!" Ben said. "The more people hate me now, the more dramatic my confession will be next Saturday!" He stood up on his seat and began waving his arms. "Hey, everyone, it's Bitter Ben Glinton!" he shouted. "Over here! I'm still alive! Remember me?!"

People looked over at Ben as they moved down the aisle, but no one seemed to believe that the real Ben Glinton, even given his history of poor decision-making, would be stupid enough to go out of his way to call attention to himself. "Sad, what someone will claim just to get on the center field camera," one fan remarked, while another went home thinking that mental illness had many faces: some people thought they were Napoleon, others thought they were disgraced baseball players. Disturbing.

"Oh, for Pete's sake, people, let me have some abuse!" Ben shouted. "Bring on the hate!" He lost his balance at one point and slipped off the seat, scraping his shin.

Earl leaned close to Roy's ear. "You don't, ah, have to put this incident in his biography, do you?" he asked him.

Roy shook his head. "I'm leaving so much stuff out for courtesy's sake," he said, "the book may wind up being twenty pages long."

Ben gave up his histrionics soon enough and they left the ballpark. In the parking lot, Ben was finally recognized by a passing spectator. It was his third grade teacher. Elderly Mrs. Sippingcorb asked him what he had gone on to do in life beyond the confines of French Rope Elementary School. Ben told her he had become a Braillist. She smiled politely and wished him good luck. On the car ride back home, she told her husband that she could have smacked that series-bungling doofus for lying to her face, and that she'd had to restrain herself from shoving her old Cannons cap right up his cavernous nose.

### 14. Whither the Curtis L. Sackler Effect?

The magic bus broke down once again in the early morning hours of the following day. They had set in for the night in the parking lot of a Wal-Mart outside Tiffin, Ohio, which thrilled Jake to no end. He had never been camping, and this was somehow even better. He stayed up till two in the morning and his father took him into the store for fifteen minutes to look at the kind of people who went to Wal-Mart at two in the morning. Before everyone went to sleep for the night, Rick told them all a ghost story so horrifying that Harold had a little trouble dozing off, imagining the vengeful spirit of The One-Eyed Octopus Hunter from Furthest Lovecraftia was galloping towards him on his six-legged horse, harpoon in his right hand, pitchfork in his left, and a chainsaw in the third hand that grew from his forehead during full moons. Templeton and Curse had nodded off sitting in the seats they'd chosen for the trip, while Jake and Earl stretched out on rickety shelves that folded out from the wall. Ben and Roy slept on the floor like bookends facing opposite ways, while Rick slouched in the dining area.

When everyone woke up, Ben was waiting for them with a nourishing McDonald's breakfast, which sealed the deal for Jake: this was the greatest trip anyone had ever taken anywhere, period. His youthful dreams of journeying to Reykjavik to explore the wonders of a country with a one hundred percent literacy rate and chessboards as far as the eye could see were all but forgotten.

"So how much success did you have with your internet media campaign?" Roy asked Ben between mouthfuls of microwaved pancake.

"I don't know, we'll have to stop at a library so I can check my e-mail," Ben told the gang. "I tried to give the whole thing a shot in the arm any way I could. I figured it wouldn't quite be enough to say that I was going to reveal my secret, so I dangled some other stuff too."

"Like what?" Earl asked, devouring a sausage patty. As long as Earl Shavey was around, unfinished sausage patties did not stand a chance in hell.

"Like I tossed Emmitt's name out there, for one thing," Ben said. "Nothing like a couple of Pulitzer Prizes to attract a loyal literary following."

Templeton stopped in mid-chew. "Ah, Ben, perhaps I never told you about my aversion to meeting with the general public. I hope you didn't promise anything extraordinary."

"Just that you'd be signing anything anyone happened to show up with," Ben said, and Templeton closed his eyes, feeling a headache come on.

"I haven't done a signing since my first book was released," Templeton said. "I have a reputation as a bit of a hermit. People were just starting to accept it."

"Apologies," Ben said. "But since we all agreed not to charge an entry fee, I was grasping at straws. Also, the cash prize will have to be paid out on the spot in twenty dollar bills. I figured that would make it all more exciting and camera-friendly."

"The nineteen thousand, four hundred and fifty dollars which we still don't have, and now have a little over five days to come up with?" Harold asked. "Do you have a plan B for getting it yet?"

"Not in the sense that there's an actual, tangible plan B you can set up on an easel and point at with a stick, no."

"What happens if it just never materializes?"

"Then I'll just have to resort to...The Call," Ben said ominously. "A call that will take every fiber of my intestinal fortitude to make. A call that carries with it risk, danger, sacrifice, and even superhuman demands on our collective physical strength—but which *will* get us the money we require. I don't ever want to have to make it, but if it comes to it, that mountain shall be climbed, oh yes."

"Ben, for a cause like this, I would be willing to put up the prize money," Templeton offered.

"Much appreciated, Emmitt," Ben replied, "but I feel it's my destiny now to make everything happen with my own hand. I don't want to tempt karma by cheating here and there. Anyway, since I'm going to be the one actually winning the prize, there's no real need to even raise that cash. If a catastrophe happens and somehow Stephen Hawking shows up and uses his big old science brain to beat me after I've gotten so good that only a freak of nature can manage it, then I'll make...the Call."

"The Call, oh, I have to write that down," Roy said, getting out his notebook. "You know, with each passing day, there's more and more here we can work with for this bio. I'm starting not to care that I got fired yesterday."

The spit take that Ben performed at the tail end of this sentence dowsed Harold, Curse, and Earl with generous eyefuls of orange juice. Though they had come to expect no better from him, their shock cost them precious microseconds and they were unable to maneuver out of the way of the deadly oncoming citrus. Jake clapped his hands and roared with delight at the sight of his father slowly wiping his glasses on his napkin while Harold and Curse took considerably longer to regain their sight and dignity.

"My bad," Ben said. "You got *fired?*" he asked Roy.

"Yeah," he said, "my editor told me I had to stay in town to cover the regional prep school indoor soccer semi-finals, and I told him I really needed to follow you for the book, so he said I could stay out in the desert, die there, and let my remains be eaten by vultures."

"That slime," Curse muttered. "When we get back there, we'll build some kind of contraption that'll pull all his limbs off in sequence but keep him alive somehow for at least a half hour or so."

"No, really, I don't mind," Roy said. "This book's gonna be great, and now I can get out of that stupid reporting game entirely and focus on the things I really want to do, aside from writing sports bios."

"What else did you have in mind?" Templeton asked him.

Roy looked at them all rather nervously. "Well, I know it might sound weird, but I sort of always thought I might be a good poet."

Ben heard this statement at the most unfortunate moment possible; he had just begun to drain the last of his orange juice when his brain forced him once again to suddenly jettison the offending liquid onto his compatriots with even more velocity than before, this time sending an arcing sunlit spray onto the defenseless foreheads of those he had already injured both physically and emotionally with his first salvo, though Curse caught only a slight bit of liquid on his left ear due to reflexes that had remained on red alert status since that initial offensive. Harold and Earl wept inside for the dryness that had once been theirs but was now just a fond memory.

"I knew it wasn't a good idea to mention it," Roy said.

"I think it's a fine and noble pursuit," Templeton said, somewhat predictably.

"There's never been a sports writer who became a great poet," Earl said supportively. "You could be the first."

"I always wanted to capture the essence of a great championship game with a poem," Roy said. "Look at *Casey at the Bat*. It's immortal."

"Most depressing thing ever written," Ben said. "What kind of a hitter lets two strikes go by in that situation? He wasn't smart enough to jump on a first pitch fast ball?"

Their circular conversation was broken when Rick opened the driver's side door and stuck his head inside the vehicle. "We've got a slight problem, dudes," he said. "The battery's dead, but that's not all."

Leaving the last vestiges of their breakfast behind, they all filed out into the bright July sunshine shafting down onto the unsightly parking lot and gathered around the RV's gigantic open hood. Rick stuck his arm into the inner workings and pointed at something. "Check it out. I actually found this stuck between the flange capacitor and the C-fold."

Ben leaned in and squinted, then reached in to dislodge a large, shiny object. It was a socket wrench. He managed to release it from its death grip on a tiny bolt beneath one of the six Harris hinges (a startlingly high number of Harris hinges, to be sure).

"That's just the beginning," Rick said. "Peer between the chassis hooks and the key wipe. You won't believe your eyes."

Earl was closest to the mechanical intestines in question, so he got the best look of any of them, and poked his fingers into the jumbly darkness. He pulled out first a screwdriver, then a claw hammer, and then, to their disbelieving eyes, a half-full pack of cigarettes that had been lodged beside a lighter in the shape of an alligator.

"Whoever was working on this thing left about half their tool box in the engine," Rick said. "I also found a carpenter's level, an old battery tester, and about fifty pages of a repair manual to a 1987 Saab. Those were curled up inside the wiper fluid reservoir. But the capper is this." From his pocket he took out a tiny flashlight he had also found inside the engine and affixed its feeble beam deep into the confused snarl of engine parts and abject darkness. The heads of the group craned, twisted, and bumped gently into one another. Curse lifted Jake up so he could get in on the gawking action.

"Is that..." Templeton began, not quite getting a good enough look below the vapor coils to make sure of what he believed he was witnessing.

"Yeah, it is," Rick said. "It's a pineapple."

"Look at the *size* of that thing," Curse said, whistling. "If you can ever get that out of there, we can eat for a week."

"The problem is, the little spines have pretty much completely scraped away the housing of the fusillator," Rick said in scary tones. "The sucker's toast. That's a nine hundred dollar repair before we can start the engine, if you can even find a replacement here in Wherever, Ohio."

"Oh, terrific," Ben said morosely. "Just what we need. There's no chance we can just pop into Wal-Mart and grab one?"

"Funny thing," Rick said, "I once replaced a fusillator in my father's speedboat with an electric can opener. Ran great for two whole hours. Then..." He trailed off. "Let's just say I don't live with my father anymore," he finished.

"Okay, okay, we gotta put our heads together," Ben said. "We can't leave the Millennium Falcon here to rot and just go on without it. It's like our Noah's Ark, or that hovercraft that carried the Partridge Family around. But at the same time, we can't afford to lose even a day. I'm due at this APBA guru's house that Fergus Hibbert clued me onto tomorrow at noon. It's absolutely the only time he agreed to see me."

"We're going to be cutting Las Vegas really close anyway," Harold noted. "You never think of Nevada being far away, but wow. It's a wonder why anybody even bothers."

They all fell silent, individually contemplating possible solutions. Rick didn't think it would be such a terrible idea for him to simply wander off toward the closest horizon and start selling hemp shoes for a living, but if he got to Vegas and was able to win the prize money, he could go back to school and finish his Indignant Forestry degree. Earl had a swift, horrifying mental image of himself living in the parking lot for the next twelve years, teaching Jake history and higher algebra inside Wal-Mart during their slowest business hours, using only the materials they could find on the store's shelves, and very slowly building up enough courage to call the boy's mother and tell her what had become of them.

Their futile huddle was interrupted by the approach of a man from the west. Ben heard footsteps clomping on the cement and he turned to see a tall, very bald, and very mean-looking gent walking towards them. The others became aware of him a couple of seconds later. The man's arms, emerging from a dirty white T-shirt, were the size of fence posts that had been soaked by rain and left out to expand and bust. He wore black jeans and scuffed steel-toed boots. Ben's hopes that this was merely parking lot security coming to give him the heave ho for dumping the ice from his cup of orange juice onto the tarmac dwindled quickly. The man stopped before them, surveying them one by one with eyes that had obviously punched many a wiseacre face in their day. His skin looked leathery, like a carpet with disciplinary problems.

"Hello there," Harold greeted him. "Nice day for, um...weather."

The intruding ruffian completely ignored him and strangely focused his gaze on Roy alone. Roy, eleven inches shorter and sixty pounds lighter, shrank under the man's lengthening shadow. When the man reached into his back pocket to draw something out, Ben's first thought was that if someone had to die on this trip, he'd always figured it would be Earl instead.

The stranger produced not a weapon but a thick wad of bills—fifties, it looked like. He reached forward suddenly, grabbed Roy's right hand, and yanked it upward, twisting it so that his palm was face up. Down came the bills, slapped onto Roy's pale flesh so hard it almost embedded the face of Ulysses S. Grant into it. Roy closed one eye, prepared for random street violence that never came.

"Take it," the man snarled at him in what was frankly a much higher-pitched voice than his physical image projected. It seemed a little like false advertising. "You won it. I hope it..." He searched for just the right words. "...Messes you up," he finished lamely, then gave them all a final disdainful once-over before turning and clomping off into the morning light. Whatever terror the brute had originally caused them dissipated completely when he mounted not a Harley Davidson but a very sensible, very affordable sky blue ten speed bicycle and pedaled east, making sure to use his hand signals when merging with traffic.

Roy just stood there, not quite as dumbfounded as they would have thought. On his face there was evidence of a secret knowledge of the situation he did not wish to impart.

"Okayyyyyyyyyy," Curse said, "go ahead and start explaining *that* one *any* old time."

"Look at all that money!" Jake said, actually pointing at it. "You could go into the Discovery Channel store and buy the biggest globe they have!"

Roy did indeed take a good look at the cash, and then, without even counting it, he turned to Ben and repeated the same act that his mysterious benefactor had performed on him, taking Ben's hand, turning his palm face up, and placing the cash directly onto it, with a little less force this time.

"You have to take this from me, Ben," Roy said. "I don't want any part of it. Let's find a mechanic, fix the engine, and get going."

"Oh no," Ben said, forcing the bills back on him, "if I take this, the cops will say I was in on the whole thing. Don't give anything to me, don't get your fingerprints on my vehicle, don't tell me the name of the deceased."

"It's not like that," Roy said. "It's...well, I...I can't tell you."

"You're among friends," Templeton said. "Surely a young man like you couldn't have gotten into too much trouble."

"Not...trouble," Roy said. "Something that...no, no, don't make me remember it!"

"Dude," Rick said. "It's obviously eating you up inside. You have to purge your blentha. Purge it right here in the parking lot."

"Yeah, that blentha's gotta go," Ben agreed.

"There's like, four thousand dollars there!" Jake said, having calculated the approximate thickness of the wad and using simple (for him) division.

"That's exactly how much I spent on mulch last year to fix my stump problem near the front walk," Harold said sadly.

"I can't talk about it," Roy said. "I knew it was a bad idea to come along on this trip...to leave my apartment where I was safe and take such a reckless chance...especially when APBA is involved...I...I...."

*January, 2002.*

*Outside, the white stuff that always accompanied a real Vermont northeaster came down hard and heavy, but no one crouched deep within the basement of the Dr. Curtis L. Sackler Humanities Building on the campus of Franklin and Murray University would be making any snow angels on this cruel night. Ten young men stood around a stolen card table set up beneath a single 25-watt light bulb, surrounded by the dank of decades. Silence hung in the air like so much expired veal.*

*The two competitors facing each other across the table had torn into each other for five straight hours now. On one side, Grog Streep, the campus's fiercest-looking senior, a communications major with a mean streak wide as the Dr. Curtis L. Sackler Memorial Walking Path, scowled and knocked back another domestic beer in just seconds. On the other side, Roy Skinla, nicknamed "The White Gherkin" for reasons of general cruelty, sat up as tall in his folding chair as his five foot seven inch frame would allow. He wasn't about to back down to this bully, oh no, not after what he had been through since dinnertime. He had methodically knocked off four of his classmates to get to the final round of this subterranean death match, and he could taste authentic victory for the first time in his life. Between the two men lay four thousand dollars in cash, absolutely all the money their parents had set aside for their miscellaneous daily purchases throughout graduate school—shampoo, laundry, the occasional candy bar, stuff like that. Now it was all riding on a single roll of the dice.*

*With the cool of a veteran gunslinger, Roy picked up his yellow dice shaker and let slip the dogs of war onto the card table. They clacked into each other once, twice, three times, then halted with the precision of a military drill team. There was a communal gasp around him as Grog Streep's head lowered with agonizing slowness.*

*"Goal," Roy whispered. "Goal."*

*As his classmates all looked at him with an awed hush, Roy stood up from his chair, his forehead gleaming with sweat, just like always, except now instead of the perspiration of a chronic glandular problem, it was the defiant moisture of a man who had climbed the highest mountain on campus.*

*"I know you're going to have difficulty getting through your internship with KTTB-45 without any spending money," he said to his slain enemy, "so I'm not going to take it now. I want you to keep it for five years, and think every day of what it must be like to be me, a true champion. Yes, Grog, think about it with every children's television show you have a hand in producing, and every night you lie awake, dreaming of what could have been. And five years from now, you'll pay up, every penny—or I'll do to you again what I did just now: make you wish you had never been born!"*

*There was a cheer from around him, and the next thing he knew, he had been lifted onto the shoulders of his comrades, who would go back to calling him The White Gherkin twenty-four hours from now and pretending they never knew him, but who for one moment looked upon Roy as the skinny, pasty-faced, dateless deity that he truly was.*

"It was my darkest moment," Roy told the group, standing in the Wal-Mart parking lot and feeling ten times smaller than he did that night. "I never played APBA Hockey again, and I promised myself I'd never go near another sports board game. And then came that night at Harold's house."

"Hardcore, man," Rick whispered, impressed. "Wild stuff."

"I shouldn't even be around anyone who plays these games," Roy said. "I could become obsessed again."

"This is terrific!" Ben exclaimed. "Who needs to go see some supposed APBA strategy expert in Indiana when I have *you* to tell me all about it!"

"I'm not any good at the baseball game," Roy said. "I only had the hockey one, and it wasn't because of skill that I won that night. It was pure luck. I felt dirty then, and this money makes me feel dirty now. So take it, Ben. It makes sense, with the karma and everything.

I can't keep the cash, but it's perfect for what you want to do." He put it one last time into Ben's hand, where it was starting to feel most welcome.

"If the whole thing's about destiny, Ben," Earl said, "this fits perfectly. A stranger comes out of nowhere..."

"You make an interesting case," Ben said, kind of hoping everyone would just get back into the RV so he could spend some time alone with the money, and maybe give it a little kiss. "Yes, this money just landed on us naturally. And if it really spooks your brain to have it, Roy—"

"It does," Roy said. "I'm in recovery, and I can't profit from my addiction. Thank goodness I don't even really like baseball, or I'd probably be hounding all of you to play the game. Please, don't anyone even teach me the rules or show me the cards if you can help it. I'll just keep writing the book and hopefully I'll be all right."

"Rick," Ben said, his chest swelling with confidence, "take this money and call around for a mechanic who'll fix the vehicle by this afternoon. Grease his palms if you need to. But first, I think we could all use another round of pancakes, this time without little pieces of Styrofoam lodged in them. "

About this there was no real consensus, but Rick took the money anyway and began his tasks while the rest of them sunned themselves in the parking lot, tossing a Frisbee around and taking turns using the freaky shower on board. The summer day rose gloriously around them, and somewhere to the east, Grog Streep rode into work at WPLJ-13 in North Tiffin on his ten speed, where, as script supervisor on the Emmy award-winning *Cap'n Candy Cane 'n' Friends,* he was only occasionally haunted my memories of the night Roy Skinla had taken him down a few pegs by rolling so many lucky sixty-sixes it wasn't even funny.


## 15. Tea and Biscuits in the Room That Was Big


"Are you sure that's the right house?" Harold asked Ben for the third time in as many minutes.

The faces of the Independent APBA Collective of Metro Harrisburg stared out from every available window of the TRAVEL

OPTION as the beast sat motionless beside a quiet curb in exurban Kokomo, Indiana. After seemingly endless hours of westerly driving, they had come to 1933 Long Arrow Lane, and had no valid reason to doubt that the address they'd zeroed in on was invalid. But it almost had to be. The house before them was a capitalistic behemoth, a four story white-bricked homage to wealth with a circular driveway, manicured hedges, and pillars, honest to God pillars, guarding the front steps. The front lawn was immaculately mown in a subtle swirl pattern, and a thick aura of intimidating cleanliness hung about the property. Ben expected to see men in white jumpsuits leap out at any moment and start scrubbing the eaves with toothbrushes.

"1933 Long Arrow Lane, that's what this definitely says," Ben said, again checking the bubble gum wrapper Fergus Hibbert had given him in Philadelphia. "It's the only house on the road anyway. It's got to be the right one."

"No gate or anything keeping us out," Earl noted. "Might as well just walk up and try the door, Ben."

Ben swallowed uneasily. Being in the presence of truly big money had always made him feel uncomfortable. In the early days of his playing career, he had contemplated blowing everything he made on a nice farmhouse in the country with four acres of slightly marshy land to roam around on, but he had chickened out on the tour the realtor gave him, made deeply queasy by the sheer floor area he would have to vacuum every couple of years or so. That misstep, combined with his one experience in a truly nice restaurant, an epic nightmare of multiple spoons, miniscule portions, and sauces that combined upwards of three different barely pronounceable ingredients, had secured his opinion of really rich people: like camels at the zoo, it was fun sometimes to pay a few bucks to peer at them in their cages, but then it was time to grab a stuffed panda at the gift shop and get the hell out of there.

"No one's going to bite you if you knock on the door, Ben," Templeton soothed him, choosing not to reveal to his friends just yet that his own house back in Harrisburg was actually a little bigger than this one. "He did agree to see you, didn't he?"

"Just in a five-word letter," Ben said. "Ah well, how obnoxious can he be if he's spending so much time playing a board game? If I'm not back in fifteen minutes, call in an air strike." He hopped out of the RV and crossed the lawn, conscious of every mark his feet made on the grass and imagining a federal judge throwing him into prison for defiling such perfection.

He expected the pushing of the doorbell to spur a cacophony of cathedral chimes and Gregorian chants, or at least "Lara's Theme," but it was just a normal doorbell, which disappointed him greatly. When the huge door opened, a shaggy-haired kid of about eighteen was standing there in torn jeans, cheap sneakers, and a T-shirt with Bob Seger on it. He rubbed his eyes as if just having awoken at noon really took a lot out of him.

"Yes?" he asked, looking past Ben at the RV, which he seemed to be somewhat impressed with.

"Fergus Hibbert gave me this address. I'm Ben Glinton, I'm here to talk to Jerzy Plenck. Are you his son?"

"Me? No. I'm his butler." The kid said this with no trace of humor. "He's been expecting you, I think. I'll holler at him that you're here. C'mon in."

The door opened wider and Ben stepped inside the flawlessly air conditioned foyer, in which hung large paintings by some of the lesser known Impressionist masters. Off to the left and right were well-decorated sitting rooms, and a spiral staircase led up to God knows where. The butler started to mount it when down from secret heights came a very diminutive man in a black turtleneck sweater and short hair so white he would have been ignored for days in a bowl of rice.

"Hey, um, this Ben Glinton guy's here," said the butler as the small man moved past him.

"Thank you, Ousmus," said Jerzy Plenck in a modest, cultured voice as he descended. "Would you arrange for Mrs. Loiles to bring us tea in the recreation room, and then you may retire for the rest of the afternoon. Oh, and I left your wages in the greenhouse beside the rhododendrons."

"Rockin'," Ousmus replied, and shambled out of sight, yawning.

Plenck came forward and offered a tiny hand to Ben. The man was maybe five feet two inches tall and perfectly symmetrical, like a child's doll. He looked like he could be broken in half by sneezing on him. His bright blue eyes twinkled. "Hello, Mr. Glinton. Good to have you."

"Thanks," Ben said. "Nice spread you have here. Fergus didn't tell me you were, you know, loaded up the ying yang." He couldn't get over how perfectly white the man's hair was. He had to fight the urge to dye it for Easter.

"Yes, I do fairly well for myself," Plenck said, motioning politely for Ben to walk with him toward the shining hallway in front of them. "It's all money that could disappear quickly, of course, so I try not to become accustomed to any of it."

"What exactly do you do?" Ben said as they turned right and walked past a huge study crammed wall to wall with bookshelves. The books which packed them looked very old, very valuable, and definitely not fake.

"I do a bit of wagering," Plenck answered. "I advance money to certain parties based on my belief that certain outcomes in the sporting world are more likely to come to pass than others, and I am rewarded if my predictions are in fact valid."

Ben did a double take. "You *gamble?* You gamble on sports? And you've won enough dough to live *here?* What's your secret?"

"Oh, there are no secrets, Ben, not in this life," Plenck said from about a foot below eye level. "Simply what we can observe and put to use. Ten years ago, when I was nothing more than the chief operating officer of a large European defense contractor, I watched a professional sporting contest for the first time. A basketball match, in fact. I became more and more intrigued by the interplay between skill and chance I witnessed that night and on subsequent nights, until I finally retired to wager on these events, baseball in particular. It's a lovely game, more suited than any other to the pace at which I prefer to live my life."

"I guess it's a little less stressful to bet on stuff when you already own Boardwalk, Park Place, and Ventnor Avenue," Ben said.

"Indeed, it has been," Plenck said as they walked through a room containing nothing but a grand piano, four velvet chairs, and opulent examples of art from the Orphist school. "I don't particularly care for stress. I have very little contact with the outside world so that I can focus my energies on my amusements."

"Can't blame you," Ben said. "Kind of hard to believe a guy like you plays APBA, though."

"Oh, I enjoy a bit of further unwinding with tabletop pursuits," Plenck told him. They had emerged into another hallway and now they stopped for a moment beside a white door at the end of a plush green carpet. "I've found that there's not quite enough of America's favorite pastime to be found on the television during the winter months, and I was happy to find a way to re-create it in relative silence." He pushed the door open and gestured for Ben to enter first.

The huge room looked out on Planck's back lawn and the hedge maze that grew there. Sunlight poured in through a large picture window. In the center of this virtually barren and pristine enclosure was a large table with two chairs on opposite sides. Laid out on the table was APBA Baseball. But this set was...different.

Ben walked over to it and looked down in amazement. At first he didn't even believe his eyes, thinking that what he was seeing was just like that fake five dollar bill the owner of Skippy's Liquors had painted on the floor beside the cash register to fool people into bending down to swipe it, a work of craftsmanship remarkable enough to achieve a 48% success rate against the general public and a 71% success rate against Ben himself. But the thing on the table before him was...ohmygod, it was real.

The pleasant-looking cardboard baseball diamond that usually came with a new APBA Baseball game had been replaced by one made of mahogany. Some unknown but extremely talented artist had reproduced an aerial shot of Lippleby's Bangers & Mash Stadium in Green Bay in dozens of vivid colors, and the markers which stood in for base runners were not red plastic discs but highly precise metal figurines painted in the colors of that city's woeful franchise. So accurate, in fact, that the players even seemed to have facial expressions depicting effort and determination.

"Ohhhhhhhhhh," Ben murmured lustily.

"I possess depictions of all current and past professional stadiums," Plenck said casually. "And base runners representing all teams, naturally."

Ben's eyes were treated next to the sight of a play results booklet Plenck had had specially made in Vienna. The book itself, bound in leather, was propped up by an oak lectern. A team of scriveners, monks actually, had been hired to transcribe the play results by hand onto each high-gloss page in a rainbow of bold inks.

The calligraphy was stunning. They had even been able to make a result of FOUL OUT, PO-C look sublimely romantic.

"Ohhhhhhhhhhhhhhhhhhhhhhh," Ben said again, feeling woozy.

The cards. For the love of Elvis, the *cards*. Plenck had been in the midst of conducting a game between the Maryland Riflesmiths and the Atlanta Clouts when Ben had arrived. Probably knowing, like all APBA competitors, that there was nothing that could replace the feeling of nice player cards in one's hand, Plenck had gone beyond the company's efforts and carved each one from...no, it couldn't be...

"Ivory," he told Ben. "Incredibly light because of the extreme thinness of each card. You can actually see light through them if you hold them up to the window. And if you turn them over, you'll notice that each features a full-color reproduction of the player's bubblegum card. That's where the real costs began to mount. I've only had the 1977 season set completed, but I have people working on others. Go ahead, pick one up."

"OHHHHHHHHHHHhhhhhhhhhhhhhhhhhhhhhhhhhhh," was the sound that for the third time emerged from Ben's mouth as he became as shell-shocked as any kid that ever took the tour of Willy Wonka's chocolate factory. If Plenck had told him to lick one of the cards because it tasted like a snozzberry, he would have bought into it entirely.

"The dice...one's gold and one's silver," Ben said in a strangled, tiny voice, picking them up off the playing field and letting them drop into a hand-carved maple shaker shaped like a baseball glove.

"Worth a pretty penny, too," said Plenck. "Try my landing lawn."

Ben poured the dice out onto a flat, green, velvet-lined cushion fenced in by little planks colored to look like outfield fences. There was a small, delicate thumping sound as the dice hit paydirt, a sound sweeter than any song Ben had ever heard, except for maybe "Running with the Devil."

"It's not velvet, actually," Plenck said. "That's real grass. It's quite a challenge to keep up, but I find that if I keep the lawn on the sill over there between games, it draws enough sunlight to both keep the grass alive and give it that wonderful summer aroma of a real field."

That did it. Game over. Ben passed the hell out.

.

When he awoke a minute later, Plenck was fanning him with his scoresheet. Ben didn't even want to look up from the floor at it for fear he might lose consciousness again. He got slowly to his feet, helped up by one of Plenck's small manicured hands. His one hundred and forty pounds didn't haul a lot of tonnage and Ben had to do most of the work of standing himself.

"Amazing, the effect this game has on people," Plenck observed. "The sight of the ultimate set had caused two of the three visitors to my estate this past year to have a similar reaction. I believe the game reaches our inner adolescent more powerfully than even a mother's cooking. Come, have a seat at the gaming table, Ben."

Ben did so, and Plenck sat across from him. Ben gazed down at the game set and tried to think of meaningless number cycles to keep himself from salivating.

"Luck, Ben," Plenck said. "It dictates so much of our lives. Where we are born, to whom, the people we encounter in our pursuits, the illnesses we suffer. And of course, one's success with APBA Baseball has much to do with luck."

"I know," Ben said. "This could be a problem. I really need to win that tournament I was talking about in my letter to you."

"An almost impossible task, if you continue to employ the managerial techniques you wrote about in your letter. I must say, I was most disturbed to hear about your lineup techniques and your woeful on-base percentage. I dare predict the competition will be over for you as soon as it begins—unless we study together, very hard."

"But I have to get going to Las Vegas," Ben said. "I was hoping you could maybe jot a few tips on an index card or something and I could keep it with me. Doesn't have to be made out of ivory. A normal index card should be fine."

"Oh, I'm afraid that won't work, Ben," said Plenck as the ancient Mrs. Loiles came into the room with tea and biscuits, just the thing to restore Ben's sense of masculinity after dropping like a brick to the floor in excitement over the components of a board game. The woman set a silver tray between them and shuffled out of the room, perhaps to go celebrate her two hundredth birthday.

"I haven't made any scientific observations about the game," Plenck explained as he poured the tea. "None that I could write down, at any rate. What I've done over the past three years is to get a strong feel for the secret interplay between the game's factors of chance and managerial acumen. I've learned the subtleties of the boards and I believe I would have a sizeable advantage over any opponent if given a team no worse than his. Quite sizeable, in fact. It has taken all my powers of observation to mentally track each game's hidden patterns instead of allowing myself to ride the wings of my imagination, so to speak, and become awed and over-stimulated by the excitement of the homeruns, the double plays, the strikeouts, the hitting streaks, the stunning endings."

"What are the chances of you being able to show me how to wallop the competition in time for the tournament if I stayed here and went through the whole Yoda treatment while the others drove on and I just caught a flight at the last second?"

"I'm afraid none," Plenck said. "For you to win given your skill level, I believe I would have to stick right by your side through every roll of the dice, counseling you as necessary."

"Oof," Ben said. "The problem is, I don't think we're gonna be allowed to have anyone coaching us."

"Did you not set up the tournament yourself?" Plenck asked, a small smile creeping onto his delicate face. "Is it not up to you to determine the rules of play?"

A light bulb switched on inside Ben's head, sputtered for a second, and then bathed his skill with a full forty, forty-five watts. "Yes!" Ben said through a mouthful of table wafer. "Yes, it's my show! Bench coaches *will* be allowed! But that means—"

"I would come with you on your journey," Plenck said. "Only by judging the ebb and flow of a particular game can I really deduce what sort of moves you will have to make, at precisely the right moments, to give yourself the best chance at victory. It is not unlike standing in a stilled forest waiting for deer to show themselves. A truly gifted hunter does not rely on fake urine and tree stands to draw his prey. He can merely sense when something is about to happen, and he acts accordingly."

"Fake urine, gotcha, good analogy," Ben asked. "But why would you want to leave Buckingham Freaking Palace to sleep on the floor of an RV with a bunch of deadbeats and no more than one Pulitzer Prize winner?" He was sure that it would be at this exact point that he would wake up from this wondrous dream, probably with the sound of the lawnmower outside the window merging cruelly into the sound of his cruddy alarm clock.

Plenck stood up, clasped his hands behind his back, and took a turn about the room, as they used to say in British novels that took place in houses exactly like this one. "Since I was a child, Ben," he said, "I have been accused by both friends and enemies alike of having been possessed of overwhelming luck. I was born to vastly wealthy parents who became only vastly wealthier when they kept winning the lottery. My company was blessed with absurd fortune when an incompetent and corrupt board of directors vanished in the Bermuda Triangle before they could run the operation into the ground. And the first twelve bets I placed on professional baseball were all freakish winners. They weren't even wagers based on research or even hunches; I laid thousands of dollars down on such gambits as predicting how many times players would spit during an inning and whether the ball girl could field a foul tap cleanly. It has done no small injury to my pride as a man to be called nothing more than a conjurer of providence. I long for a moment when I can engage in a pursuit founded on the luck of the dice, and somehow use nothing more than my intelligence to obviate their influence. I want to be able to help you win that tournament based on my observations of the game's tightrope walk between mental acumen and chance, and my ability to impart those enigmas to a willing student. Then, and only then, can I sleep easy at night, immune to the opinions of my contemporaries, knowing I accomplished something real and incontrovertible."

Ben stood up from his chair in tacit support of this great man's decision. "Then you will ride along with us to Vegas and there we will all triumph!" he announced. "Any chance you'd want to fund the rest of the prize money if everything else falls through?"

For the first time, the small man made a sound like a laugh. "Don't be absurd, Benjamin," he said. "I didn't make fifty million dollars in my life by throwing money around. Why don't you finish your chamomile while I pack a few things for the voyage."

## 16. Savage Brutes, Encountered by the Roadside, are Dispatched Before Injurious Blows to the Self-Esteem are Suffered

So then it was nine of them headed across the country in an RV that seemed more cramped with each passing mile, though no one really minded so terribly. Each man aboard the ship had his own dealings to attend to, and between all the activity and the sightseeing, time passed quickly. By Wednesday they were in Missouri, admiring the open prairies and eating at roadside diners never mentioned in any AAA guides, or any phone books for that matter. Jerzy Plenck had actually brought along his own specially prepared macrobiotic meals, packed inside a black leather suitcase and consisting mostly of kelp fingers and collapsible whey, but he enjoyed free ice water with lemon when the rest of the Collective decided to hit such places as Aunt Grammy's Calorie Sack in Sikeston and Four Losers Subs and Fried Chicken in Belleville (where a twelve inch meatball hoagie came with a side of dry Raisin Bran). Like Mr. Rogers, Plenck wore the same thing pretty much all the time, changing at night into silk pajamas which were basically identical to his daytime clothing before he good-naturedly stretched out on the floor, where he always slept when he was at home anyway.

He and Ben played a great deal of APBA as the miles passed, with Plenck often pausing in the middle of games to lecture Ben, and anyone else who happened to be interested, on the mystical role of the dice and the subtle tendencies of the playing boards. The fellas lapped it all up, though Ben wasn't sure he needed all this arcane information, especially the long tangents about mathematical probability and why a tabletop manager should always be conservative on the base paths with two outs and a runner on second—or was it that he should be extra aggressive? Ben, already pestered by an inability to learn a new phone number without forgetting the name of a close relative, just couldn't keep it all straight. One thing became certain, though: Plenck's tiny Polish head was absolutely teeming with a talent for knowing when to make the best moves to secure victory. He beat Ben eleven times in a row at one point using a team of lesser strength, something he simply shouldn't have been able to do. At critical junctures during the games, Plenck would stop to examine the scoresheet in great detail, and then pore over the player ratings for minutes on end before announcing a strategic decision—or holding off on one—that inevitably won the game. None of them had ever seen anything like it. They were all dying to have him pick baseball games for them so they could cash in like mad, but he told them he was currently on sabbatical from gambling, wishing to focus his energies entirely on helping Ben win the upcoming tournament. In his few off hours from explaining to Ben why a botched double play wasn't necessarily reason to forfeit a game in disgust, or why it wasn't such a good idea to send a player to third on a sac fly simply out of spite, he read the novels of Thomas Mann and listened to the choral music of Australian pygmies.

Meanwhile, Jake was working on a summer extra credit project assigned to him by one of his soon-to-be professors at Hofstra. When he wasn't playing APBA or gazing at the constantly fascinating sights out the window, he was collecting common field spiders for an intensive study on whether they seemed to want something better from life. The extent of this pursuit was made fully known to his fellow travelers only in the middle of the night when Curse suddenly jumped up from his spot on the floor, practically dove out of the RV, and ran in his shorts down a newly paved highway outside Carthage, yelling that his brain was being eaten. One of Jake's specimens had gotten out of its tiny plastic case and done a little moonlight hiking inside Curse's nose. Unfortunately, Curse became so hysterical that he inhaled the spider entirely, a realization so unpleasant that he felt only by striking himself over the head a dozen times with Jerzy Plenck's ceramic teapot could he distract himself from the desire to seek out the nearest vacant electric chair and sizzle himself off into the next life.

Two books were being written during this time. Emmitt Templeton jotted down page upon page of descriptions of the minutiae of everything they passed, having decided that his observations during this week's trip would comprise chapter one of a ten chapter prologue of a book-length essay that would run at least 1500 pages. Meanwhile, Roy continued to press on with Ben's biography. Reading all the old scouting reports on Ben, which the Kentucky Cannons had only been too happy to dump on him, he discovered that Ben's entire career had essentially begun with a spontaneous wager between two scouts, one of whom bet the other that "the trout-looking left fielder with the goofy walk" would be the first to slip on an especially deceptive patch of ice lingering outside the Montreal Edmontons' winter practice facility—a gymnasium attached to a senior citizens center. When Ben went down on his butt "flailing his arms like a retarded penguin trying to fly," according to the notes, the outcome of the bet was that Ben's contract was fobbed off on a British team, where he suddenly played surprisingly well, beginning to make his way slowly to the big leagues. Roy debated for a while whether or not to include this story in the biography and then went ahead and did it, trying to be as honest as possible, though in the end he did replace the words "retarded penguin" with "challenged seabird." The only part of the story Ben disputed was the physical dimensions of the gymnasium.

Harold Pillick tried to improve himself by using a stop at a shopping mall to pick up some classics of western literature which Templeton had recommended, but the first part of *Dracula* scared him so badly that he had to resort to imagining all the characters as players on his old Cannons team to get through the rest of it. Only by picturing the Count being brushed back by a high inside fastball as Renfield broke for second base, which was being covered by Mina Harker, could he go on. He stopped halfway through the scene where Dracula preys on poor Lucy Westenra to imagine the Prince of Darkness hauling ass around third on a hard single to right only to have Doctor Van Helsing reach out and yank him down to the turf by his cape, instigating a bench-clearing brawl. In the end, Harold missed out on much of the sense of foreboding that Bram Stoker had created, but at least he finished a real novel for the first time since college. In his breaks from reading, he took the wheel of the TRAVEL OPTION so Rick could compose more harmonica songs for a future album about mercury poisoning in Atlantic cod.

Once, and only once, Ben consented to give an impromptu performance on the clarinet with which he had taught his students back in the day, and which he'd brought along to pawn at some point. He played Chopin's *Sonata in B Flat Minor*. Three of the men wept openly at his evocative, heartrending performance. Their names shall never be revealed.

On Thursday, the RV pulled up in front of a laundromat so everyone could wash their clothes. Jerzy Plenck was fascinated both with the public cleaning process and the atmosphere inside Mr. Shirtpantashorts, where locals from the town gathered with a real sense of community to be hypnotized by whatever soap opera was showing on the black-and-white TV set bolted to the wall. Because the change machine was broken, Earl and Jake went on a mile hike down the road to the closest bank, soaking up the hot sun. While everyone waited for their return, they shot a little pool in a dungeon-like and barely air-conditioned bar next door called T. C. McCrudd's. Plenck hadn't played since he was in his twenties, so naturally he nearly ran the table the very first time he broke and went on to demolish everyone, never changing his bemused, apologetic expression.

Ben collapsed onto a bar stool beside Curse Williger as they waited their turns to be beaten again. "What are you listening to?" he asked Curse, who had a pair of earphones jammed into his head.

Curse removed one of the earpieces. "Death metal," he said. "A band called The Punched and the Slapped. Good stuff."

"Don't know them. Hey, I forgot to ask you, what did your wife say about you coming out here with us?"

Curse pulled the other earphone out of his head and sipped his beer. "Aw, that marriage is pretty much over. Me going on this trip was the last straw for her."

"Whoops," Ben said. "Sorry."

Curse just shook his head. "Doesn't matter. You remember what I'm like to be around. Didn't figure it'd last. Didn't figure it'd go up in flames so quick though. Turns out, people I know were taking bets on it behind my back. Real nice." He stared out the only clean window in the place and adjusted the brim of his ball cap.

"Women," Ben said, grimacing. "Always walking around, doing things. They just don't get...stuff."

"Yup," Curse agreed. "Man, you said it. Now I just want one thing, and that's to win that tournament in Vegas."

"I didn't think you'd care so much about something like that."

"Everybody wants some kind of championship ring in life," Curse told him. "Doesn't have to be anything grand. Just something you were able to win. I win this thing, I'll bet you I won't even think about baseball anymore. It was my father who wanted me to play, anyway. I wanted to work construction. Build stuff. That's what I'm doing as soon as we get back east. No more radio work for the Sky Turks. What do I really know about the game anyway?"

"Oh, but no one's as good as you when it comes to describing a batter getting plunked by a pitch," Ben said. "Last year when Dan Sonoda took that slider right in the elbow and charged the mound and you talked about his nostrils flaring and little bits of spit coming out of his mouth when he tripped on the rosin bag? *That* was poetry."

Curse thought about it. "Yeah, that was pretty good," he agreed. "I got nice letters about that one."

Earl and Jake Shavey came into the pool hall at that moment, drenched from head to toe in sweat. Earl's bald head was dizzyingly shiny and Jake had lost about four pounds, roughly half his body weight. "We got quarters," Earl announced, panting. "But there's a ton of soap suds spilling out over the sidewalk outside and the police roped the whole place off. I think one of the machines blew up!"

"Wait a second," Ben said, rising from his stool, "Roy stayed over there to watch the end of *Cops!*"

The Roy in question appeared in the doorway a second later, feeling his way into the pool hall on shaky legs. Clinging to the left side of his ashen face was a big puffy balloon of white suds which had begun to slide silently down his cheek like an exhausted climber who just couldn't hang on to a crag on Mount Sinai one moment longer. Roy's legs were be-sudsed from the waist down.

"Thought one more pair of boxers could fit..." he began, but couldn't go on, leaning on one of the pool tables for support.

"Oh my God, let's get out of here before they make us pay for that!" Ben said, hurriedly tossing a few dollar bills on the bar. "I've got a bad history with small claims courts in this state!" He made a mad dash for the door and everyone followed.

"Is the Midwest like this all the time, because if it is, I'm living here when I grow up," Jake announced as they piled out. The suds made a bold move on them out on the sidewalk, but to no avail.


The trekkers encountered infamy and controversy on Friday morning.

It happened in the middle of a most atypical game between Ben and Jerzy Plenck. Through an almost legendary streak of opportune dice rolls, Ben had leapt ahead big and stayed ahead big into the seventh inning. Managing the woeful Alberta Whippets of the defunct Seniors League of Western Canada, Plenck had to go through five pitchers just to hang on for dear life, never trailing by less than six runs. Ben was certain that his lunch today would possess the sweet lemony aftertaste of his first victory against Plenck in the last seven tries. He was tired of nodding knowingly at all of Plenck's managerial advice, most of which bent his cerebellum beyond repair. He was getting to the point where just beating this insanely polite and pleasant little finger puppet of a man would make the whole crazy trip worthwhile.

"Strikeout!" Ben blurted as another one of Plenck's batters went down haplessly with runners on the corners. "The tide is turnin', pal! The tide is turnin'! I'm ready for the big time!" Beside him, Harold slapped him on the back. Curse, taking a nap just a few feet away, opened one eye and closed it again, certain he must be dreaming. There was no way he could be inside a decrepit RV with Ben Glinton as a billboard hawking discounted potatoes flashed by on the highway. The scene made no sense whatsoever.

Plenck calmly collected his dice and put them back into his shaker. "Indeed, the sun is shining brightly on your hopes today, Ben," he said. "I must make a brief pinch hitting maneuver. Excuse me just a moment while I locate a suitable candidate for the task."

He sorted through his player cards and Ben suddenly found himself getting nervous. Almost anytime Plenck stopped the proceedings to make a move, the course of the game flip-flopped dramatically.

"Maybe I'll...maybe I'll just bring in my closer," Ben said, fixing his gaze on Plenck and looking for the slightest crack in that poker-faced exterior. There was none. There was *never* a crack. The man was like a stainless steel frying pan with arms.

"Regardless of whom you choose to bring in, I think I shall send the estimable Mr. Rodney Lootenbake to the plate," Plenck said, and Ben penciled him onto the scoresheet with a shaky right hand. Rodney Lootenbake? Rodney Lootenbake? Who the hell was Rodney *Lootenbake?*

Rodney Lootenbake homered to right.

"Ah, perfect," Plenck said mildly, pushing his plastic discs around the base paths, a simple act he never seemed to stop enjoying.

"Okay, 9-6," Ben said. "9-6. Two outs though, good luck."

Plenck's next batter reached base on an error thanks to the infield's iffy defense, which Ben should have fixed an inning ago. Plenck then stole second on the catcher's weak arm—a catcher Ben had stuck with because he had been foolishly seduced by the look of his power numbers. He refused to issue an intentional walk to someone named Billy Cadaco in order to get Plenck's weakest hitter up to the plate, and a quick single brought the runner home.

His stomach beginning to churn, Ben brought in a new pitcher. Plenck singled again and decided not to send his very fast runner to third for reasons that just didn't make any sense in Ben's cluttered mind.

"Why aren't you sending him? *Why aren't you sending him?"* Ben asked, sweating.

"Listen to the dice," Plenck counseled. "Listen to the dice, Ben, and they will tell you what to do. I've told you many times."

"But they're stupid!" Ben protested. "They have no idea what the hell's going on! They're made out of plastic!"

"Don't they?" Plenck wondered. He rolled again and his next batter knocked a triple into the left field corner.

"Jiminy jumping beans," Harold said. "Wipeout. Tie game."

"It's almost supernatural," Earl said. "Jake, put down *Death in Venice* and take a look at what's going on here."

"I can't take it anymore!" Ben said. "There is no way this bunch of Canadian losers can beat me! They finished last in a seventy-six team league!"

"I believe you are correct, Ben," Plenck said softly. "I sense that my fortune has expired for the time being. The gods have been too favorable in too brief a time window, I fear. Perhaps they'll return to my side in extra innings." He brought his next batter to the top of his lineup stack and rolled the dice.

"Oh my...I was wrong," Plenck said 2.6 seconds later. "Another homerun."

Ben pitched forward and his head clonked on the surface of the table, rattling his Hooters mug. Harold patted his shoulder gently.

When Ben lifted his head again, plastic discs were stuck to his forehead and right cheek.

They were jettisoned off violently when the RV suddenly skidded to a halt. Curse rolled off his shelf and onto the floor with a heavy thump. Jake grabbed onto his father's legs for dear life. Roy had been on his cell phone trying to secretly call the First Catholic Church of Altoona in an attempt to get to the bottom of a crazy but disturbingly convincing rumor that Ben had once been deeply involved in the attempted exorcism of a chicken, and the phone flew out of Roy's hand and hit Ben in the gums.

"We're okay, we're okay!" Templeton called back to the group from the driver's seat, having taken over for a few hours so Rick could get some more sleep. Templeton had been having the time of his life behind the wheel from west Missouri into Kansas, besotted with middle-aged daydreams of buying his own RV, changing his name to Frederick A. Herschler, and never returning to Pennsylvania. Now he threw The Many-Wheeled Creature Which Obeyed Only the Wind into park and killed the engine while everyone gathered themselves.

"What happened?" Roy asked, rushing over to peer out the windshield.

"These people in front of us stopped a little short and I had to bring us down fast," Templeton said. "It took about a hundred yards for us to actually stop. Sort of a worrying testament to the brakes."

"Oh," said Ben, climbing to his feet, "I should have told you that the dealer warned me never to push on them too soft or too hard, or to use them too much before ten a.m."

The group filed out of the vehicle to see if the one they were following sustained any damage when the RV had tapped its fender ever so lightly. It happened to be another motor home, a sleeker, cleaner, more expensive product than Ben's, and this one had valid license plates. Four or five guys had gotten out of it and now crowded around the fender for a casual inspection. Nothing seemed to be out of whack.

"Sorry about that," Templeton said to the strangers. "Hope I didn't scare you too badly."

"Oh, that's okay," said a short man of about forty. "We had to stop to avoid hitting a prairie dog. Not surprising we almost had a bit of a smash-up."

"How funny," Earl said. "Nothing but guys on board for you too, eh?"

"That's right," said a red-headed fellow in a leather jacket. "Just a bunch of dudes hitting the open road. Do you by any chance know if we're still headed more or less toward Sublette?"

"You'll have to go back a mile and take a left at that rotting bathtub someone left in the road," Templeton told them.

"Much appreciated," said the short man. "Say, it looks like your windshield's hit more than a few bugs along your trip. All out of washer fluid?"

"Yeah, we are," Ben said before Rick could volunteer the information that the reservoir was quite full, but with fluid so old it had actually turned into a minty gel.

"We'll be happy to squeegee it for you," a guy in his twenties offered, and turned to head back into the RV to get the needed supplies.

"That's really neighborly of you," Harold said. "Where are you fellas headed, anyway?"

"Strat-O-Matic Baseball tournament in San Jose," the redhead said. "How about yourself?"

"How serendipitous," Jerzy Plenck said. "We happen to be traveling toward a self-created tournament in which the game of APBA will be the featured catalyst."

A heavy silence fell over the dusty intersection. The man who had been heading into the vehicle to grab a squeegee stopped in his tracks and turned slowly, as if Butch Cassidy and the Sundance Kid had asked him to kindly put his hands up in the air. The others in his party seemed to step closer together in unconscious solidarity.

"APBA, huh?" the oldest of them asked rhetorically, rubbing his hairless chin. There was a definite twinge of sarcasm in his voice.

"That's right," Earl Shavey said, stepping forward, not liking the sound of the man's tone. Jake followed suit.

"Terrific," Shorty said with disdain. "I guess, ah, you come from a place where Strat-O-Matic can't be easily bought? One of the Benelux countries, maybe, or Micronesia?"

"Oh, we've all had our chances to buy that particular game," Earl said, taking off his glasses. "I guess we were just too busy admiring all of APBA's far more attractive and well-designed components."

A murmur went through the other group, and the APBA Collective closed ranks behind Earl in response to it. Red put his hands in the pockets of his leather jacket and tongued the inside of his cheek.

"Yeah, APBA sure has nice...*parts,*" he said with dripping derision. "I hear they're a nice distraction from Strat-O-Matic's superior statistical accuracy."

Rick's jaw dropped. He had heard some foul, foul things spoken in his twenty-six years on Mother Earth, but these guys were shooting flaming arrows.

"Obviously you're not aware of what you're saying," Earl responded, trying to swell up his chest inside his brown J.C. Penney sweater vest. "That's okay; you must be really tired from throwing around that *twenty-sided die* all day." Behind him, Jake and Rick giggled, knowing Earl had scored a direct hit that must have shredded the strangers' very souls.

Red stuck a piece of sugarless gum in his mouth and began to chew it very, very slowly as his eyes narrowed to little slits. "Not as tired as I am from sorting through the cards of *every player who had any sort of measurable playing time during any given year,*" he said, his voice low and guttural. The men on his side seconded his opinion with grunts in the affirmative.

"Now, gentlemen, isn't this a bit silly?" Jerzy Plenck asked. "Coming to loggerheads over the pros and cons of pursuits so inconsequential in the grand scheme of the universe? Let's not squander this opportunity to forge new friendshi—"

"How do you keep all those player cards together, by the way?" Earl asked. "Oh, did you say 'With sad little rubber bands instead of tasteful envelopes and only after spending half my youth perforating them from big bulky sheets?' What a shame. By the way, make sure you keep an eye on the side of the road as you drive for some interesting rain-out results, because, heh, because they sure as heck aren't included with *your* game."

"That's *got* to hurt," Curse whispered admiringly, seeing Earl in a whole new light.

"Included in *our* game is the biggest fan base in all of tabletop sports, Mr. I'm-So-Cool-Just-Because-I-Can-See-A-Player's-City-of-Birth-on-His-Card," Red spat. "You all are nothing but a bunch of chart-flippers!"

"Charts filled with play descriptions a little more vivid than a bunch of *acronyms and hyphens!*" Earl shouted, somewhat erroneously, but everyone more or less got the point.

"Yeah, that's right, Dad!" Jake said, bonding with his father more in the past twelve seconds than in their entire decade of watching *Nova* together.

"We just *love* your lonnnnnng, flaaaaat boxes," Rick chimed in. "Hope you have room for them in the back of your closet, where they'll all wind up!"

"If you're all such hot stuff," Red challenged them, "how come you're not at the actual APBA convention? What's the matter, did you get too bogged down having to laboriously add up the individual fielding ratings of your lineup to determine the defense's overall strength? Ha!"

Earl started to respond to this, almost getting a whole word out of his mouth, but then stopped. His attention shifted to Ben, who seemed completely unaware that the argument had ground to a sudden halt. His eyes were a-sparkle with excitement and he motioned with his head to Earl to let fly another entertaining insult.

"APBA convention?" Harold said, frowning. "The annual APBA convention is *this* weekend?"

"Of course, you ninnies," said the short man. "Your goofy-named game has the spotlight all to itself for a few lousy days, and you're gonna miss it. Good work!"

"Ben, why did you schedule our tournament on the same weekend as the convention?" Templeton asked. "All the most serious players will already be obligated to that and not some last-minute event."

"I didn't know there *was* such a thing as an APBA convention," Ben said, really disappointed that the delightful shouting match had to come to an end because of such trifling little details. "If it's so huge, why didn't any of *you* guys know about it?"

"We told you at that first meeting in your apartment, Ben, none of us are hardcore fanatics," Earl said. "We just like to play a whole heck of a lot."

"I wonder what this is gonna do to attendance," Curse wondered aloud.

"What a bunch of rubes," said Red, shaking his head sadly. "Come on, guys, let's get rolling before they try to sell us their old Statis Pro games."

Earl gasped. "You could do a *heck* of a lot worse than to simulate all the major sports using Statis Pro!" he shouted, shaking a fist. "Go back to Glen Head, you losers!"

Someone in the Strat-O-Matic group yelled something back about the pathetic lack of bold, sharp edges to APBA's player cards and in seconds they were all back aboard their RV and pulling quickly away from the intersection, leaving the Collective standing in the sun. When their pulses got back to normal after the bloody encounter, they headed back into their own craft and Ben started to dig out some cold cuts from the cooler he'd brought, trying to distract them all with the promise of lunch.

"Don't worry about a thing," Ben told them. "I checked my e-mail at the library in Neodesha while you guys were trying to fix our taillights. There's been plenty of response to the tournament. No TV stations are committed yet, but at least six players are confirmed. Curse, I may have promised everyone that you'd give them three or four free pitching lessons and a personal invitation to that cool little cabin in the Shenandoahs you've been showing us pictures of, and we may want to start thinking of how we're going to fit a water slide into the conference center. But your faith in me and in every single aspect of this trip will, as I have always maintained, be completely rewarded. Now, for lunch we have meatloaf sandwiches that to *me* still smell perfectly fine. Jake, come here and smell these and tell me there's anything so terribly wrong with them. Come on, I dare you."

## 17. The Designer of *4th & 19 Football* Airs a Long-Harbored Grievance

By Friday afternoon, they were all getting just a wee bit sick of each other as cabin fever reared its ugly head. Ben had kept his promise not to refer to Harold as Turkey Boat anymore, but had fallen into the habit of calling him "Grassy Pete" for no reason whatsoever. Curse had grown tired of Rick's constant admonitions to recycle, to buy a hybrid car, and to learn to make his own toothpaste.

Templeton often composed lengthy passages of future works of fiction in his sleep, mumbling the words while he kept a tape recorder running in order to transcribe them when he awoke. Sometimes the compositions had some literary value, but just as often, Templeton's helpless sleep-self lapsed into inventing the weakly plotted tale of a sixteenth century female pirate named Eleanor Scantyclad, whose erotic adventures on the Galapagos Islands threatened Jake Shavey's innocence somewhat. Earl, in charge of the News of the Zany section of his company newsletter back at work, had taken to proofreading the messy chapters Roy had drafted for Ben's biography, and Roy didn't especially care for the way Earl kept criticizing his handwriting. Earl couldn't help it; as a child his parents had stressed the vital importance of good penmanship to the point where his failed cursive Qs were sent to the local newspaper in an attempt to shame him. Meanwhile, everyone was more or less baffled by Jerzy Plenck and his odd habits. His meditation hour always had to take place outdoors, so they had to pull over just after dawn and just before sunset so he could sit atop a picnic table and repeatedly nod with increasing head speed until he suddenly stopped and appeared to sleep with his eyes open for exactly fifty-six minutes. Grackles landed on his shoulders and perched there during these sessions. Afterwards, Jerzy would suggest they all drink weak chai with him while he told them some Chinese fable about blacksmiths or something. Meanwhile, it remained only mildly amusing to watch him clobber Ben at APBA, sometimes taking advantage of Ben's distressing managerial predictability, other times staring at the dice intently and almost able to predict from looking at the box score what numbers would come up on them next. He called this process "divining the exo-rhythms of the F range." Whatever he called it, Ben seemed to be getting worse rather than better, despite his own insistence that he felt on the verge of a breakthrough. He spoke of this alleged breakthrough with slightly less conviction than Paul McCartney telling Ringo Starr that they couldn't have done it without him.

Then there was the TRAVEL OPTION. As of Thursday night, the list of activities they could no longer perform lest the doleful creature suffer mechanical collapse and strand them in rural Utah included: showering, using two of the three electrical outlets, changing lanes too suddenly, filling the tank with gas without letting it sit for a few minutes about halfway through, rolling down the driver's side window, adjusting the driver's side mirror, changing the presets on the radio (what was left of it after four of the buttons had fallen off going around a curve in the city of Beaver), tapping on the windows, and yielding to pedestrians. They each had their own ideas as to what should become of the ship after the Vegas tournament, since it was completely clear that it would never make it back across the country and was basically unsellable. They took a secret vote on everybody's suggestions. In last place came Jerzy Plenck's idea to donate the RV to the Nevada Arts Commission as possible gallery space for promising young artists working in ceramics and beadwork. Everyone else voted to burn it in a field. Exactly what kind of field varied from person to person, but yeah, that was what was going to happen.

Dusk on Friday saw the diminishment of the ranks of the Independent APBA Collective of Metro Harrisburg by one.

For about two hours, they had all been scanning the passing landscape for a spot where Plenck could sit on top of something and meditate as he faced northwest, but the land had been barren of any objects remotely resembling a perch for this purpose. Instead, against the dramatic backdrop of the La Sal Mountains, Utah had revealed to them a shadowy desert wonderland of gentle rolling hills and deceptively exotic flora. The sun hanging low over the horizon threw it all into breathtakingly beautiful relief. They turned the radio off and only the sound of the engine complemented the rhapsodic silence of the countryside. No cars even went past them anymore, telling them that 1) out here in the land where God's creation was still not yet finished, nature still wielded benign dominance, and 2) they were kind of lost. They chose to ignore this second fact and Jake started to snap pictures of the approaching sunset which he would upload to his website if they ever saw a computer again.

"Wow," Jake said, working his digital camera like a pro, "we never see anything like this in Harrisburg."

"Makes the whole trip worthwhile, pretty much," Curse said, gazing at the horizon's colorful palette.

"Truly awe-inspiring," Templeton said, feeling another chapter of his book drop into place.

"Try not to gather too much on one side of the vehicle," Ben said, "or the struts could cave in again."

Finally they saw a stump. It would have to do for Plenck. It sat in the middle of yet another infinite stretch of hardpan near another meaningless milepost. They pulled over, got out of the RV, and took a few steps off the shoulder, feeling the cool wind ruffle their hair and clothes, smelling the untainted air that promised nothing but health and tranquility. The road disappeared both ways into the distance. A transcendent dark blue glow had settled over the earth. Many miles away, the La Sals crouched like a gathering of stoic judges, great blocks of ancient darkness, immobile, daunting.

"This will do nicely," Plenck said with a respectful lack of volume.

"Hey, why isn't Rick coming out?" Jake asked, pointing back at the RV.

Rick was staring through the windshield, hypnotized, his mouth hanging open. After a couple of seconds, he managed to slide off the driver's seat and exit the vehicle slowly, never taking his eyes off the mountains, as if the sights before him were displayed on an old battery-operated TV and he was afraid that any sudden movement would irreparably jostle the antenna and lose the image. He took a few shaky steps forward, not quite able yet to make his mouth close.

"Nice, huh?" Roy asked him, a little freaked out by Rick's stupor.

"It's the *dream,*" Rick said, ignoring him. He turned his head left and right, taking in every little detail of the roadside view. "The *dream.*"

"To what do you refer?" Plenck asked politely.

"All my life, I've had this recurring dream," Rick told them, his knees weak. "It's this exact setting, to the last detail."

"Hmmm, not a whole lot of detail," Ben said. "Just a whole lot of nothing in every direction, pretty much."

"No, no, you're wrong," Rick said, leaving them and walking in a wide circle. "Everything's the same, including the stump there. And look, see that power grid out there? You can just barely see it. I've dreamed about that, too." They looked. Indeed, a row of silvery towers crouched at the very far reaches of their vision, touched by orange sunlight, beautiful somehow, appearing almost as natural as any of the other wonders around them.

"I used to draw this place when I was a kid, without ever having even seen it," Rick told them. "I knew I had to make it here before I died."

"Well, you've done it, and you probably have about fifty years to spare," Curse congratulated him. "Good job, yo."

Rick closed his eyes briefly, then opened them again. The landscape had not disappeared. "All my life," he said, "I've wanted to find a place of total tranquility where I could start all over again. A place away from the things of man, where nothing had been ruined."

"Start all over again?" Harold asked. "What do you mean?"

"Just that," Rick said, turning the face them. "To just walk off and forget everything, and become one with the earth, reborn, naked."

"Naked, yes," Ben said. "You just mean spiritually, right?"

"Um...surrrre," Rick said, eyes shifting from side to side. "But *this* is the place, I know it. It's the first time I've ever been west of Chicago. Maybe the time is now."

"You're not really serious, are you?" Earl asked. "You mean you really want to..."

"Head for the mountains with just my soul in my hand," Rick said bravely. "And the stars above for nourishment."

"Oh, please," Ben said. "There's scorpions out here, man. They'll pick your bones clean."

"I want to be really brave just once," Rick said. "I want to put what I preach into practice. I want to blend my blethna with my ja."

"Easier said than done, young man," Plenck advised. "But I fully support your decision."

"No one's going anywhere," Ben said. "We have a tournament to get to. You shouldn't be making any major decisions until we see what kind of buffets we're in for in Vegas."

"Sorry, Ben," Rick said. "The moment is just too perfect. Something's speaking to me from beyond. I must walk on."

"But why not take it to the next level and find someplace *really* remote, like the Outback or something?" Harold asked, fascinated.

"Yeah, good luck affording *that* plane ticket," Rick said. "This will do just fine. So...I guess this is goodbye, dudes. Thanks for everything."

"What's gonna happen to you?" Jake asked, rather frightened.

"I'll be okay, Jake," Rick told him. "I'll just merge with the wild for a time, and then I suppose I'll come out of it and live like anybody else. But it'll be a new me. A wiser me. A cleansed me."

"Like when I tried to become a switch-hitter in '97," Ben said, nodding, finally beginning to understand.

"I guess," Rick said.

"You don't want to take your stuff?" Roy asked. "Your harmonica? Your copy of *High Times* that Dick Van Dyke signed?"

"Absolutely nothing," Rick said, gazing at the mountains, feeling his spirit becoming lighter and lighter.

"But you'll go insane out here with nothing to do but astral project," Ben said. "Take *something.*"

Rick considered this viewpoint. "I suppose if..." he began, then motioned for Jake to come over to him. He whispered something into the kid's ear, and Jake disappeared into the RV for a minute. When he emerged, he was holding Rick's APBA Baseball set. He gave it to the crazy adventurer and retreated again respectfully. The group had organically created a little symbolic circle around Rick, and holding his game, he turned to the south and began to walk, taking easy, confident steps across the scrubland, becoming a silhouette in no time at all. He turned to wave before he got too small in their vision, and everyone waved back.

"Now there goes a true hero," Jerzy Plenck said.

"He was already talking a half hour ago about how he was a little hungry," Earl said. "Where's he going to eat?"

"I think he said the stars were gonna feed him," Jake said, continuing to wave after all the others had stopped.

"I can't believe he's choosing the wild over Las Vegas," Ben mused, shaking his head. "There's no spiritual cleansing quite like losing a hundred bucks on a single spin at the nickel slots. I'll never understand the tree-huggers."

Jerzy Plenck decided to forgo his meditation time out of respect for the moment. It was a good ten minutes before the group could bring themselves to get back into the RV. In Ben's biography, Roy would describe the scene of Rick's fearless departure like this:

*Just as the phoenix of legend rose exultant from the ashes, so too did Richard Leahy Nippthorpe rise from the wreckage of modern day civilization to reclaim his true identity as a man untainted by society's expectations of what comprises an employable individual.*

*His largeness was never bigger than when he abandoned Ben's vehicle to chart his own sacred path beyond the tree stump that had been the reason for their movement's cessation. Did some part of Ben's heart reach a five-fingered hand out to join him, sensing that the trip to the west could not possibly end as well as he was hoping, given his seeming inability to make his intelligence grow enough to compete in his penultimate tournament? No one would ever know, just as no one would ever know what became of Rick after he became a part of the late summer sunset which he loved more than even the song of the hummingbird, or the song of the blue jay, or the song of the sparrow, or the song of the seagull, or the song of the robin, or the song of the majestic bald eagle that perhaps swooped down from the sky to guide his feet as they carried him into the hazy future.*

The book's editor would later excise this entire passage except for the part about the stump. But Roy felt he had at least captured for himself the mood of the moment. None of them realized that as the RV pulled back onto the road and motored away, Rick was waving his arms frantically at them from a distance, hollering that he had left his entire card set in the vehicle, rendering his game useless, and that he'd decided it might be better to begin his pious journey after they had stopped to grab some good complex carbohydrates someplace, and maybe even a milk shake. They never heard him over the sound of the engine and the untrammeled beauty of the landscape—which, yes, was so disgustingly beautiful that it produced actual musical notes. Nor did they ever find out what became of young Rick, remaining forever unaware of his ten-hour struggle to get two lousy seconds of decent shut-eye in the desert cold, his discovery at dawn of a Burger King, Barnes and Noble, Nike Outlet, and Target Superstore just a mile or so past the electrical towers, and his decision that he maybe wasn't really up for spiritual purity just now and was more suited to bussing tables for a while at a vegan restaurant beside the state's largest Red Lobster. He was sure he would have another go at the whole desert scenario at some point, but as summer turned to autumn, he became slightly more entranced by the idea of dating one of his co-workers, a seriously hot feminist who not only played the bewitching music of the Austrian one-stringed echospiel, but published her own underground 'zine about dumpster diving.

The Collective drove on through the soft night with Templeton at the wheel, though the mood inside the RV was not terribly upbeat. It was Jerzy Plenck who finally decided to get the boys back into a proper frame of mind twenty minutes after they dropped that long-haired fella off in the middle of nowhere.

"I've got a notion," he said as the others gazed out the windows. "Why not try out a new game, this one of my own design? That should take our minds off our sudden loss of manpower, and perhaps teach us some new skills as well."

Ben raised an eyebrow. "New game?"

"Yes indeed," Jerzy said, and opened his ever-surprising black leather suitcase, from which had already emerged everything from a six-pack of Thai noodle cups to a water filtration system to a copy of the Declaration of Independence. Now he produced a small wooden box with a gold-plated latch and placed it on the table in the dining area, or "eat part" as Ben called it. The Collective gathered around as the box was opened delicately.

Inside was what looked like a very rudimentary board game, a baseball sim whose components were made of nothing more fancy than cardboard and typing paper and a pair of dice that were worth only what a pair of normal dice would fetch on the open market (about thirty cents). Ben and the others had expected to see some sort of ruby dice, or maybe game boards carved from the original wood that built Noah's Ark, or something that would make them at least mildly envious of Plenck's magic fountain of cash. He placed the game on the table in front of him and sat down, adding to the mix a couple of little pencils swiped from a miniature golf course in Kansas City.

"I give you Thwack-a-Dinger Baseball," Plenck said, rolling up the sleeves of his expensive turtleneck sweater. "It has not yet been introduced to the general public, but soon, very soon, I will begin to market it. It is the result of almost a decade of design and testing."

"It doesn't look like much," Jake said, "Where are the player cards?"

"There are none, young man," Plenck said. "I found that the use of doppelgangers distracted from the central theme of the game."

"And what is that?" Curse asked, puzzled.

"Ah, you shall soon see. Who would like to be my opponent?"

"I'll give it a shot," Harold said, squishing himself behind the dining table.

"Very well, Mr. Pillick. Why don't you play the role of the visiting team, and I shall play the host."

"Can I be the Cannons?" Harold asked.

"No team names shall be brought into the game," Plenck said in the tone of a headmaster disciplining a fourth grader for asking to go to the bathroom thirty seconds after an exam had started.

"Um, okay," Harold said. "What are the rules?"

"Simply roll the dice," Plenck said, "and they shall be revealed to you. Oh, I am so glad I could share this game with you, gentlemen."

Everyone leaned over the shoulders of the gamers as Harold picked up the blue and green dice and rolled them carefully so the movement of the RV wouldn't send them off the table, as had been a major developing problem on the trip.

"That's a 36, or just a 9, depending on which numerical system this game uses," Jake volunteered.

"Or is it neither?" Plenck asked the air. "In Thwack-a-Dinger Baseball, we append the sum of seventy to all additive results, and then we multiply by nineteen. Thus, you just rolled a 1501 to begin our contest."

"Why do you do that?" Roy asked.

Plenck looked at him as if he had asked why you shouldn't eat expired ham. "Well, it sharpens the math skills, of course," he said, and lifted a thin chart on which a few dozen play results had been printed using an ink cartridge that had obviously been on its last legs. He read from it in theatrical tones. " 'The batter reaches first base due mostly to a marked lack of concentration by not just one player, but the opposing team as a whole.' Congratulations on your early advantage, Harold."

"All right, sounds good, though I'm not sure how we would score that exactly," Harold said. "Um, where are the base runner markers?"

Plenck chuckled without smiling. "I think we are adults enough to keep track of the progress of base runners using nothing more than our interior abaci," he commented dismissively.

"All right. Next batter up." Harold picked up the dice and prepared to roll again, shaking the moody cubes in a right hand that had become more and more effete since his retirement from the game. Instead of *chicka-chicka-chicka,* there was more of a *doop-doop-doop* sound.

"Just a moment," Plenck said, holding a hand up. "We must consult the Sacrifice Bunt table."

"I don't want to bunt," Harold said.

"Yeah, you swing for the fences, Grassy Pete," Ben said, clapping him on the shoulder. "Bunting. Even the sound of the word is ugly."

"Bunting is mandatory, I'm afraid," Plenck warned. "It is essential to the theme of the game."

"The theme of the game," Earl repeated. "I can't wait to see what it is. Mandatory bunting seems kind of strange."

Nevertheless, Harold, not wanting to be impolite, rolled the dice, and after some quick jottings on a slip of paper, came up with a result of 1387. The type was quite small on the sac bunt table, and Plenck had to don his teeny European reading glasses to make out what he had put there.

" 'The batter fails to bunt successfully,' " he read, " 'due to insufficient time spent visualizing successful outcomes during practice. Double play.' "

"This game seems kind of, you know, critical of people," Jake noted.

"Ah indeed," Plenck said. "It's the first baseball simulation that reflects the harshest truths of the mental game rather than our pie-eyed view of the physical abilities of its heroes. Here we see the decline of bunting ability as a consequence not of corporeal miscalculations, but of uneven interior states."

"Is that really necessary?" Harold asked. "I mean, aren't we supposed to just have fun?"

Again, Plenck gave him the Has-Your-Melon-Gone-Mushy look. "Fun is for ingesters of beer and swallowers of corn chips," he said. "Thwack-a-Dinger Baseball is about the realities of the deep cerebral game which we must confront now, lest the lack of true awareness on the part of its participants become a plague on all major leagues."

"When do you start thwacking dingers?" Ben asked.

"Homeruns? I think you'll find that their utter absence from my simulation will force us into a refreshing re-appraisal of defense, speed, critical thought, and above all, the mental conditioning of every man on the field."

"So the name is supposed to be ironic," Curse said.

Plenck frowned once again. "No, it's just a really exciting name," he said humorlessly. "Let's play on."

They did. With each minute that passed, the mood inside the RV darkened further as the APBA guru's board game reminded them again and again of human weakness and malaise. Outfielders were late with cut-off throws because they 'didn't truly understand that they were but one link in a chain of field functions necessary to the organism.' Batters fouled off pitch after pitch after pitch because they were 'lived more in terror of failure than in embrace of accomplishment.' When Harold asked if there was the possibility of replacing his pitcher, Plenck told him it was futile to do so; a side roll of the dice revealed that Harold's bullpen had 'simply left their essential desire behind' that day and would be completely ineffective.

"This game is weird," Jake said in the third inning, finally expressing the thoughts of everyone else standing around the table.

Plenck reacted with a bitterness none of them had seen from him before. "The 'weirdness,' as you call it, is entirely by design," he said.

"Is *this* by design?" Ben asked, pointing at something on the main result chart. "It looks like if you try to steal third, the only thing that can happen is that your runner trips halfway there and gets seriously hurt."

"A lesson for us all," Plenck said, a cautionary finger raised into the air.

"Let me guess," Templeton called back from the driver's seat, having monitored the game's progress as he drove. "Not even the seemingly simple navigation of the base paths is a given if one is lost in a grander sense."

"Oh boy," Earl said.

"Actually, I just think it's foolish to try to steal third," Plenck corrected him. "A manager should be grateful his runner got as far as second."

As the scoreless game slogged on and the RV rolled west through the Nevada darkness, more and more basic design flaws were revealed, and Plenck's veneer of grace and culture was alarmingly chipped away as he reacted to criticisms with more and more hostility. An absurd number of pop flies were lost in the sun in shallow left and became triples. If a batter struck out, the catcher inevitably tried to pick off the lead runner only to throw the ball into the stands and injure a spectator's kidney. No matter what happened, though, no one could seem to get safely to home plate. The chances of a man scoring from second on a single were about two percent, and even singles to the gap with a runner on third tended to result in the guy deciding it was 'more prudent' to stay where he was. Either that, or the third base coach held the runner 'in order to make the next batter prove his true worth to the team' by bringing him home with a hit.

"Oh, for goodness sakes!" Harold cried when, after loading the bases with nobody out, all three of his next batters fouled out harmlessly to the catcher. "Whenever the bases are loaded, *every* out is a foul out to the catcher!"

"Yeah, what gives there, Mr. Plenck?" Roy asked.

"I am growing very tired of hearing your churlish attacks on my game," Plenck snarled, his face displaying a little bit of color for the first time since they'd known him. "I suppose you'd rather be playing APBA."

"Well, duh," Curse said. "It actually makes some sense."

"You know nothing of the definition of the word!" Plenck shouted. "I give you a work of genius, and you do nothing but naysay and pshaw!"

"We don't mean to pshaw," Roy said apologetically, "but—"

Plenck held up a hand to shush him and struggled to work his way out from behind the table. It took a while, but he finally managed to stand up, not quite looming over all of them. "But nothing!" he said loudly. "Thwack-a-Dinger Baseball is a superior simulation, and that's all there is to it! I cannot be blamed if your puny minds aren't able to grasp my theme!"

"What was that again?" Ben asked.

Plenck riveted his hands to his hips. "The theme is Shutup!" he snapped.

"Well, *that's* kind of childish," Jake said.

"You seem different suddenly," Earl observed. "Are you feeling all right?"

"I'll tell you how I'm feeling!" the guru shouted. "I'm not feeling myself at all—in fact, I'm feeling like a different person entirely! Gentlemen, meet your true fellow traveler—a man known in the sports gaming underworld as *Hentley Harkaby!*" With that, he reached up to his scalp and shockingly tore away his carefully tailored white wig to reveal a shock of slightly grayer hair underneath. Everyone gasped. Templeton, looking in the rearview mirror, applied what was left of the RV's brakes and swerved over to the shoulder.

"Yes, it's me!" the impostor bellowed. "Hentley Harkaby in the flesh!"

"Who?" asked Curse.

"He's the guy who invented some game called Hey Batter Hey Batter Hey Batter Hey Batter *Swing,*" Ben said, taking two fearful steps back. "It sucked so bad he went crazy and tried to sabotage other company's games!"

"My game did *not* suck, and *none* of my efforts has ever sucked!" Harkaby defended himself. "Not Gentlemanly Stroll Golf, not Beware the Rim Basketball, and certainly not Thwack-a-Dinger Baseball! Is it *my* failing that this fetid society can't embrace any board game which invariably ends in a tie in order to teach the participants a much-needed tutorial in sportsmanship? *You're* all the problem, not me! Everyone in this noxious world is against me! But now, I have exacted a most curious revenge—you, Ben Glinton, have spent this trip learning absolutely *nothing* of value for your tournament. All the advice I've given you is useless. Useless! Everything I've taught is the exact *opposite* of what you should know to win at APBA!"

"Well, then I should just do the opposite of *that,* and I'll win, right?" Ben asked.

Harkaby hesitated and looked uncertainly down at his shoes. "No, no, no, nothing will work for you, so just forget about doing that," he warned, recovering himself. "You're hopeless. Hopeless! I know absolutely nothing about your stupid game!"

"I don't get it," Earl said. "You were certainly winning a lot for someone who claims to not know anything about it."

"I was *cheating,* you lackwits!" Harkaby revealed, pulling a pair of dice from his pocket. "These are loaded! You didn't even once think that all that nonsense about exo-rhythms and the 'truth of the numerological handprint' was total rubbish?"

They all looked at each other and shrugged.

"What a bunch of blundering tatterdemalions," Harkaby alleged. "Well, good luck winning your precious tournament now, Mr. Glinton, when you've improved not a single trifle!"

"Boy, no offense, but you must be really insane, Mr. Harkaby," Harold said. "You went to all the trouble of tricking Fergus Hibbert into thinking you were some kind of Zen master, creating some incredible ultimate APBA set, making a wig even though none of us had any idea what you looked like anyway...all to prevent someone you don't even know from winning a tournament that's completely meaningless to you?"

"Quite insane," seconded Templeton, having turned off the RV's engine and come back to join the others in case somebody needed the help of an ex-Marine and National Book Award finalist to defuse this unpredictable madman.

"Don't forget deceiving you into thinking my riches were gained by betting on sports instead of how I really attained my wealth: through bringing nuisance lawsuits against the Mormon church!" Plenck said. "But it was all worth it, I assure you. I'll travel to any lengths and continue to do whatever it takes to make you people realize the intellectual futility of playing any other board game than the ones I create. Acknowledge my brilliance here and now, or you shall suffer even greater consequences!"

"We'll take our chances, you nutjob," Curse said. "Wow, you are seriously loony tunes. How come you just don't use all that money you have to advertise your lousy game and sell it online or something?"

"I've tried, ingrates, and I've been rewarded with sales figures more insulting to me than even you are. The public is too busy listening to that infernal rock music and playing Space Man Invasion on their television sets to appreciate the enrichment I have to offer!"

"Mr. Harkaby, could you give me your place of birth?" Roy asked, taking notes for Ben's bio. "And is Harkaby spelled with two Ks or just one?"

"Kudos on your master plan to make me look stupid and all, Hannibal Lecter," Ben said. "Now, um, where can we drop you?"

"Oh, I didn't just make you look foolish, Glinton," Plenck said, rubbing his hands together. "I went into your wallet my first night here and found the tattered Arby's coupon on which you had written all the e-mail addresses you used to alert people to your puerile tournament, plus the names of the media outlets you attempted to inform. Let's just say they all got a second e-mail yesterday...one which surely guarantees you'll be playing APBA only amongst yourselves tomorrow!"

"You total wanker!" Ben cried. "What did you tell them?"

"Simply that the tournament's only prize would be not twenty thousand dollars, but a single tube of generic denture polish," said the smiling spy. "Game, set, and match, fellows. Now if you'll excuse me, I'll be getting out right here, if you don't mind." He pushed his puny way past them all, leaving his suitcase behind, and turned to issue a final insult. "And thank you, Mr. Pillick, for boring me to tears these past two nights with a laundry list of your secret ambitions. I hope finding and killing the Loch Ness Monster will bring you every happiness!" With that, he stepped out of the RV and started walking down the dark, empty highway.

They all peered through the windshield, and Templeton switched the headlights on to see him better. Plenck didn't turn back. He moved swiftly away from them with that style of walking of his which was so incredibly irritating for no particular reason.

"Yikes," Roy said. "How are we going to get word back to all those people in time to get them to change their minds about the tournament? It starts tomorrow at one!"

"We'll stop somewhere and I'll try to reverse the damage, maybe make some calls," Ben said, shoulders sagging as if he were a beach ball recently poked with a hairpin. "Wow, I guess I'm not going to be able to win this thing after all. I'm as dumb as I ever was."

"Don't say that, Ben," Harold said. "If we start now, we can all help you."

"I'm not even in the mood to play," Ben sighed. "Now where in the world is that guy *going?* Does he realize we're still in the desert?"

"He'll be all right," Curse said. "He's rich. He'll call a cab from a pay phone or something, or maybe he'll bump into Rick."

Templeton started the engine and they rolled slowly forward, eventually pulling up beside Harkaby. The window rolled down and Earl's head poked out.

"Mr. Harkaby, do you want us to use the cell phone to maybe call you a cab somehow?" he asked.

"Silence!" Harkaby said, not looking at them. "Go lick the substantial wounds I've inflicted, lowly peasants!"

Roy's head poked out too. "Do you at least want your wig back?" he asked.

"Just toss it, please," Harkaby instructed. Roy threw it out towards him and it fell to the pavement. Harkaby picked it up, never stopping, and put it crookedly on his head. After that, they drove on, leaving the saboteur, who come to think of it was virtually a senior citizen, to his own sinister devices. As fate would have it, not only would he be just fine, but an hour later he would find another two hundred and twelve thousand dollars in a paper bag along the side of the road. Fate just didn't know what to make of the man named Hentley Harkaby.

"The place feels kind of empty," Roy said when they had all sat down again, bumping along at fifty miles per hour. It was time to start forgetting this embarrassing episode and start thinking about what would comprise their last dinner on the trip west.

"No one else gets off this bus or reveals their true identity until we get to where we're going," Ben told them. "No more surprises. I need a nice cheeseburger, and I need it now."

"At least we're less than twelve hours away from Las Vegas," Templeton said, noticing a road sign fly past them. "Won't be long now!"

Ben put a quizzical finger to his lips. "Wait a second...did I say Las Vegas? Is that what I've been saying? Oh shoot, I meant Reno, I'm sorry. Yeah, I should have been saying Reno all this time. That's where we're going. The site of the tournament is Reno. Duh. Totally my mistake. Totally."

Once again, the odds were defied when Ben's kind-hearted peers refrained from pummeling him with towels wrapped around heavy bars of soap, though any non-partisan judge would have ruled that the justification to do so was certainly there. Seeing how down Ben was after Plenck's revelation that his lessons had been a total waste of time, they refrained from even poisoning his ginger snaps.

Templeton took the next right turn and they motored on into the night, noticeably lighter but no wiser than they were an hour before.

## 18. Lexington Redemption, an Unwelcome Intruder, and the Girl with the Tarantula Tattoo

Their arrival in the sort-of fabled city of dreams at eleven a.m. the next morning would have caused much celebration if the treasonous wreck that brought them there didn't finally up and die twelve feet short of the city line. The TRAVEL OPTION made a sound like a donkey choking on a pancake just as they all laid grateful eyes on the WELCOME TO RENO sign, and the next thing they knew, the exhaust system fell off. They got out of the RV, kicked the pipes into a ditch, and gazed longingly ahead of them, where buildings beckoned in the distance.

"All right, boys," Ben said, "grab whatever you can out of the house. We're walking."

Some personal possessions were gathered, but not too many beyond the APBA sets. Templeton started the engine just long enough to move the RV well off the road into the cracked and weedy parking lot of Helvetico Roulette and Coat Check Supply, and Jake took a last picture of the heap for the scrapbook. Ben saluted it and they turned to begin walking the last one and three-quarters miles that would dump them into the lobby of the Lucky Ape Hotel and Casino, built in 1997 with money that never actually existed, a fact that would eventually come as quite a surprise to its Lebanese investors.

The desert sun bore down on them like hot butter on a dinner roll. No one passing them by in their luxurious, fully inspected and insured vehicles bothered to stop. As soon as the Collective got to the first sign of real civilization, which in this case happened to be a condemned massage parlor, they rested on a bench in the shade while Ben lugged his sweaty self across the street to a pay phone. The others watched him dial number after number and gesticulate madly into the handset in an attempt to convince whoever he could that the tournament was indeed on and that the prize money was a go, although even the cost of the promised generic tube of denture polish was somewhat beyond him at this point. When he had completed four or five calls, he made another mad, jaywalk-laden dash across the busy street, clipped only once by a passing Volvo. Despite their fear that Ben would meet an untimely end just trying to get from one side of the road to another, the group's spirits were buoyed by the sounds of traffic and activity and the sights of people everywhere, whereas during the last few days, two clumps of tumbleweed bumping into each other was considered rush hour.

"Doesn't look like you had much luck," Templeton said to Ben. He was taking the heat especially hard, owning a writer's mostly sedentary body.

"I gave it a shot," Ben said. "I got a good feeling about the local public affairs station maybe sending a guy over."

"We only have two hours left till the tournament starts," Harold said. "Let's just hope for the best."

They marched onward, past a check cashing outlet, an off-track betting joint, a store that sold irregular sunglasses, a $3.99 lobster buffet (the restaurant defined "lobster" in very small print as "any hard-shelled ocean or creek mollusk"), an RV dealer specializing in lightly used TRAVEL OPTIONs, the Optimistic Hooker Lounge and Gaming Parlor, and a wig outlet. Beyond it all, at the very outer limits of their endurance, lay the Lucky Ape, its entrance guarded by a giant metal replica of the jungle's favorite son. Visitors and guests were obligated to walk through the ape's gaping mouth in order to reach the air conditioning within.

"We made it!" Harold beamed.

"How are you doing, Jake?" Earl asked his son.

"These irregular sunglasses smell like feet," Jake replied. Other than that, he had more energy than anyone, as usual.

"This heat reminds me of that four-game series we played that August in Arizona a few years back," Curse said. "Greeny made me pitch on short rest. I swore I'd never spend a day in a hot climate again."

"I remember that series," Ben said. "Greeny swore he'd never use me in center field again."

Entering the modestly decorated hotel was like diving into the icy waters of the Atlantic. Someone had decided to crank the air conditioning up to a level commonly referred to in the cooling and heating industry as "Doomsday Scenario." They were thoroughly popsicled by the time they got to the front desk.

"The last name's Glinton, checking in," Ben said to the clerk. "And I'm running the APBA tournament too, such as it is."

"Welcome, Mr. Glinton," the clerk greeted him perkily, typing a few keystrokes on his secondhand computer. His nametag bore a single word: TODDY. "Your room for a one-night stay is ready for you."

"Room, not rooms?" Roy asked despairingly.

"And the gathering in the conference center to your left will be most happy to begin the tournament," Toddy added. "I'm only sorry that the room can barely hold the crowd."

"Say what?" Ben asked. "Crowd? Barely?"

"Yes," Toddy said. "Had we known there would be such a massive turnout, we could have made arrangements to open up the Mad Monkey Ballroom."

Dumbfounded, Ben and the others looked off to the left. A tall pair of double doors was sealed tight, bearing a single hand-lettered sign that read APBA THING IN HERE. Earl crossed the lobby and pulled one of the doors open.

"Scent my socks!" Earl gasped. "It's a mob scene!"

Templeton, Curse, Harold, Roy, Jake, and Ben all rushed over to the entrance and stood there, shell-shocked. Inside the nondescript room, which was no bigger than a junior high school auditorium, were hundreds of people, milling around, socializing, and already playing exhibition games on the dozen or so cheap cafeteria tables set up for the purpose. Many of the people wore APBA shirts and caps, and gamers were examining each other's card sets and chattering excitedly. Far more shocking than the huge crowd of APBAites, though, was the sight of so many TV cameras and media types dotting the room, looking for all the world like they were getting ready for the Emmys to begin.

"What the hell..." Ben stammered, both delighted and terrified.

"Looks like you said the right things on the phone somehow," Roy said.

"What, are you kidding?" Ben said. "That was only fifteen minutes ago, and anyway, I was so depressed that I was just miming conversations. I didn't call anybody. It wouldn't have done any good. Something crazy is going on here."

Earl was the first to realize what had happened. He noticed the small and misspelled banner that the hotel had hung over the dented and somewhat charred lectern at the front of the room. It welcomed all APBA players, and gave a special Lucky Ape embrace to...

"Oh, no," Ben said, closing his eyes.

"He's here!" a delirious voice said behind him, and a teenaged APBA fan nudged Ben aside to penetrate the crowd. "There he is!"

From a side entrance came none other than Spike Vail, surrounded by his usual entourage of agents, biographers, and media flunkies. Grinning like a contented eel, Spike began shaking hands left and right as flashbulbs snapped. He was wearing what Ben usually wore in public: sweatpants, old sneakers, and a T-shirt whose ownership was actually a point of some dispute. When Spike Vail wore this stuff, it was considered cool. He looked like he had just rolled out of bed, but his smile was Hollywood perfection.

"Why is *he* here?" Templeton asked no one in particular.

"Mr. Vail called the hotel last night and expressed an interest in participating in the tournament," said Toddy the hotel clerk from behind him, having covertly sidled up when no one was paying attention. "He signed up to play just like everyone else. Just in the last few hours, we started getting reservations by the truckload. By the way, gentlemen, is there a Mr. Walter Williger in your group?"

"Yeah, that's me," Curse said.

"We have a phone message for you at the desk, Mr. Williger," Toddy told him.

"Oh. Okay. I'll be back, guys." He followed Toddy back out into the lobby.

"Spike Vail," Ben said, teeth gritted. "Figures he'd have to show up and steal all our thunder."

"I was just reading in the paper last night that his new CD isn't selling very well," Earl said. "Maybe he's desperate for a little promotion."

"That CD is really bad," Jake said. "A kid at space camp had it. Spike talks about all his statistics in every song. He didn't leave out a single year."

"What he's desperate for, if I know Spike Vail, is to win anything and everything," Ben said, watching the man chat up a Thunder Dunk anchor for a live camera. "Well, I may go down today in typically disgraceful fashion, but no *way* am I gonna lose to *that* guy."

"I'm going to get a little closer to see if I can maybe get a quote for the book," Roy said, taking out a fresh pencil.

"You, um, might want to shower first," Templeton suggested. "We all should, if we want to be in human condition when the tournament starts."

"Yeah, let's go up to the room and clean up and maybe grab a nap before one o'clock," Harold said. "If Deenie were to somehow materialize right now and see me like this, she'd use the hose on me."

"I wonder how good these players are," Earl wondered. "Oh no...there's Darla Volume."

"Darla? You mean a girl?" Ben asked, following Earl's gaze. In the center of the room, sitting alone at one of the cafeteria tables and smoking a cigarette in clear violation of conference center policy, was a striking young woman of about twenty, dressed all in stylish black with hair to match. Even her lipstick was the color of midnight.

"I saw her on the front page of an APBA newsletter last year," Earl said. "She's a wizard at the game. She doesn't even like it. She just plays it because no one expects a girl to be any good."

"She's pretty," Roy said, drooling a little. "Pretty girl is pretty."

"I think she might be a bit out of your league there, Fargo," Ben said, noticing Darla's intense green eyes and general aura of disdain for all creatures great and small, especially APBA types. She bore a tarantula tattoo on her long thin neck. Unlike most of the attendees, she hadn't brought anything game-related with her.

"And look, there's the Davis brothers, Chris and Brian," Jake said, pointing. "I played them last year in a competition in Pottsville, remember, Dad? They got into that fist fight with each other about whether or not to try to throw one of my runners out at home plate or cut the throw off from right field."

"They were still really good, as I recall," Earl said. "This should be a pretty intense day."

"I'll show these people some intensity," Ben vowed, completely infused with the sense of purpose that had been seemingly lost as they crossed the Midwest. The murmur of the crowd, the lights, the cameras, the knowledge that an unworthy athlete intended to steal the glory which by all rights was his alone...it all took Ben back to his wide-eyed early days in the big leagues when he thought he could be a superstar if only he could get a lot better at hitting, throwing, catching, and running.

"Looks like everyone's already agreed to a tournament format," Templeton noted, gesturing at an easel set up near the lectern. Someone had drawn up rudimentary brackets, and it appeared that the names of the Collective were already penciled in, having been taken right off the sign-up sheet at the front desk.

"So there's nothing we need to do but get into the Zone," Ben said. "All right, let's pop up to the room, change, and then seize our destiny." He turned and they all followed him through the tall doors again as Spike Vail began signing autographs. Virtually everyone in attendance began to form a line.

Curse was standing right outside the conference center, looking down at a tiny slip of paper. He looked like someone had conked him over the head with the butt end of a rake.

"What's up, Curse?" Ben asked him.

"The Cannons called," Curse said wonderingly. "Jim Byrne got dive-bombed by a pigeon on the mound last night. He's out for six weeks. The Cannons want to sign me."

"That's amazing!" said Roy. "Don't they know you called your retirement 'one hundred percent, in-your-face, get-off-my-lawn permanent'?"

"They do, yeah," Curse said. "But they're desperate. They think they have a shot to get back into the playoffs if they have a solid number two guy behind Phil Graham. They have Peter Ventura as their pitching coach now, and he remembers me from my rookie year with the Tight Sox."

"What's the money like?" Earl asked. "Big bucks?"

"Huh? Oh, um, I didn't really ask. I was so blown away that they'd ask me back."

"Playing for the Cannons again," Harold mused. "Imagine that."

"Do you really want to, though?" Ben asked. "You just told me the other day that you were ready to never think about it again."

"I guess that was when I figured it could never happen," Curse said. "I said so many bad things about the umpires...they might make it hard for me."

"The Cannons are a pretty well-rounded team this year," Templeton said. "It wouldn't surprise me if they were able to put a run together and squeak into the playoffs. You'd be a better lefty than Michael Cieslinski, I bet. His curve ball is getting weaker and weaker."

"And his placement is getting worse and worse," Curse said, looking down at the floor for answers. He looked like a little kid about to start his very first day of kindergarten after hearing that it was filled with dragons and mummies and werewolves. "Oh man, they want to send a car to take me to the airport in fifteen minutes. I have to call them back now or never."

"I say do it, Curse," Ben said. "Win a few games, get them into the Series again, get that nickname of yours wiped out."

"Seriously, that's your opinion?"

"Yeah. You can't turn down a chance at the big time. That's a what-if situation you don't want hanging over your head for the rest of your days."

"What do you think, Harold?" Curse asked. "Would you go back if they wanted you?"

"In a heartbeat," Harold said, nodding. "Nobody ever really gets a second chance in life to go back and write their own ending. You should take it. We're baseball players. We should try to stay baseball players until they throw us out kicking and screaming. We weren't ever supposed to be anything else. Well, I'm an exception, maybe, but you know what I mean."

"You'll be great, Walter," Templeton said. "You're still in excellent shape, and you know more about pitching now than you ever did."

"I haven't thrown in so long, I could really make a fool out of myself," Curse worried. "Sometimes I get these aches in my foot, too. I doubt I can plant hard enough to get my velocity up as much as I need to."

"That championship ring might not come any other way," Earl said. "Darla Volume's in that room. She's going to eat us all alive."

Curse was silent for a moment, but it didn't seem like there was much of a decision to be made. "Athletes," he said simply, shaking his head. "We can't stay away. Just don't know what's good for us."

Ben slapped him on the arm. "If it seems like the hitters have an edge over you because you're rusty, you know what to do, pal," he said.

"Throw completely wild, put a few of them down, scare the bejesus out of everybody," Curse said.

"That's right."

"Okay. I'll try. I'll give it a shot." He cradled his APBA set under one arm. "Gonna take this with me on the plane. I'll be rooting for you guys. Especially you, Ben."

"Thanks, man."

Curse shook all their hands in turn. He told Jake not to push his relievers too hard during the tournament, and thanked Templeton for signing a book for him, which he would read during the Cannons' upcoming road trip to Sacramento, where, if things went according to plan, he would be taking the mound once again after a three year absence from the game.

"I must be crazy, or just a total hypocrite," Curse said in the end, chuckling a little as he walked away from the Collective. "I'll have tickets waiting for everybody when we play Philadelphia, if I'm still on the team."

"You will be," Ben called after him. "Go destroy some people."

Curse placed a very brief call back to the Cannons' front office and then walked out of the lobby, through the mouth of the metal ape, and into the bright late morning sunlight to wait for his ride. It seemed to the gang that he walked with the same cocky stride he used to have whenever he took the mound in the first inning, before his anger at the umpires and the game in general ruined everything. Maybe it was just their imagination. Or maybe the air conditioning was turned up so freaking high that their very visual perception had become unreliable.

"The hour of victory approaches," Ben said, taking their room key out of his pocket, and everyone headed for the elevator.

"Ah, Ben, you told me to remind you as soon as we got to the hotel that we still don't have the rest of the prize money yet," Roy said.

*"The hour of victory approaches,"* Ben said again as the elevator doors closed shut. "One hurdle at a time, Roy."

At 12:45 p.m., when the Collective descended from the seventh floor of the Lucky Ape and entered the Dangling Vine Conference Center, the ever-helpful Toddy informed Ben that the lectern set up at the front of the room was for his benefit, placed there so he could give a little introduction to the tournament and award the day's grand prize after everything finished up. At 12:57, after mingling some with the crowd, which had thinned just a little bit after signatures had been secured from Spike Vail, Ben went over to the star. One of his flunkies started to hold a hand up but Spike maneuvered around him to greet Ben.

"Hey, Ben Glinton!" he said cheerfully. "Man, I haven't seen you since we took the Series! You kind of checked out early, know what I mean? Last thing I saw, you were jumping off the top of a fence and a bus almost creamed you."

"Yeah, how ya doing," Ben said. "How'd you suddenly get so interested in this scene?"

"Oh, I have to make sure the name of Spike Vail is getting treated right, you know. Plus I'm gonna be managing someday soon, and I want to get my feet wet, oh yeah."

"Great, great. So, no endorsement deals at all going on here? You're not pitching anything to the crowd?"

"Now that you mentioned it, I do have a super deal going on with the good people at Cyclops Cola," Spike said, finally letting go of Ben's hand. Ben's fillings would continue to rattle for another three minutes. "I've been signing empty six-packs. Ever tried Cyclops? It's good, tastes a little like chocolate milk. Plus if I win the tournament, I'm giving half my prize money to my charity, Cigarettes for Seniors."

"Well, good luck," Ben said. "I'm sure you'll keep things low key."

"Low key, yeah, right!" Spike said. "Let's get this mother revved up!"

Ben walked over to the lectern and tapped the microphone, producing an impressive whine of feedback. The gamers who had been comparing card sets and swapping gossip looked over.

"Hi, everyone, and welcome to the Nineteen Thousand, Four Hundred and Fifty Dollar Tournament of Valiants. I'm Ben Glinton."

There was scattered applause, and a solitary jeer from somewhere in the crowd. Ben scanned it to isolate the villain, but he couldn't pick him out. Still, not a bad reaction overall. The feeling inside the room was just too good to produce any serious booing.

"Speaking of the nineteen grand," he went on, "the grand prize will definitely be every bit of that money, not just some kind of ointment that a crazy person told you about in some unauthorized e-mail."

"Oh, we all know about Hentley Harkaby," someone near the front said. "He made the mistake of signing his e-mails. We know he's crazier than crap." A titter ran through the crowd.

"Excellent. Everyone just select teams of roughly equal records," Ben instructed, "and let's begin. Advice from co-managers is allowed. Find your opponent on the match-up chart, grab a table, and just start rolling. I've arranged for the Lucky Ape to provide snacks and finger foods. Looks like it's mostly just three kinds of saltless pretzels, but I think I spotted some bologna in there somewhere, and apparently Cyclops Cola put a case of something out."

"There's ice if you go down the hall, up two flights of stairs, take a left, then a right, and then one more left," said Toddy, who wouldn't go away. He was sitting at one of the cafeteria tables beside the crazy Davis brothers, who both bore bandages on their faces from a noontime scuffle over which font was the best one APBA had ever used on the player cards.

"Thanks," Ben said. "Okay, APBA-heads, go to it!"

There was some applause, and people began to crowd around the easel on which the pairings had been written. Most already knew who they were going up against and seats were taken, scoresheets broken out, and player envelopes unclasped. Ben, stomach filled with not only butterflies but what felt like some tiny manic-depressive dude playing the bongoes, felt a tap on his shoulder. He turned around to see a mild-mannered school-teacherish fellow smiling at him shyly. "Hello, my name is Ron Pisarz," he said. "I believe I'm your opponent in the first round. I should tell you, I've never played APBA before. I thought this was a Jenga tournament. But I'm willing to learn if you can bring me along slowly."

Secretly, Ben did a clumsy cartwheel inside his brain, almost knocking over a lamp. Finally, here was someone he could roll over with ease. "Sure thing," he said. "Let's find a seat."

It was going to be an interesting first round for everyone in the collective. Jake was matched against a twenty-five year old chap named Ivo, who was from Chechnya. An American relative had sent him one of the original versions of APBA Baseball years ago and he had taught himself the game even as his war-torn country fell apart around him. "I am so grinning to be here in your nation's capital, playing this wonderful game," he told Jake, fairly busting with excitement. "I've never played against another. Will I be defeated?"

"I dunno," Jake said. "Your country isn't going to, um, not let you back in if you lose, right?"

"Oh no," Ivo assured him, "I have much too vast importance to my government's internal security to be sent away."

On the other side of the room, Templeton had drawn a name that was quite familiar to him. T.L. Harris was the author of the acclaimed series of Napoleonic war novels which had been recently turned into a quite terrible CBS mini-series. Even more recently, he had written a scathing review of Templeton's *The Dying Cloud Whispereth,* calling it "a masterpiece, to be sure, but just barely, filled with parts that have difficulty even qualifying as excellent." The two men sat across from each other and shook hands tersely.

"Good to see you, Harris," Templeton said. "I hope our game won't bore you as much as my writing apparently does."

"Oh, Templeton, come off it," Harris retorted. "I'm sure you do the best you can with your public school education."

Templeton shoved his dice into his shaker with extreme prejudice and pulled from his card set the team envelope containing his beloved 1977 Connecticut Corduroys. "You're going down, hoser," he warned, and they began.

Earl was sitting right beside them. Right off the bat, he had drawn one of the more whispered-about competitors in the building. This man gave his name only as Phineus. He spoke with a thick Austrian accent and was decked out in a sharp dark blue suit. Phineus seemed like the sort of man who might win the tournament handily and then throw a single memory-erasing cloud pellet onto the table before somersaulting out the nearest window into a waiting black van with tinted windows. He was always looking over his shoulder and kept feeling around beneath the cafeteria tables when he thought no one was watching, as if probing for evidence of covert audio surveillance. He never said a word unless he absolutely had to, and most unsettling of all, the sole card set he had shown up with (the power-heavy, speed-challenged 1988 Trenton Potstickers) was more than a little spotted with dried blood.

Harold and Roy walked from table to table as everyone played, happy to just be spectators, though it was somewhat difficult for Roy, who had to chew a great deal of spearmint gum to suppress the urge to join in on the action. He used Templeton's mini-cassette recorder to document the sounds of the games and the chatter of the players. It would all go into the last chapter of Ben's biography, whose title, he had decided, would be *Please Don't Call Me 'The Blemish' Anymore; It's Really, Really Hurtful.* They did their best not to get drawn into the gathering which watched Spike Vail square off against a fifteen year old kid who seemed far too star-struck to make sound baseball decisions, but there was such a buzz around their game that they couldn't resist taking in at least a few innings. Height-challenged Roy had a lot of trouble seeing over the shoulders of the media people who peppered Spike with questions about his most recent trade demands as he rolled his dice and began to easily trounce his opponent, managing his own team from the season before, with himself batting cleanup. To Spike Vail, everything about baseball came naturally, and APBA seemed to be no exception. He didn't need to make smart moves; the dice pretty much won the game for him. The spectators applauded with every base hit that sealed his victory. Ben looked up from his own game once in a while, irritated.

Ron, the guy who had never even played the game before, took Ben into the ninth inning tied and with a runner on first and nobody out. Ben was ready to dowse himself in kerosene and light a match. Ron, who really was a schoolteacher, didn't even understand the rules of baseball itself, much less the board game version, but Ben had gotten overconfident early and tried to squash the man by sending in his best two relievers at the slightest sign that a run might score. Errors and walks had kept things close, and right around the time Ben had explained to Mr. Pisarz what a double play was, the guy's dice had gotten absurdly hot. He never made a managerial move not forced upon him and stuck with his starter even after the guy was completely gassed. And yet, still there was a chance Ben was going to get bounced. He survived the ninth and when the game went into extra innings, Templeton and Jake came over to lend him moral support, having survived the first round. Earl went down in defeat to Phineus, 2-1, on a late ground rule double with the bases loaded, and the man of mystery remained sitting at the table as Earl slunk off.

"I'm certain we shall meet again," Phineus told him cryptically, putting his player cards away. "Perhaps in a battle of another sort...eh, Mr. Kelshnikov?"

"My name is Earl, Earl Shavey," Earl said.

Phineus looked at him knowingly. "Yes...as you say," he whispered. Then, without another word, he stood, walked over to the fire exit, and looking around him furtively, pushed the door open by backing into it. He made a strange sign with his hands, sort of a circular cross on his forearm meant to be seen by Earl and no one else, and then disappeared. Earl was left to figure out what sort of crackpot he had been playing against...or had his opponent not been a crackpot at all, but a man with secret knowledge of the shadowy history of Earl B. Shavey, and of a former life ruled not by a wife, son, and steady job with a major American soy sauce concern, but by the dagger, false passport, and cleverly constructed falsehood? What name had been whispered between them in a Dutch café in 1977 to seal the fate of three counterspies who had made the deadly mistake of underestimating Earl's facility with psychological torture? What had happened to the microfilm he and Phineus buried in an empty field in Berdsk a year later, leaving alliances in ruin and the Cold War itself burning more brightly than ever? The answers to these questions were actually quite moot: As usual, Phineus had completely mistaken Earl for somebody else. His eyesight was just plain awful, and he simply refused to admit he needed contacts. Earl, whose closest brush to the world of espionage came when he rented *All the President's Men*, burped quietly, wiped his glasses on the bottom of his sweater, and moseyed over to Ben's game to lend a hand.

"Whooooo-hoooooo!" Ben exclaimed just as he got over there. "Single to left! Victory is mine!" He let out a whooshing sigh of relief as the man across from him snapped his fingers in good-natured frustration.

"Well, it's no Jenga, but it's still a really good game," Ron Pisarz said. "See you later, Mr. Glinton."

"All right, who's next on the hit list?" Ben asked anyone who happened to be nearby. "Let's keep the 1:40 Glinton train to Nirvana moving!"

Round two was more of a test, and only through an act of divine providence did Ben live to see another hour. Playing a relentlessly dour man, who at age 75 was the oldest player in the tournament, Ben made a couple of tactical errors that wiped out a couple of two-run homers by the fairly mediocre first baseman for the 2001 San Diego Sweepies, Darrin Hunter. The senior citizen who grunted loudly after every dice roll, no matter what the result, climbed back into the game with ease and Ben felt the hand of doom smoosh its long bony fingers in his hair again. But when Darrin Hunter connected for a *third* homerun, Ben just knew he was going to win again.

"Good God, that's man's on fire!" shouted an anonymous spectator who had lost in round one. Ben couldn't be absolutely sure he was merely talking about Darrin Hunter, so he assumed the compliment was directed at himself.

The old man grunted. For the fifth or sixth time during the game, he demanded that Ben verify the board result giving him a homerun, as if a '1' on a player's card could possibly mean anything else.

"Unfair, unfair," muttered the old man. "I've been playing this game for fifty years, and no one that bad has *ever* hit three homeruns."

Ben realized he had a point. If they had played five hundred games, Hunter probably would never again have been able to poke three into the cheap seats during any one of them. His card was festooned with 13s (almost always strikeouts) and 24s (hello, double plays), but his APBA self had chosen to grab one moment of glory at the most opportune time available. Ben hoped that wherever he was, Hunter felt the good karma; his career had ended in 2003 after an accident with an Easy Bake oven had ruined his left knee. Ben led the game 7-5 going into the top of the ninth, and the old man went down feebly on three rolls.

"I didn't lie about my age to fight in World War II to be beaten like this, sonny," he growled. "If you ever need help from the men of the 41st Infantry, you can forget about it."

"God bless America," Ben said consolingly, but as soon as the veteran had left the table, Ben threw his hands up in elation. "I got it all today!" he blurted, but no one was really listening. Just a few feet away, Spike Vail was absolutely clobbering a guy who actually played in the Mexican minor leagues by a score of 13-0. Darla Volume was coolly taking apart her second opponent managing no one better than the 1988 Madison Mushies, a team that had formed and disbanded within the same season. She rolled the dice with her right hand while in her left she never stopped cycling through the songs in her CD collection, which she stacked beside the playing field. All the CDs were by women, and all those women recorded with feminist record labels, and all those record labels donated money to liberal causes, and all those liberal causes got five hours of volunteer time per week from Darla Volume. She made her strategic moves effortlessly and merely shrugged when she won, as if beating her invariably male opponents was the easiest thing in the world. She had been asked on four dates since 12:30 and accepted none of them. Her heart was dedicated to one goal: showing up the male species which thought it owned APBA just like it supposedly owned everything else. Everyone was dreading what she was going to say when she took the lectern to claim her prize money. The last time she'd won a competition, she'd gone off on a half hour rant against society's unwillingness to pay midwives a living wage.

Templeton got through round two in his inimitable fashion, stretching the game out with unbearably slow decisions which eventually grated on his opponent enough to the point where the poor guy simply lost his concentration. Jake won again as well, zipping through his game a mile a minute, bouncing up and down on his chair, performing difficult mathematical calculations in his head during the roll of the dice and out-managing a man four times older than he in half the time of a normal game. After game two, Jake galloped to stuff his face with pretzels and console his Dad, whom he secretly knew didn't have a chance in heck to win it all anyway.

There was a ten-minute break, the crowd thinning out a bit with some of the losers heading off to the corners of the room to engage in more casual contests. Then round three began. It went as follows:

Jake beat a computer program called The Inscrutable Skipper which someone had installed onto a PC and let loose against the field. It set its lineups by poring over years of APBA data and then made managerial moves by having a third party (in this case, Roy) type in the current situation and score, after which it spat out its desires in hot pink text on a black screen. It gave Jake a scare but nothing more. When it lost, 8-4, it was wheeled harmlessly away and sat forgotten in a corner. The man who had spent eleven years designing the software hung his head low and drank deeply from a bottle of gin.

Templeton lost exactly the kind of game he should have won, a fairly boring, low-scoring affair in which his bullpen let him down in the end. He would describe the loss in excruciating detail a year later in one of the longest essays ever written for *Harper's* magazine, using it to illustrate many points about why the Tet cease fire did not hold in 1968. His only consolation was that the man who beat him received a phone call in the seventh inning from his wife, telling him she had found out where he had snuck off to, and a divorce filing was now imminent. The guy had to suddenly dash home, forfeiting his place in the tournament.

Spike Vail won again, this time on a homerun in the bottom of the ninth inning by some player he'd never heard of, even though he'd actually played with the man for two years. When that last dinger sailed into the stands, Spike stood up, made both a two-handed swinging motion and a thwacking sound by popping his finger in his cheek, then literally jogged around the cafeteria table to simulate a homer trot. The cameras ate it up. Every minute that Spike was in the tournament meant more advertising dollars for the Thunder Dunk Sports Network, who broadcasted it all live. Ben made it into one of the camera shots exactly once, when he got up to go to the bathroom.

Ben was losing his game three in the fifth inning when he had a revelation. He had made virtually no proactive moves to win his first two games, and it occurred to him that this was exactly how the uneducated Ron Pisarz had managed to stay competitive for so long. So, in full panic mode after falling behind 4-2 with the 2005 Memphis Cymbal Crashes, Ben decided to go completely minimalist and do...nothing. He refused to even think about endangering his team by attempting a steal, putting on a hit and run, playing the infield in, or even changing his pitcher. For the first time in his life, he decided to clamp down on his traitorous brain entirely. He was ever so tempted to insert a pinch runner with a man on second and two outs, and to bring in Keith Avallone to stare down three consecutive lefties in the other guy's lineup, but instead he did absolutely nada. And the next thing he knew, he was ahead 5-4. His mind told him to bring his closer in with one out in the ninth, but he didn't. He didn't even make a most obvious defensive substitution. He just rolled the dice and watched the dice be rolled. And the next thing he knew, he had advanced to round four.

"Did you just do what I think you just did?" Harold asked him as Ben took a long, exhausted sip from a warm Cyclops Cola.

"I did," Ben said. "I put up a No Trespassing sign on my brain. Roy, you may not want to write this down for the biography, but as of this date, I have officially issued a vote of no confidence to my own head. I am now completely ready to accept the fact that, though I'm sure God loves me, I'm just not terribly bright."

"I think that's quite brave of you, Ben," Templeton said, walking over from his loss. "And probably the smartest move you could ever make. No offense."

"None taken, Emmitt my man," Ben said. "My God, am I close to winning it all? Is this possible?"

"Semi-finals next round," Harold said. "Ben, what was that you were saying about...The Call?"

"Ah yes," Ben said. "The prize money. Tell you what, get a couple of quarters ready. If I make it through round four, I'll find a phone. Until then, I'm just going to sit here and Zen out, if you don't mind."

Templeton rubbed one of Ben's shoulders and Earl rubbed the other. Some people standing around the brackets board had transferred the names of the third round winners to the next level.

"Spike Vail will play...Ben Glinton!" someone announced, and Ben felt another rush of adrenalin surge through his system, followed by a surge of imitation sugar as he drained the last of his Cyclops Cola. No liquid as disgusting had ever entered his system, but the fake sugar, banned in nine states, was going to be of some definite use, oh yes, indeed, very much so, yes, definitely, for sure, no doubt about it, indeed.


## 20. Wuthering Dice, *or* Spike's Near-Death Experience Inspires Him to Appreciate the Simple Beauty of, You Know, Leaves and Stuff


"Greeny? What are *you* doing here?"

Ben had taken his seat opposite Spike Vail, and, looking to his left where Darla Volume was about to take on Jake Shavey, saw his old Cannons manager sitting down gruffly beside the kid. He had trouble recognizing Greeny St. Clair in any sort of clothing other than a saggy baseball uniform, and the man looked mighty awkward in a sweater and slacks, with what remained of his hair combed for possibly the first time ever.

"I gotta fill up my retirement somehow," Greeny said. "I got bounced out of the first round thanks to some young punk who got lucky."

"So why did the Cannons fire you?" Ben asked him as Spike selected his starting lineup from his old Guardians teammates. "I hope it had nothing to do with what I did in '02."

"Naw, it wasn't that. They got a bunch of stat geeks running the front office now. They ran some numbers on me and found out that I spent the most time arguing, ordered the most bean balls, and handed out more fines for dripping water all over the damn clubhouse than any other manager. Then they claimed that any prospect I taught immediately got seventy-five percent worse. Bunch of garbage. My son bought me this APBA game after I got canned and I re-did the 2002 season and we won the damn Series in five games. All right, kid," he said to Jake, "I'm gonna help you take this tournament." He looked across the table at Darla Volume. "Young lady, who's *your* co-manager?"

"Thanks but no thanks on *that* sad concept," Darla said, rolling her eyes. "I don't need someone looking over my shoulder. If it takes more than one person's brain cells to win this game, I just feel sad for you."

Ben sorted his 1994 Salt Lake Salt Licks out in front of him, more than a little distracted by the media goofballs hovering behind Spike Vail. The rest of the crowd was divided neatly between the two games; some people pulled up chairs while others just stood.

"Ha ha, you ready to bring it on, Glinton?" Spike asked as Ben filled in the lineups on the scoresheet. "You're writing down all the right ratings for me, right? I'm seven for fifteen today so far, gotta keep the juices flowing." He winked at one of the cameras.

"We're all set. Your team won a couple more games than mine, so I'll be playing at home, if you don't mind."

"Not at all," Spike said. "It makes no difference to me where we play. I like to bat first, get a few runs on the board before you know what hit you."

"Then go ahead," Ben said. "Want a co-manager?"

"Oh, my lovely wife Shelley will be my light and inspiration," Spike said with ultimate sensitivity, reaching out for his wife's hand. Shelley Vail yawned and checked her watch. (To everyone's shock, the famous baseball player had chosen to marry a thin blonde. Darla Volume stared her down, her disapproval a potent death ray.)

"Roll it up," Ben commanded, taking a deep breath. Instead of just giving his dice a quick and meaningless courtesy rattle, like a hitter waving his bat a bit before settling in to take a pitch, Spike shook them violently and hurled them with brutal velocity into an overturned APBA box. They slammed against one edge and bounced backwards, revealing a 33.

"And my good friend Jim Barnes doubles to lead off the game!" Spike announced in a loud voice, receiving some nice applause as he pushed a red disc around first base and onto second. "Slide, Jim, slide!" he yelled, and everyone laughed except Ben and Darla Volume, who had donned her headphones once again and started her game against Jake more or less oblivious to any sounds but those of Kate Bush and any sights other than the player cards in front of her.

Spike wasn't able to score in the first, and in fact his first three innings against Ben produced no runs. Thunder Dunk's completely unstructured, unhosted TV coverage of Spike Vail's doings occasionally caught the Darla/Jake game in one corner of the frame, but never actually went over there. Most of the human speech in the room was to be heard on that side of the table, as Greeny constantly advised Jake on matters of strategy, which the somewhat overawed Jake unfortunately took, becoming absurdly conservative. He and his Dad were far more on the same wavelength managing-wise, but Earl had wanted to get a lot of photos of his son being counseled by a big league play-caller and didn't really notice that the man was tanking the game for Jake.

"Do I really want to give up a run for an out here, sir?" Jake asked Greeny in the top of the fifth. "Her hitter is so slow and weak, I could bring the infield in..."

"No no, kid, trust me on this one," Greeny assured him. "Take the double play possibility. The big inning will kill you. Ever see what happened to the Cannons in the '96 wildcard?"

"I wasn't born then," Jake told him.

"Trust me, it was a nightmare," Greeny said. "Come on, roll those dice, young lady. The kid's playing his infield deep. Do your worst."

Darla read Greeny's lips, turning the volume on her CD player up a little louder, and spilled a 62 onto the playing field. The ball was knocked to third base, a run scored, and one out was safely secured. The next batter, though, quickly doubled.

"Oh no!" Jake said, slapping his forehead. "It backfired!"

"Not your fault," Greeny said. "You gotta play the percentages."

"I think the percentages were the other way," Jake insisted as Darla jotted down the new stats on the scoresheet.

Darla cruised into the ninth leading 4 to 1. Jake got two runners on base and wanted to bring in a man with a lousy on-base percentage but some potent power to pinch hit. Greeny almost had a fit.

"This girl ain't got no serious closer," Greeny advised. "Who is it, Richard Berg? Coached him in the minors for six months. Had a fast ball like pushing a marble through cottage cheese. You can chip away for a while. Don't bring in some lunkhead who won't get anyone over to third."

"Okay, Greeny, sir," Jake obeyed. The decision ended the game in less than sixty seconds.

"Snails, double snails, and snail tails with pistachio ice cream!" Jake erupted, stamping his feet. "I played it too safe!"

"No...baseball got too risky," Greeny said, a statement with more logical holes than there were words in the sentence. (It was this exact statement, actually, that had finally gotten him fired from the Cannons.) Earl collected Jake and took him outside briefly to try to impart some fatherly knowledge about life and loss. He blew it as usual, and decided to just buy Jake some new constellation observation software instead. He was pretty sure he could find some in Reno.

So the semi-finals came down to just Ben and Spike Vail. Darla couldn't be bothered to stick around and watch, choosing instead to nibble on some carrot sticks in the corner to wait for the finals, but everyone else in the conference center saw everything that happened, including The Incident.

Ben's strategy of having no strategy whatsoever had been working beautifully once again. He entered the seventh inning up 8-6 after a few very stressful innings in which his pitchers just couldn't slam the door with two outs, after his hitters had almost buried Vail for good. Spike's managerial methods consisted entirely of swinging for the fences every time, playing for the three-run homer. He was good enough to provide one himself in the sixth, his card once again performing up to the ridiculous standard set by his actual body. When he rolled his 66 and the crowd cheered, Spike jumped up and did twenty jumping jacks. He asked his wife to count them out, and she did the first seven half-heartedly before excusing herself to go buy some Tic Tacs. Spike jumped on, accidentally knocking Roy in the face on number twenty when Roy leaned forward to note the score of the game for his notes. Ben sat there and stewed. He turned to Harold as Spike accepted the crowd's congratulations.

"All right, Harold, I need you to jump in here if I really need to make a decision to save myself," he said. "I've been on auto-pilot for a lot of innings now. I'm getting itchy to do something."

"I don't know, Ben, I think you should trust the whole hands-off thing," Harold said. "I'll bet Spike beats himself somehow. I've noticed that he doesn't ever put in any reliever who's pitched well against him in real life. He should have put Steve Le Shay in by now, but the poor guy's rotting in the envelope. This could really work for you."

The seventh inning was scoreless, with Spike Vail's card failing to come through with a man on third. The crowd oohed and aahed as Ben's starter, still in the game, battling on through inning after inning, struck him out.

"Must have been a bee on me or something," Spike joked. "You'll see me again at the plate, though, oh yeah."

Ben led off the bottom of the eighth with a pair of walks, and Spike, already down by two runs, became noticeably worried. He decided to insert his third reliever of the game—the supposedly forgotten Steve Le Shay.

"Hey, remember that time Le Shay got you to pop out in the 2000 Series?" Ben asked Spike. "Wow, I thought you were going to charge the mound. That was the infamous 0 for 7 game, wasn't it?"

"I remember," Spike said, trying to keep it light. "My elbow was killing me that night, oh yeah."

"I think you've gone something like 4 for 40 against ole S.S. these past two years," Ben said.

"4 for 42," Jake said from behind him. The APBA folk which had let him through to stand close to the action voiced their confirmation of this critical statistic.

Spike had taken Le Shay's card halfway out of the envelope, but then he slid it back inside. "I'm not liking the lack of a Z on that card," he told the closest camera. "Better get more of a control guy in there to shut this inning down."

Seventeen hundred miles away, the real Steve Le Shay, having just been bombarded on the mound in a 1 p.m. game against New Jersey, stood in his otherwise empty locker room, toweling off and watching the tournament. "You moron!" he shouted at the screen. "You're gonna fall for the cheapest reverse psychology ruse in the history of mankind?! Put me in the game, you overpaid clown! That's Ben Glinton talking to you! You're getting outsmarted by BEN GLINTON!!"

Ben made a note of Spike's new pitcher, Chris Palermo, on the scoresheet, and nodded knowingly to Harold, who tried to keep his face neutral. There was some concerned mumbling in the crowd. Spike seemed to reconsider his choice at the last second, but his pride wouldn't let him be anything other than what he was. He stuck with Palermo.

"Oh, I am so gonna throw a slider right at your face the next time you get in that batter's box!" Steve Le Shay cried to the little

Spike Vail on TV set. "You think Curse Williger's a dangerous pitcher?! Let's play a little ShayBall, you bonehead!"

"Roll those dice, Glinton," Spike said in Reno, leaning forward. "Do it to it."

*Chicka-chicka-chicka-chicka-chicka-chicka-chicka-chicka.*

Ben spilled the dice out onto the field. The white one skittered all the way across it and landed an inch in front of Spike's chest.

"A 51 on Lance Haffner's card becomes a...41," Ben said, suddenly very concerned, as any board result over 35 could mean a very strange kind of trouble. "What happened? What happened?"

Both he and Spike made a grab for the results booklet. Spike got there first and he raised his arms in the air. "*Triple play,* boyo!" he erupted. "Triple play! Manager's best friend! Third to short to first, that's three outs and you are *done in the ninth!*"

The crowd stomped, laughed, hooted, even belched at this amazing APBA rarity. Ben shook his head and looked at Harold.

"Okay, so *anything* I try is a bad idea," he said. "I get it now."

Back east, Steve Le Shay bit into his towel. "You still should've put me in there, Vail," he said. "I would've just struck everybody out, niiiiiiiiiiiiiiiiice and slow."

Le Shay's bench coach walked in. "Talking to the TV again," he said disgustedly. "That's it, you psycho. You are *so* being sent down tomorrow."

At the Lucky Ape, Spike sent for a bottle of spring water before the bottom of the ninth began. The Cyclops Cola rep standing nearby cried a little inside.

"Two runs, Spike, surely you can get two measly runs," Ben teased. "Could you imagine losing to *Ben Glinton?* The biggest idiot in baseball history? Oof, I wouldn't want to be you when I go home tonight."

"Okay, Blemish, watch this," Spike said.

*Chicka-chicka-chicka-chicka-chicka-chicka-chicka-chicka.*

Infield single.

*Chicka-chicka-chicka-chicka-chicka-chicka-chicka-chicka.*

Single to right.

"Okay, Harold," Ben said out of the side of his mouth. "I'm getting Lee Harris out of this game. He's shot."

"Three of his runs were unearned," Harold said. "Come on, Ben, give him just one more batter. You have a good match-up, arm-wise."

"Vail's on deck, Pillick!" Ben hissed. "I need an out right now!"

"One more," Harold pleaded. "Ben, every second you don't make a decision is one more step towards not having to give away twenty thousand dollars."

Ben held his tongue. Spike sent Wayne Poniwaz into the batter's box. He thrust the dice into the overturned APBA box with more obnoxious force than he ever had, as if he were trying to punish the tiny suckers for making him sweat this one out.

This was The Incident, as seen on live TV in twenty-one states:

The red die smashed into the box and ricocheted back towards Spike. His mouth was partially open when the object in question began its aggressive trajectory back towards him. He had no time to react. Slow motion instant replays of the television image showed a tiny red blur entering his mouth. He swallowed out of pure reflex. The die vanished.

Silence. No one was sure exactly what had happened, kind of like when the Oscar for Best Sound Effects Editing of 1983 was announced and the words "Jay Boekelheide" somehow dropped from the presenter's lips instead of "Ben Burtt."

"Did...did you just swallow that?" Ben asked.

Spike looked at him and blinked once, twice, three times. "Uh-huh," he said queasily.

"You're not supposed to do that," Jake told him.

Spike put his hands on the edge of the cafeteria table and gripped it tightly, his burly arms bulging. "There's been...some lodging," he croaked in a deeply strange voice. It kind of sounded like a squishy banana had gotten stuck in a garbage disposal. His wife felt his forehead.

"You, ah, you gonna be okay there, Spikey?" Ben asked. Someone leaned into Spike's face and snapped a photograph. His eyes did a drunken cartwheel in their sockets.

"Need to lie down. Me. Now." Spike got up and his wife and his agent snuck under his arms to support him. He didn't do so hot when it came to walking under his own power, so he was mostly just dragged aside.

As the spectators all around whispered and clasped their hands together in concern, a stretcher appeared out of nowhere, rolled forward by the Lucky Ape's ubiquitous Toddy. They'd had a stretcher ready to go ever since some of the Quack Quack quarter slots in the lobby delivered a series of near-fatal electrical shocks to a church youth group from Ely. Spike was helped onto it as the media swarmed around, jamming microphones in his face. Quite unnecessarily, Todd closed the stretcher's arm and head clamps and Spike was more or less immobilized.

"We'll have an ambulance outside in three minutes!" Toddy announced. "I need some room to move him, people, let's form a gap, let's form a gap!"

"Glurp," Spike burped. A reporter from a local station bent over him and asked him if he regretted skipping out on his team's game in Texas to be here today. Roy even tried to get a question in, but as usual when in the presence of even the most mildly prominent athletes, he couldn't get his words out correctly and wound up emitting only the following string of completely useless syllables: "Hey, yes, okay, nice."

The gap that Toddy had demanded was formed and the stretcher was rolled hurriedly through it. Ever the lionheart, Spike managed to raise his forearm into the air, giving the crowd a defiant thumbs-up. Somewhere in the recesses of his mind, a triumphant violin and brass combination played a hero's theme. There was applause, and perhaps a little poorly contained laughter. Some of Spike's most diehard fans followed him out into the lobby, as did all of the television cameras. As he slipped into a wholly gratuitous unconsciousness, he found the strength to retreat into a wondrous fantasy world where he ruled a race of elfin warlocks engaged in a never-ending battle against the Sinister Lemon People of Clavius-9. It was a scenario he often embraced when confronted by an instance of even momentary failure. The golden land of Fancytown was a sweet and forgiving place to be. After his departure, the conference center got a lot quieter, and more hospitable in general.

"Well, what happens now?" Jake asked everyone around him, looking from face to face for an answer.

"I think we have ourselves a forfeit," someone in the crowd said. "I think Glinton wins."

"You're right," said Earl. "The tournaments Jake and I have played in, if someone can't finish, they forfeit the game."

"Glinton wins!" shouted a fellow wearing an APBA T-shirt and an APBA ball cap. The assuredness of his tone seemed to convince the hundred or so people left in the room of his statement's validity, and Harold suddenly grabbed Ben's arm and lifted it skyward, grinning.

"I'll take whatever I can get!" Ben said, the sentiment of a true warrior. He got to his feet and high-fived everyone in the Collective and then everyone standing behind them. The more games he won, the more people had started to warm up to him. He may have destroyed the Cannons' 2002 season, but to the folks in the room, he seemed smaller and goofier in person, just like somebody off the street—a dim-witted next door neighbor, maybe, or a twelve year old who still believed in Santa Claus. His commonness made him at least fifty percent less odious.

"All right," Darla Volume said in a bored voice from two cafeteria tables over, "let's not waste too much time before we start the final game. I do, like, have a life to lead outside the Lucky Ape Hotel and Casino."

"Twenty minutes, twenty minutes till the championship game!" announced the Cyclops Cola rep, who seemed on the surface to have really gotten into the APBA vibe over the past hour or so. Little did anyone realize he had merely seen an opportunity to take a few bets on the increasingly intense action, seizing the chance in true corporate fashion to line his pockets with the money of innocents.

Everyone dispersed for a breath of fresh air. Ben went to the bathroom around the corner from the front desk. to splash some cold water on his face. When he emerged into the lobby again, Harold, Templeton, Earl, Jake, and Roy were waiting for him silently. They all looked very worried.

"Okay," Ben said, exhaling, "who's got those fifty cents I asked for?"

As Templeton dug out two quarters from his slacks, Harold glanced anxiously at the conference center, where people were already filing back in to get the best possible view of the upcoming action. "Ben, even if you somehow made The Call and *somehow* got the money, you told everyone it would be paid out in cash as soon as the final game was over. How—"

"Thank you, Emmitt," Ben said, interrupting Harold and accepting the coins. "I'm going to walk over to that pay phone in the corner now. Feel free to follow me if you wish. Please keep me in your thoughts and prayers as I do this. And cross as many fingers as you can afford to."

Ben knew that he would chicken out if he took any time to think of what he was about to do, so he went to the pay phone briskly, so briskly he almost left the rest of the Collective in the dust. They caught up to him and gave him all of thirty-six inches of breathing space as he dialed a number from heart. Roy's pen was poised above a fresh notepad, ready to transcribe. He had realized a half hour ago that the events which had taken place since one o'clock would in all likelihood comprise about fifty percent of Ben's biography, and maybe more than that if things just kept getting weirder.

Someone on the other end of the line answered Ben's call.

"Hi, it's me," Ben said, not even having to give his name. "Um...I'm in a bit of a spot. I need money. Nineteen th—ah, twenty-two thousand dollars. In twenty dollar bills." He listened for a moment. "Yes," he said in response to a simple question. To another he answered yes a second time. He then gave the location of the pay phone, listened for another ten seconds, and said, "I understand." Then, with no further ado, he hung up the phone and turned to the Collective, shrugging.

Earl was flabbergasted. "That's it, Ben? There's no second call?"

"Yeah, basically," Ben said. "Whoo, that took a lot out of me."

"How in the world is that going to amount to anything?" Harold asked. "It sure didn't seem—"

"Wait for it," Ben stopped him, holding up an index finger and turning toward the front entrance. The ticking of Templeton's watch seemed very loud indeed.

Through the glass doors and into the lobby came a man they had seen before. It was the enigmatic Phineus! Now wearing dark sunglasses, he walked stiffly over to Ben, carrying a small brown valise. Sometime between his icy 9-3 first round victory in the tournament and now, he had re-slicked his hair and had his shoes shined. His unreadable face was like a blank chalkboard, or, more specifically, the fancy kind that you could write on with a felt-tipped marker and erase with your shirt sleeve if you wanted.

"Mr. Cloud wishes you a pleasant day," Phineus said, seeming bored. He set the valise at Ben's feet, turned, and walked away. Thinking of the Roy vs. Grog Streep incident, the others had to try hard to remember the last time so many people had appeared from nowhere to offer up big hunks of cash for no immediately apparent reason. The last they saw of Phineus, his ankles were being nipped at by some old lady's yipping Chihuahua even as he tried to help her and her gigantic pair of cello cases through the doors under her crushing criticism of his upper arm strength.

Ben picked up the valise and opened it. He took out two stacks of twenty dollar bills, bound in rubber hands with cheery red polka dots on them.

"Problem solved," he said. "Now, who's got the team envelope for the 2002 Cannons? I think it's time I started thinking about setting a starting lineup."

Earl began to take the envelope from his breast pocket, but Templeton stopped him.

"Ah...Ben?" he said.

"Oh, how I got the money, yes," Ben said. "Of course I was going to explain The Call before we went back inside. I'd never leave you guys hanging like that. Well, gather around and you will hear a tale that you'll be repeating to your grandchildren until you flop over dead someday. The story begins on a sleety Pennsylvania day as a recently retired ballplayer by the name of Ben Glinton was innocently eating a chicken pot pie in his apartment when there came a mysterious knock on his door. When he opened it, he saw an absolutely gorgeous, stunningly sexy woman who introduced herself as NOTE TO THE READER: THE FOLLOWING EXPLANATION OF THE CHAIN OF EVENTS THAT LED TO THE INSTANT FULFILLMENT OF THE SUM OF THE APBA TOURNAMENT PRIZE MONEY HAS BEEN DELETED BY THE PUBLISHER IN ACCORDANCE WITH THE GUIDELINES SET DOWN BY THE STEENER-BRIARTHUMB READER FAIRNESS ACT OF 2004, WHICH DEMANDS THAT FINANCIAL RESTITUTION BE PROVIDED TO ANY CONSUMER WHO FINDS THAT A WORK OF FICTION UNFAIRLY REQUIRES A SUDDEN SUSPENSION OF

DISBELIEF FAR ABOVE ANY RATIONAL STANDARD, DEFINED IN THE WORDING OF THE ACT AS ANY PLOT TWIST OR DEVELOPMENT WHICH WOULD GRAVELY INSULT THE INTELLIGENCE OF A PERSON OF EVEN BELOW AVERAGE COGNITIVE ABILITIES. THE MISSING PASSAGE HAS BEEN FOUND BY THE MINNESOTA CIRCUIT COURT TO BE IN CLEAR VIOLATION OF THE 2004 ACT, AND THE PUBLISHER, IN ORDER TO AVOID ARBITRATION AND POSSIBLE FINES AND/OR PAYMENTS TO COMPLAINTANTS, HAS CHOSEN TO REMOVE THE OFFENDING TEXT, WHICH SHALL REMAIN ON FILE ON THE FOURTEENTH FLOOR OF ITS CENTRAL DOCUMENTS WAREHOUSE AND BE AVAILABLE FOR INSPECTION UPON NOTARIZED WRITTEN REQUEST UNTIL THE THIRTIETH DAY OF MAY, 2006.

"...and that's why Phineus wasn't wearing any socks today, and hasn't been physically able to since that night in Dayton," Ben finished. He handed the money to Templeton for safekeeping, then clapped his hands in front of him as he turned to the conference center once again. "Now who's going to be my co-manager so we can take the prize that's rightfully ours? Harold, are you game again?"

"Sure, Ben," Harold said, flattered. "I'm with you all the way. But if there's a chance that the director of the Bronx Zoo might show up and take the money back—"

"If you'd listened closely to what I just told you, Harold, you'd realize that he's not ever going to be a problem for us, if he knows what's good for him," Ben said. "Now, I am completely focused on winning just one more game of APBA Baseball to take us to the promised land. Anyone who's got his mind on other things should just head off to the casino for some watered-down ginger ale and germ-filled coin cups. Are we all together?"

They were. Ben Glinton, Emmitt Templeton, Earl Shavey, Jake Shavey, Roy Skinla, and Harold "Grassy Pete" Pillick went forward to make their final stand.

## 21. The Ending in Which Everything Turns Out Relatively Okay for Everybody, but Just Relatively

As hard as it might be to believe, the championship game went right down to the wire.

4-3 was the ninth inning score, on the edge of their seats were the spectators, and agonizingly silent was the room as Ben stared defeat in the face with just three outs left before the tournament would officially belong to the ages. It wasn't that his old teammates, the 2002 Cannons whom he'd failed so badly four years before, hadn't played well. Curse Williger had pitched solidly and gotten himself out of a couple of tight jams, coming up with big strikeouts at the most opportune moments, and Joe Costa had batted as heroically as his .332 average that year dictated. And it wasn't that Ben's own managerial incompetence had caused any problems— Harold had made darn sure never to say anything in his ear that even remotely sounded like a suggestion to make a move of any kind. Mostly it was Darla Volume and her specially created San Andreas Suffragettes, a fictional women's team set she'd had carefully made a couple of weeks before by an APBA specialist back in her home city of East Whippany, that put Ben's back against a very painful wall. The Suffragettes all bore the names of oppressed and iconoclastic women throughout American history; Harriet Tubman had pitched seven strong innings against the Cannons before giving way to fierce set-up artist Emma Goldman, while Beryl Markham and Margaret Bourke-White had come through with clutch singles to give Darla the lead since the fourth. Ben could feel his heart drop into his feet when Darla brought out her biggest gun, Anne Morrow Lindbergh, to close out the ninth with her gaudy A & C rating. The crowd in the conference center felt the chances of Ben being able to tie the game sink from slim to virtually none. Those who weren't deeply infatuated with Darla Volume and who would gladly do her every bidding found themselves genuinely saddened by the obvious impending outcome of Ben's Cinderella run for the grand prize. Only one TV camera remained, not even one operated by Thunder Dunk. This camera was operated by a nineteen year old sophomore from Reno Community College as part of a live feed back to the campus, where the only one watching the proceedings was his course advisor.

Thunder Dunk had cleared out as soon as Spike Vail went down, following him throughout his brief stay in the hospital and his wheelchair-bound exit from same. He was cleared to return to his team immediately and vowed to return to the APBA table as soon as his trachea felt a little better. Thunder Dunk decided that sticking around to hear Ben's promised revelations about game seven of the 2002 Series would not be quite as compelling to the average viewer as tape-delayed coverage of the 2006 Professional Water Polo Skills Challenge, so they switched over to that as soon as Spike disappeared into a stretch limo and left Reno altogether.

"Harold, I don't think I can get Jason on base against this Anne Lindbergh freak," Ben said in an aside to his co-manager near the end, referring to Jason Blaze. "It's time to get creative."

"You might be right," Harold said, biting his fingernails. Templeton, Earl, Jake, and Roy were right beside him. "But that injury to Dan Patterson, and you keeping yourself on the bench, has really made the team thin. No one else can hit worth a lick."

In the crowd, someone coughed. Across the table, Darla Volume adjusted the treble controls on her portable CD player. She stifled a yawn and restrained herself from jotting down some notes about how she wanted to divvy up her prize money. It seemed like every time she turned around, there was a new charity devoted to providing female filmmakers with affordable housing, and they were all knocking at her door.

Ben got a crazy gleam in his eye. He picked up the Cannons' team envelope and blew into it. "I'm making a decision," he said. "I just don't have nothing to lose anymore."

Harold sat up straight quickly, "Oh gosh, oh gosh...let me think just a second...we're not on the clock here..."

The crowd murmured in fear as Ben pulled from the team envelope the card of one Harold Pillick.

"What are you doing, Ben?" Harold asked, aghast. "That's my card! That's *my* card!"

"I know, Harold," he said. "I have faith in you." He began to write Harold's name into the lineup. Darla seemed disinterested. She shook her dice gently to keep her wrist in practice.

"I know what he's doing!" Templeton whispered to Earl. "It just might work!"

Ben rolled his dice. They gave him a 64.

Harold grinned.

"Batter hit by the pitch," Ben said, reading from the Bases Empty chart. "Harold takes first!"

As he pushed a base runner toward first base, the crowd applauded. Harold Pillick had led his league in exactly one category during his lifetime: the ratio of getting plunked to total plate appearances, and his APBA card reflected this in spades. No one had ever been sure why Harold had been so damn adept at drawing pitches right into his puny side or even at his bubble head, since there was nothing at all unusual about his stance, and he never really even figured out how to work a count during his brief stay in the bigs. Some baseball experts had theorized—strictly in hushed tones among themselves—that Harold had possessed something called The Bullying Bastard Factor. That is, whenever he stepped into the box, he presented an image of such physical weakness and ineptitude that pitchers just couldn't resist sending one off his skeleton, simply to be mean.

"Thanks, Ben," Harold said, humbled. "I never knew you believed in me a little."

"Don't mention it, pal," Ben replied. "It's time you got some payback for keeping me on the straight and narrow these past few years. All right, who do we have next? Clyde Ringo? Oh boy. Okay, okay, no need to panic. He had a few hits in '02, right? I must have missed seeing them somehow, but I seem to recall him coming back to the dugout sometimes with a smile on his face. Didn't he? Just a few times, wasn't he smiling?"

"Easy, Ben," Roy said. "Hold on."

"Right, hold on," he said, and put his dice back in their maternal shaker. He spilled them out on the table again immediately.

Clyde Ringo would have singled, but Anne Morrow Lindbergh's superior pitching rating mathematically reduced his mighty blow to a scrawny fly out to right field. Ben's left eyelid began to twitch. Darla crossed her arms in front of her, getting a very satisfied look on her face.

Now, Ben thought, now was the time to put his own card into the lineup.

If John Kuchar grounded into a double play, the game was over. He had to act now. Harold knew it too. But he did nothing. John had almost never grounded into DPs in 2002, or any other year for that matter. If Ben was going to have faith in Harold Pillick's anemic abilities, he could certainly give a few props to John.

*Chicka-chicka-chicka.*

John singled to center! The crowd gasped!

"Are you going to try to send your little buddy there over to third?" Darla asked. "Do you want to know Helen Keller's arm rating?"

"I don't need to know Helen Keller's sad, tired arm rating," Ben challenged her. "My pal Harold is going to third, all right. Do the calculations, sister."

Darla consulted the Master symbols, and the odds of Harold's successful slide into third base, based on his speed versus Helen Keller's bony but probably underrated cannon, were figured in seconds. They were not so hot. Harold had never possessed much horsepower. Ben shook his dice anyway and began to tilt his wrist.

"Don't do it!" someone in the crowd said, unable to help themselves. "Suicide!"

Too late. The dice came out. Darla Volume's cool exterior cracked just a hair when she realized  that Harold was not only safe, but safe by a country mile.

"I did it!" Harold shouted, slamming a hand onto the cafeteria table. "So *that's* what it feels like to make it to third on a single to center!"

"I never had any doubt," Ben said firmly as the little men inside his brain quickly shoveled the fifty-seven pounds of doubt he'd actually had into a dark pit somewhere near his left ear so no Feds snooping around would ever find it. "One out, tying run on third, Darla. Looks like Mrs. Lindbergh could write some fine Peter Rabbit books, but she can't slam the door on Lexington's second favorite baseball team."

"You're thinking of Beatrix Potter," Jake said.

Finally, the moment Ben had been waiting for had arrived. There was no more time to muck around with destiny. He reached into the Cannons' envelope and took his own card out.

"Now entering the game as a pinch hitter, number 31, Benjamin Doris Glinton of Mount Airy, Maryland," Ben announced, and there was a smattering of applause. Darla's eyes dropped ever so briefly to her roster of Suffragettes, which she had spread out on the cafeteria table for easy consultation. She made no move to make a pitching change, confident that Ben had no particular edge over Mrs. Lindbergh. And boy, was she ever right.

"I'll be playing the infield deep," Darla said. "For the double play. Do I smell cigar smoke? I will absolutely freak if someone's smoking a cigar within five hundred feet of this room."

"Okay, Ben," Harold said softly, leaning in extra close, "I know you're not going to want to hear this, but the situation has never been more perfect for a squ—"

"I don't want to hear it," Ben interrupted.

"Yeah, but a squee—"

"Silence, Harold."

"I know, Ben, but jeez, will you just lis—"

"Nopenopenopenopenope."

"Sure, you want to get a big hit and bring me home, but mathematically, I'm saying, you really have to be open to bun—"

"Open to bunnies?" Ben asked. "Of course I am. How could I not be? They're gray and furry and adorable."

Harold hung his head. "Ben...a squeeze play...even if it fails, you have such a good hitter on deck...John will be on second..."

"Harold," Ben said, "I don't care if Secretariat will be on second base and home plate is made out of hay. I don't bunt. *No* real man bunts, *ever.* I didn't drive across most of this country in a rolling cheese grater to stick myself into the lineup and not take a swing at the fences. Fergus Hibbert assured me that the printing error on my card gives me a better shot at winning this game for us than usual. So I'm gonna take it. You only live once. Everything's aligned perfectly for the first time ever."

Harold fell silent, and the others in the Collective uttered not a word. Greeny St. Clair was about to say something incredibly negative, but he decided it would be far easier to simply harangue his wife with his objectionable opinions later in the evening.

"Printing error?" Toddy the desk clerk asked from the middle of the crowd. "I know nothing of this game, but that doesn't seem completely fair. Maybe we should discuss the validity of Mr. Glinton's—"

"Here comes your pitch, Darla," Ben said, as the *chicka-chicka-chicka* of his dice drowned Toddy out. "I'm going to send it into the cheap seats in left for my Cannons, for Greeny St. Clair, for Curse Williger, for Rick Nippthorpe, and for my friends who made it here with me today. I hope you don't mind. When the homerun is official, please deposit your trash in the proper receptacle and exit through the doors at the back of the room."

The sole camera in the room zoomed slowly in on Ben's face as his mind filled with images of touching home plate and being hoisted into the air by so many of the teammates whom he would probably never see again in this lifetime, of people pouring out of the stands to celebrate everything he had ever tried to give to the game of baseball, of the home scoreboard lighting up like a Christmas tree, spelling out the words WE WIN!!!! again and again before letting all remaining fans know that they'd get twenty-five percent off a large pizza from King Saucy's with the presentation of their ticket stub, limit four toppings. Darla Volume pressed STOP on her CD player, removed her headphones, and watched, her hands clenching subconsciously into gentle fists.

The dice tumbled out onto the table. The red die showed a 1— half of an 11, which would end the game with an extra base hit of virtually any kind. The white one, though...the white one...

"A 2," Jake said, whistling. "Uh-oh."

"The 12 becomes a 25 on his card," Ivo from Chechnya told everyone, looking over Ben's shoulder.

"Double play, second to short to first," Darla said. "I'll take that nineteen thousand dollars now."

*"GYYYYYYAAAAAAAAAAAHHHHHHHHHHHHHHHHHHHHHHHH HHHHHHHHHHHHHHHHHHDOP!!!!!!"* Ben screamed, leaping up from the table, his face red as a beet, his eyes practically bungee-jumping out of their sockets. With one quick whipping of his head from left to right, his previously undiscovered psychic talents announced themselves in a shrieking line of flame which ignited the walls and rushed in a resounding flume across the conference center. The room filled with high-pitched screams of terror as a stampede began, while Ben walked calmly toward the lectern, sending out wave after wave of hot, deadly fireballs using nothing more than his vengeance-craving brain. One by one, all those who had opposed him were felled by the bright balloons of flame, causing Ben to cackle triumphantly. His lethal power surged within him and soon the entire hotel was nothing more than a charred ruin littered with unidentifiable bodies, leaving him alone in the center of Reno, all sentient creatures vanquished, all old scores settled. Soon, he knew,

the armies of the imperialist government would arrive in a fruitless attempt to stop him from claiming the Earth itself with his unrepentant destructive urges. But their helicopters, their tanks, their missiles were no more a harm to Ben Glinton now than the indifferent rain which had begun to fall mournfully from the blood red sky. Just as in the days when he had called himself a mere human and not a lordly merchant of annihilation, there was only one known weapon on the planet powerful enough to stop his thirst for carnage and bring him to his knees: the single tear of a hungry child.

By the time Ben came grudgingly back to reality, Templeton had already taken care of the transfer of the prize money to Darla Volume, who took it with a brief nod and decided to forgo her speech entirely. She hadn't planned on her ultimate victory taking quite this long, so she crumpled up her notes about the sorry state of women in science fiction, stuffed the cash into her purse, and vamoosed before more dweebs could try to verbally paw at her. About thirty people were left in the conference center when Ben began to slowly get to his feet. Earl and Jake had cleared the game away and discreetly disposed of the scoresheet which had recorded the hideous final round loss. Ben took a sip from his can of soda and stood bravely before the few considerate and mildly curious souls who had decided to stick around for his confession.

"Friends," Ben began with a heavy heart, "four years ago in Kentucky, I imploded and ruined the championship series for myself and my teammates. Never before had I committed such atrocious atrocities over the span of a single inning. Obviously, external forces had a massive hand in what happened that night. No one person could ever stage such a thorough meltdown unless he was under the influence of heavy and conflicting medications.

"I have never revealed to anyone, not even my teammates, my true state of mind on that October night," he went on, making sure to look directly into the one operational camera from time to time. "It was pretty darn abnormal, let me tell you. I was becoming very, um, what do you call it, disenchanted with the game of baseball. I had just been through a rough contract negotiation which made me look very selfish to the public, a nagging toe injury had been slowing me down for months, and there were rumors that the Cannons were considering leaving Lexington entirely and splitting their games between Tijuana and wherever it is that they hold Burning Man every year. Nobody seemed to be getting along in the clubhouse even though we were on the verge of winning the title, and that massive art forgery scandal continued to threaten the very integrity of the game.

"In short, a life in baseball had become something far, far different from how I'd imagined it when I was a kid. Sometimes as an adult, too, I had dreams about an innocent sports world where nothing else mattered but the thwack of the bat and the whoop of the ball hitting my mitt as I leapt against the wall in the outfield. On the morning of the seventh game of the series, I was told not only that one of our best players had just been arrested for impersonating a priest, but that we'd all have to wear a big ugly patch on the left shoulder of our uniforms to promote a new reality show called *Escape from the Stench.* Something in me just snapped. I had no concentration when I took the field that night. My mind was racing. Somehow I knew that this was my last game as a professional no matter what. The realization hit me like a rickshaw full of pies. After the first inning, I was as depressed as I have ever been. All I could think about was how there must be some way to preserve the essence of the great game of baseball and throw out all the lousy distractions and controversies that sucked all the pure enjoyment out of it.

"Do you want to know what was going through my brain during the half hour or so when I ruined everything? I was imagining myself as just a pawn on a wooden board that represented a baseball diamond, being moved around by the roll of dice as two opposing fans had more fun simulating the game than watching it. Everything they wanted out of baseball was right in front of them, including a little Me who had been reduced to my name, my position, and my statistics, and could help either one of them win if they used me just right. Nothing else mattered; not my contract, not my squabbles with my manager, not the naming rights to the stadium I played in, not the re-alignment of our division, not the water pressure problem in our clubhouse which had driven our best pinch hitter into retirement.

"If I had known about the existence of APBA Baseball that night, maybe I would have been able to keep myself from totally losing myself in a fantasy about a game just like it, which I wanted to create myself as soon as I got off the field that night. My life suddenly had more purpose. The baseball I was playing in the late innings of October 21st seemed like a fraud to me, and I became consumed with getting back to its purity, even if it was only in board game form. In the end, I suppose I just retired mentally a couple of innings too soon, and the Cannons paid a big price for it. That's pretty much the extent of my explanation, I guess, and it's mighty weak one, I know, but there it is.

"Now I stand here before you today a failure all over again, but this time I've failed at baseball as it really should be. Here in this poorly ventilated conference center, every player represented by these little cards is enthusiastic, team-oriented, and giving his all day after day not for money, but for the love of the sport. No one is demanding any raises or trades, or refusing to play a new position, or embarrassing themselves in public, and best of all, no one ever really has to retire. The best and the brightest play on as long as we want to manage them, oblivious to the calendar, no matter what the years are doing to us personally. Even the ones who probably had no business ever being issued a uniform to begin with, like my friend Harold here, get to keep trying to earn the fans' respect. And they play under a cloudless sky, without endless commercial breaks, and having no conception of what a labor strike is, much less a six hundred-dollar-a-night hooker who manages to steal all a team's signals *and* get videotape of a certain pitcher, whose name won't be dragged through the mud here, fondling grape gelatin while wearing a mermaid outfit.

"In short, friends, very few of us baseball players should ever have been anything more than a hopeful APBA card ready to serve whatever manager comes along on a Sunday afternoon to simulate the match-up of his dreams. You can keep hating Ben Glinton the man and the moron, but please give *this* Ben Glinton"—here he held up his card to the crowd—"a chance to redeem himself whenever you can. He's not a statistical giant, but he's perfect in his own way, and he'll do his best to win your game for you, maybe not with his speed or his defense, but with one key swing on a certain fortunate roll of the dice. Whatever you do, keep rolling them, because every time APBA Baseball is set up on a tabletop, the sport becomes the perfect daydream it can never quite be in real life, and people need all the daydreams they can get."

Applause, not angry jeers, were what followed Ben out of the Lucky Ape at 5:48 p.m. that muggy Reno day. For the first time in a long time, he was able to hold his head high as he left a baseball competition, having moved everyone with his speech. It would be a good ten to twelve minutes before the gamers in the room started to figure out just how truly shaky his reasoning, his logic, and even his vocabulary had truly been, and why the only part of the speech that held any honest weight whatsoever had been the pro-APBA part. Everything else he had myopically spouted about why he had blighted the game in 2002 quickly started to seem like total compost. But he was long gone by then, his friends following him respectfully as he strode out of the hotel, so dazzled by the golden moment that Ben's pre-tournament reminder to swipe all the pretzels they could on the way out was entirely forgotten.

"So he took his freaking jersey off in the middle of a freaking play because he couldn't *concentrate?*" Toddy asked Greeny St. Clair. *"That's* the explanation? Yeah, yeah, that makes a *hell* of a lot of sense."


Outside on the sidewalk, the Collective stood in the late afternoon light and mused about this and that for a time, feeling relieved, cleansed, and happy to have met so many people who shared their passion for a hobby that now and forever would unite them no matter where they dispersed to, and all the while costing just a fraction of other pursuits like woodworking or drug addiction. The bond they now felt with each other and their fellow APBAheads back inside the hotel would last long after the janitorial staff had swept up the conference center and the Lucky Ape had gone completely bankrupt, its board of directors fired wholesale after their curious decision to change the name of the place to The Tower of Lies and Nothingness.

"Fellas, you should feel free to stay the night in this swingin' town and enjoy all it has to offer," Ben said to his friends, "but I don't think I can join you. This whole experience has left me with the need to do...something. And go...somewhere. I'm tired but wide awake, if you know what I'm saying. I can't explain it, but I want to keep moving."

"We understand, Ben," Earl said, putting his arm around his son. "Jake and I are going down the street to rent a car. I'd really like him to see the Hoover Dam before we head back to Pennsylvania. We're not sure what it is about a big dam that attracts us, or makes us feel so obligated to drive all the way out there to look at it, but so many brochures keep telling us that we should go, I guess we will."

"Yeah, I've been there three times, and I can't for the life of me figure out why," Harold said. "I mean...it's just a big dam. Weird."

"Oh well. I guess we'll see everybody in Harrisburg soon, right? Ben, are we going to keep having APBA night in your apartment?"

"Maybe not in my apartment, since I think the wrecking ball should have reduced it to pudding by now," Ben said. "But we'll figure something out."

"So long, Mr. Glinton," Jake said, donning his irregular sunglasses once again. "Thanks for the awesome bus ride. That was the best time I ever had!"

"Later, Jake. Keep an eye on your Pa."

Earl and the boy walked off down the sidewalk companionably. Ben turned to Templeton.

"So, Emmitt," he said. "What are your plans? Wanna take a chance on some aimless western wandering?"

"No thanks, Ben," came the reply. "I've actually arranged to get a ride out to San Jose."

"San Jose? What for?"

Bashfully, Templeton turned his head toward the end of the block, where a large, disturbingly familiar RV was parked at the curb. Standing in front of it were Red and Shorty from the Strat-O-Matic Gang. Arms crossed, they nodded curtly in the Collective's direction. Red tried to spit intimidatingly on the sidewalk but it kind of just dribbled out awkwardly, missing the pavement by a foot and landing on a passing caterpillar.

"What are they doing here?" Harold asked. "What did they do, follow us?"

"They just stopped here on their way to California to play a little Keno, and I happened to see them in the lobby during the break," Templeton said. "We got to talking, and...ah, the thing is..."

"No, Emmitt, *no,*" Ben said, horror-struck. "You're not thinking of...of crossing to the *other side,* are you?"

Templeton took a few steps in the direction of the RV. "I've been playing APBA for almost thirty years," he explained. "These gentlemen showed me some of their card sets...I just thought it might be a nice change...just for a while...to see what sort of different ideas another game might have..."

"Holy smoke, if Earl turns around now and his innocent eyes see what you're contemplating," Ben said, "he'll melt into heartbroken icky blue goo right here on the sidewalk. But first he'll get your books banned from every library in America. Oh, Emmitt. The *humanity.*"

"I'll be back in Harrisburg soon, and I'll have all sorts of tales to tell," Templeton assuaged them, continuing to inch away toward the Others like a thief in the night. "We'll all share a good laugh over it."

"This conversation never existed," Ben said. "I only hope we'll be able to recognize you when you knock on our door again."

Templeton chuckled and walked on. Red opened the door for him and the famous writer climbed aboard, waving back at Ben and smiling. The Strat-O-Matics smirked and disappeared inside their Strat-O-Matic-smelling vehicle, which coughed out Strat-O-Matic-colored exhaust as it rumbled down the street toward whatever demented Strat-O-Matic destiny lay in store for them.

"Were you taking notes on that, Roy?" Ben asked. "You heard Emmitt; he turned his back on the game which brought him here and told us all to go suck on a shovel. That's a direct quote, too. Roy? Roy?"

Ben and Harold turned this way and that, but Roy was nowhere to be seen. At least at first. Finally they saw someone who looked very much like him across the street, leaning against a severely dented and bruised green station wagon and engaged in a most amorous embrace with a member of the opposite sex.

"You have GOT to be YANKING my YAM," Ben stuttered as their initial identification of the target was confirmed when Roy's notebook fell out of his back pocket, totally unnoticed. Darla Volume's passionate kisses jostled Roy Skinla this way and that and it was all the poor guy could do to stay on his feet and not flop helplessly backwards on the station wagon's hood.

"Way to go, Roy!" Harold heard himself shout, and the two lovebirds separated for the briefest of moments. Roy gave Ben and Harold a thumbs-up and apologized briefly to Darla for hitting the pause button on their public display of whatever the hell it was they could possibly be doing in a universe that was supposedly governed by immutable laws and reason.

"Hey, guys!" Roy yelled over the sound of the passing traffic. "I finally got a date! Darla actually *likes* unmanly men! She says I'm more like a woman than anyone who showed up at the tournament! We're going to spend some time together, if it's okay with you!"

"Sure, Roy!" Ben yelled back. "Just don't forget to finish the biography!"

"Oh, I won't, Ben! Darla says she wants to look it over to make sure I'm not giving you the benefit of a disgusting masculine bias, and then I'll have the first draft ready for you by the time I get back to Harrisburg!"

"Well, there goes *that* book down the toilet," Ben said out of the side of his mouth. Across the street, Darla grabbed Roy again and smooshed her angry, predatory lips against his, causing constellations to explode in his head, fireworks to detonate in his heart, and Christmas to be declared a year-round holiday in his tingling toes. He held on for dear life as Darla claimed him as her love muffin, and tried his damnedest to blot out any recollections of the nature footage he once saw in junior high school of what female black widows did to their mates. She eventually let him go just long enough to shove him in the passenger's seat of her beater and drive them away. The bumper stickers on the back of the station wagon insulted everything from the current presidential administration to the simple act of combing one's hair.

"I guess that leaves just you and me, champ," Ben said to Harold.

"Yeah, looks like," Harold said, rubbing his bald pate, starting to sweat again. "But whatever you feel like doing is fine. I don't have to be back to Deenie yet. We could be like kids on summer vacation or something. Hey, remember that time we had that three-game series in Minnesota, my rookie year? And you took me to the Mall of America and we ate Chinese at the food court and the security guy in Borders thought you stole a copy of *Penthouse?* That was a great day. Anything like that, I'm in. But we can have a whole forty-eight hours of it!"

"You're good people, Pillick," Ben said, and shook Harold's hand for the first time in his life. "If I had any money on me whatsoever, or even any prospects for the future at all, I'd take you down to Hamburger Vampire this very minute and go in halfsies with you on a Dripping Fang Salad."

"Oh yeah...money," Harold said. "You really have nothing left, do you? What are you going to do?"

Ben reached into his back pocket and took out his wallet, tapping it and smiling. "Remember, I did wangle a little extra pocket change when I made The Call. That should be enough to get us back home and to snag myself a temporary room in the second nicest flophouse in Harrisburg. After that...well, I guess yet another miracle could somehow intercede and stave off my otherwise inevitable demise..."

"Ben Glinton! Ben!" a voice cried out, becoming louder as its owner emerged from the shadows of the ape's mouth into the sunlight. They turned to behold a well-muscled man in a white shirt, khaki pants, and hip shades smiling at them and offering his hand to them for the second time in less than a month. It was none other than Thor Rollins from TDSN. "Sorry I got here so late," he said, "but I had no idea that what would happen here today would be so...so totally *make*. It was the most make thing I've seen in a long time! I was on the edge of my seat!"

"Make, yes, it was definitely make," Ben said. "How did you get here?"

"I was in Vegas for the 2006 pro snowboarding draft and I happened to catch your tournament on the network—well, the Spike Vail part anyway. I gotta say, I was riveted. It was good—Australian rules football good. I hopped on the first ultrasonic passenger jet to Reno. Boys, let me tell you, I've had an idea which is so make, it's gonna blow your socks off and send them screaming down the street with their nostrils on fire. An idea that's gonna give TDSN a virtual stranglehold over that elusive 1:30 a.m. to 2:30 a.m. Tuesday time slot which I've been trying to figure out for years. An idea, by the way, that's gonna score *you* a not inconsiderable number of Benjamins."

"Speak on, corporate media cow," Ben said. "I'm all ears."


October.

"Welcome back to Thunder Dunk's live coverage of the Autumn Dreams Celebrity APBA Square-Off," Ben said into camera four as his artificially tanned, Armani-suited body turned to his co-anchor. "I'm Ben Glinton here with our color man, Harold Pillick, and when we broke for commercial, the back-and-forth here at Madison Square Garden was getting bookmark-worthy indeed."

"That's right, Ben," Harold said, looking uncomfortable but excited under the hot lights of the stadium. "Roger Daltrey's last gambit to turn things around in the seventh for his Liverpool Heavybricks fell just short when Holly Hunter brought her infield charging in to make a key out at home plate. Now it looks as though Roger's valiant effort to raise ten thousand dollars for his chosen charity, The Thumbless Folk of Chelsea, might come to a crashing end."

"Looks like he's changed his pitcher again," Ben commented as camera five picked up a wide shot of the ornate gaming table, around which two hundred people sat in makeshift bleachers to watch the action. "Curse Williger, what's Roger's rationale here?"

"I'm not real sure, Ben," Curse reported as he roved the sidelines, leaning over the participants' shoulders, "maybe he's thinking that Brian Geisel's XY rating will completely shut Holly's lineup down until he can hand things over to someone with some actual pitching skill, but to me this is a boneheaded mistake. I swear to God, decisions like this one make me want to start slapping people." Viewers at home were treated to a bright flash in the lower right hand corner of their screens as a digital image of Brian Geisel's APBA card materialized out of nowhere, his key ratings flashing orange.

"Do you think Roger's wishing he had played today's game using the '06 Cannons," Ben asked, "so he could have put you on the mound to stifle Holly like you stifled the Ice Eaters twice a couple of weeks ago to get that ugly beast of a championship ring on your finger?"

Curse chuckled. "I don't know, Ben," he said. "I think I may have outperformed myself a little at the end there, and my APBA card would surely pick that up."

Holly Hunter picked up her shaker and emptied its contents onto the table. Two large microphones nudged past her head, irritating the hell out of her, to zero in on the sound of the dice striking the landing pad, the audio cranked way up and tinged with a blatant echo for the TV audience. When the dice came to a stop, showing a 22, the crowd clapped as they had been trained to do and Juan Varga's card appeared on the screen. The number 22 glowed and sparkled and an electronic readout of the appropriate chart result typed itself magically across the screen.

"That's a double to left!" Ben said. "Holly's next base runner will be represented by the star of Thunder Dunk's new hard-hitting drama series about the backroom dealings, locker room clashes, and bedroom love affairs that pulse deep in the heart of America's favorite new TDSN-branded sport, which, as of this moment, is still called Foot Tennis while the marketing department gets its act together. Ladies and gentlemen, say hello to Mr. Don Cheadle!"

The crowd applauded as Cheadle, wearing the uniform of Holly's New York Guardians, trotted onto a stretch of green carpet on which a baseball diamond had been reproduced. He touched first base and playfully took a two-step lead, which brought him about halfway to second.

"Is this the beginning of the end for Roger Daltrey, Harold?" Ben asked. "I figure you have to be looking for a steal attempt here. Holly's proven herself to be a ruthless savage when it comes to being aggressive on the big green beltway."

Harold nodded. "I think your intuition here is correct, Ben. Even with nobody out, she's going to run. And my *Broadcast News* for today is that it won't be *The Piano* Holly will play next week, but Mr. David Ogden Stiers as she veers ever closer to the 2006 Celebrity APBA title." A TDSN intern lowered the cue card and Harold breathed an interior sigh of relief that he had gotten the jokes right.

"Let's not jump the gun, Harold," Ben cautioned. "There's still some time left for Roger to redeem himself. And Stiers still has to get past J.K. Rowling in the semis. Looks like there's going to be a quick time-out on the field here as the lead singer of The Who sorts through his roster looking for an answer to his many bullpen troubles, so let's break for sixty seconds for another quick update from our studios in Pittsburgh about the Pool Skimmer Strangler's amazing escape from custody and his abduction of Spike Vail in an attempt to cross the border into Canada. Take it away, Linda."

*Roll! the crowd cried as the batter dug in fast,*
*His heart singing low at the mess of his past*

*While the pitcher looked in for the cue to attack,*
*Obsessed with an inning he could never get back.*
*The dice went forward to make them both new...*
*The real disappeared; the impossible shone through.*

—From Roy Skinla's poorly received book of poetry, *Caring Has a Voice That Sounds Like Your Eyes,* self-published with financial assistance from the Independent APBA Collective of Metro Harrisburg in July of 2019.

**Also by Soren Narnia**

Whatever You Find Within You

3:13 a.m.

Song of the Living Dead

Sicko, I Set You Free: A Treasury of Erotica for the Easily Amused

Tyrant, Draw Thy Sword

A Listing of the Holdings of the National Museum of Romance

Made in United States
Orlando, FL
23 September 2022

22735839R00114